David Coubrough founded the specialist hospitality firm Portfolio Recruitment in the 1980s and twice sold it to public companies, on the second occasion becoming chief executive of the PLC. He is on the board of governors of the Royal Academy of Culinary Arts and is a past chairman of Bespoke Hotels and the Castle Hotel at Taunton. He is a director of Maldon Sea Salt and is on the board of Bloomsbury Properties. He co-owns the Beehive pub and restaurant in Berkshire and is currently working on his second novel.

# HALF A POUND OF TUPPENNY RICE

DAVID
COUBROUGH

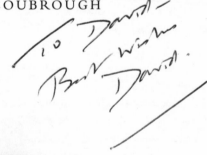

PETER OWEN PUBLISHERS
London and Chicago

PETER OWEN PUBLISHERS
81 Ridge Road, London N8 9NP

Peter Owen books are distributed in the USA and Canada by
Independent Publishers Group/Trafalgar Square,
814 North Franklin Street, Chicago, IL 60610, USA

First published in Great Britain 2016
© David Coubrough 2016

Paperback ISBN 978-0-7206-1881-5
Epub ISBN 978-0-7206-1882-2
Mobipocket ISBN 978-0-7206-1883-9
PDF ISBN 978-0-7206-1884-6

A catalogue record for this book is available from the British Library.

Every effort has been made to trace copyright holders and to obtain
their permission for the use of copyright material. The author
apologizes for any errors or omissions and would be grateful to be
notified of any corrections that should be incorporated in future
reprints or editions of this book.

Printed and bound by CPI Group (UK) Ltd, Croydon, CR0 4YY

## ACKNOWLEDGEMENTS

The author wishes to acknowledge the support and assistance of the following people: David Godwin, my literary agent, whose support and advice has played such a crucial part throughout; Richard Whitehouse; Natalie Guerin; Geoff Helliwell; Eleanor Randall; Kit Chapman; Chris Sheppardson; Richard Mitchell; Jonathan Barnes; Michael Parslew; Jackie Kane; David Wiltshire; Mike Seymour; Sarah Phillips; Philip Sisson, Barbara Gurlach and David Gabriel; my four children Olivia, Alice, Emily and Jonathan, my sister Pauline and the de Galleani family. Finally all at Peter Owen Publishers, especially Nick Kent and Antonia Owen.

## MAIN CHARACTERS

*The Morrison Family*
Grant Morrison, solicitor
Brigit Morrison, wife of Grant and mother of their two grown-up
    daughters; head of an IT recruitment consultancy firm
Rose Morrison, mother of Grant
Dennis Morrison, father of Grant
Glen Morrison, brother of Grant; married to Mandy
Gina Morrison, aunt of Grant and twin sister of Rose

*The Hughes-Webb Family*
Richard Hughes-Webb, cardiologist
Estelle Hughes-Webb, first wife of Richard
Yvie Hughes-Webb, second wife of Richard
Suzie Hughes-Webb (married name Barber),
    daughter of Richard and Yvie
Tony Hughes-Webb, son of Richard and Yvie
Frank Barber, husband of Suzie

*The Galvin Family*
Paul Galvin, accountant and property speculator
Alison Galvin, wife of Paul
Danny Galvin, son of Paul and Alison
Sharon Galvin, daughter of Paul and Alison

*The Jessops Family*
Ted Jessops, factory owner
Anne Jessops, wife of Ted
Caroline Jessops, daughter of Ted and Anne (married name Howe-Jessops)
Steve Jessops, son of Ted and Anne
Joanna, illegitimate daughter of Ted

### The Charnley Family
Arnie Charnley, entrepreneur
Lucy 'the Duchess' Charnley, wife of Arnie
Nick Charnley, son of Arnie and Lucy
Jenny Charnley, daughter of Arnie and Lucy

### The Silver Family
Bob Silver, merchant banker
Margaret Silver, wife of Bob; GP
Fiona Silver, daughter of Bob and Margaret
Henry Silver, older son of Bob and Margaret
Justyn Silver, younger son of Bob and Margaret

### The Wallace Family
Agatha Wallace, benefactor of Hector
Hector Wallace, nephew of Agatha

### The Vernon Family
Mark Vernon, owner of a bank
Robert Vernon, son of Mark

### The Simpkins Family
James Simpkins, hotel manager
Jean Simpkins, wife of James

### The Youlen Family
Tom Youlen, hotel night porter
Ivan Youlen, nephew of Tom
Tom Youlen Junior, son of Ivan
Dickie Youlen, brother of Tom, plasterer at Sandersons

### The Holford Family
Ken Holford, itinerant
Mary Holford, said to be wife of Ken
Clive Holford, son of Ken and Mary

### Other Characters
Trevor Mullings, fisherman
Robin Sanderson, founder of Sandersons, Penzance
Inspector Roy Higham, senior investigating police officer
PC Gary Stobart, junior investigating police officer

# 1

## THE RECENT PAST

'I nearly died last night.' Grant spoke with his head bowed. Brigit, his wife, sitting at the breakfast table a few feet away, looked across at him. Had he made a statement requiring a response, had he simply made a statement, or had he made an announcement? She held her look, observing him closely.

'What?' she eventually felt compelled to ask. And so he revealed his dream. He told her he thought he was back in Zennor. He didn't know what time of night it started. It began, he said, with the same tapping on the door he had heard that night staying at the bed-and-breakfast by the Cornish coast. Next it changed to loud knocking, and the noise from the corridor outside increased substantially. Before long his door was being thumped and splintered open, wood crashing in a heap on the floor. He was petrified, unable to utter a word, even though he was trying to shout. His room was suddenly filled with shadowy figures, one of whom said, 'We're police officers, and we're arresting you, Grant Morrison, for the poisoning of Tom Youlen in 1972, leading to his death in 1977, and for the murder by drowning of Hector Wallace in 1972.'

Brigit arched an eyebrow; a look he knew betrayed anxiety on her part.

He continued. 'When I woke up I couldn't breathe. I could see, I could move, but I thought I was in limbo between life and death. I genuinely thought for a few moments I had actually died, that I was on the other side and that this was the beginning of the afterlife; this was my fate.'

'Then what?' Brigit tried to play it cool.

'It took a few seconds before my respiratory system started working again – before I could breathe normally. I've never experienced anything quite like it. After several minutes I'd calmed myself enough to realize it had been a horrific dream, but it was the waking from it that scared the living daylights out of me – quite literally.'

She restrained a giggle. Grant could take himself very seriously and wouldn't see the oddness of his last remark. Only he could be more scared waking from a nightmare than having one.

'You see,' he continued, 'for several minutes I just lay there taking short intakes of breath and exhaling from the pit of my stomach. Gradually my breathing returned to normal and I could feel the blood flow in my head.' He stopped and stared ahead once more.

She was unsure of whether to cuddle and reassure him or just to let him be for a while. She was unsettled by his story, and she didn't really want to touch him right then; he seemed different, distant. She wondered about the recent trip to Cornwall he had undertaken alone. He had said, 'I've got to find out the truth, Brig. I've got to know what happened.' And now he had returned home apparently scared out of his wits by the two nights of extraordinary, sinister events he had experienced during his stay in the village of Zennor.

At length Grant went on. 'When I was in Zennor, one night at some unearthly hour, just as I was drifting of to sleep, I heard it.'

'What?'

'A soft voice that I thought at first was a woman's. Singing "Half a pound of tuppenny rice, half a pound of treacle . . ."

I heard the first line in a dreamy haze, the second wide awake. "That's the way the money goes . . ." I jumped out of bed, reaching for the door. Then I stopped myself, fearing I might be walking into a trap.'

'Who was it?'

'I don't know. I have no idea, Brig. But there was something else that freaked me out. It seemed to be a child's voice. And there was an echo – as if the words were being sung by a child in a cathedral choir.'

His wife observed him. She had heard bits and pieces of his experiences as a teenager in Cornwall over the past few months, but during the previous twenty-five years she had known him he had never mentioned it at all. 'D'you mean this is connected to what you have been banging on about for months now? And that this relates to the stuff that occurred forty years back?'

Grant didn't appear to hear her, but he told her more about his disturbed nights in Zennor. How music from the bar below his bedroom had woken him at four in the morning, with 'Good Morning, Starshine' from the 1960s' musical *Hair* playing at high volume. At that time of night it had given him quite a start.

'There were other things, Brig. There was the message.'

'What message?'

'I was in Porthcurno and came across Trevor Mullings, the fisherman who got drunk with Hector Wallace the night Hector drowned.'

'So there was a real Hector Wallace – not just in your dream.'

'Yes, there was. He used to stay with us at the hotel, and he left a message for his aunt, who was his companion and bene-factor. "Dear Aunt Agatha, I will love you always . . ." They said it was written in blood and that he had added in ink,

"Tonight I am not alone." When he returned from the sea, cold and dead to the world, no one knew he had left a message. I recently discovered it in a bottle.'

Brigit was becoming disoriented. 'Are you sure you want to pursue this? I mean, why does it matter forty years on, for goodness' sake?'

'Oh, it does matter. It matters very much indeed.'

# 2

## 20 AUGUST 1972

'It was him.'

'Who?' the doctor whispered urgently, kneeling beside the stricken man who was lying on the grassy verge of the narrow lane. His face was shadowed by the hedge above, as she raised his right arm, feeling for his pulse.

'Him from the hotel,' he gasped, barely audibly. 'He said he would . . . if I spoke.' The words died on the man's lips as his head fell back on to the ground; he was exhausted by the effort of forming the last words he would ever speak. The doctor lifted the man's head, supporting the back of his neck. She examined his dull, lifeless eyes and without a backward glance said, 'Call an ambulance. He's suffered a stroke or heart attack.' Margaret Silver's voice held steadier than her thoughts.

Aware that the man was close to death, the doctor was extremely concerned. She had recognized him as the night porter from the hotel near by where her family and a group of others returned every year in August for a fortnight's holiday. His name was Tom Youlen. A short, squat local from Zennor, his face looked as if it had been chiselled from the craggy rocks that edged the nearby Cornish shoreline; his voice was so deep it could have challenged the foghorns of merchant ships plying their trade on the inhospitable waves below.

That Sunday morning she had been on her way back from church with three fellow hotel guests. They had been driving down a tiny lane the width of a single car; their windows were open partly so they could listen out for oncoming vehicles. The passengers were silent, anxious that the driver should maintain full concentration, particularly as the road was growing increasingly narrow. However, their attention was arrested not by a vehicle but by a cry of 'Puffin, shag, herring gull, gannet and chough' from beyond the next sharp bend. Despite the driver, Mark Vernon, braking, their car only just avoided knocking down the unanticipated pedestrian. Had they not heard him first they probably would have hit him. The four watched in horror as the man staggered within a few inches of the bonnet before collapsing backwards into a hedgerow of thick thorn. Margaret was the first to reach him, and she helped him lie down on the grass, with Mark close behind her.

At her command to summon an ambulance, Mark set off to make an emergency call from the nearest house. He wheezed with asthma as he rushed back to the car as fast as his spindly frame would permit. He drove off erratically, nearly sending the vehicle off the road when he hit a large pothole on his way. He thumped on the door of the first building he came across. Seagulls squalled, and a cool gust of fresh air swept in from the coast, causing him to shiver as he waited impatiently. Slowly the oak-panelled door opened and an elderly man peered out suspiciously.

'So sorry. Someone . . . Someone's collapsed in the lane. I urgently need to use your phone to call an ambulance. Please, this is an emergency.' He struggled to articulate, but the old man led him straight to the telephone in the hallway, and his 999 call was answered speedily.

The ambulance raced from Penzance, shuddering to a halt and blocking the entire lane, its siren still blaring. The collapsed night porter stared vacantly at the senior paramedic, his eyes resembling green marbles. He tried desperately to lift his head to speak, but his lips would not part, and no sound could be heard.

Margaret addressed the paramedic. 'I'm a doctor, and we found the man in the lane in a terribly confused state. He collapsed into the hedge after we braked to avoid hitting him. His name is Tom, I think. He works at our hotel. He said a few words just before you arrived.' She told him the words the man had uttered.

'What?' The ambulance man, a rotund individual with overgrown white sideburns, had hitherto appeared rather indifferent to the drama unfolding but now looked somewhat intrigued despite himself.

One of the other passengers chipped in. 'We know him. Tom's the night porter at our hotel.' The man's jaunty Home Counties accent jarred with the Cornish paramedic.

'I'm calling the police. Thanks for all your help,' he said to the assembled group in the manner of a head teacher dismissing his pupils. 'They may wish to take statements from you, so stick around, if you will, until they arrive.'

As for Tom, he never said anything again. Margaret was right. He had suffered a stroke, and he died five years later without regaining his ability to speak.

These events, some ten days into the families' two-week holiday, were to have repercussions for the next forty years and disturbed seventeen-year-old Grant Morrison in particular. Grant had also discovered around this time that his mother, Rose, had been having an affair with the father of one of the other families. He was Richard Hughes-Webb, a heart surgeon who returned each year to the hotel and who owned a cottage in Zennor. He used his holiday cottage for storing toxic materials that he used in experiments on animals and also, Grant was to discover to his dismay, for extramarital assignations.

As the years had gone by, Grant's preoccupation with these events, far from diminishing, had become more prominent, to the point where the business of Tom's accident came to haunt him profoundly. He couldn't disconnect it from his mother's involvement with Hughes-Webb, who had used the porter Tom as his caretaker and made him a complicit pawn. Tom, who minded the cottage for Hughes-Webb, never betrayed his boss and had been known to remark, 'No one needs to know what goes on behind closed doors.' Tom was paid handsomely for both his caretaking and his discretion, but he was to die prematurely some five years later.

*'It was him. Him from the hotel. He said he would . . . if I spoke.'*

For over forty years Tom's words had been hard-wired into Grant's brain. How had Hughes-Webb got away with it? Forensic reports had confirmed the cause of Tom's death as ascariasis, a life-threatening infection caused by contaminated parasitic roundworm eggs, presumably ingested at Hughes-Webb's cottage, but how the hotel porter came to ingest the eggs was never explained. Grant feared there had been either a botched, inadequate investigation or a cover-up. Either way, he could never banish the unsettling and unpleasant thoughts from his mind, particularly as his parents' marriage had deteriorated so significantly after that holiday in 1972. Despite knowing that his father, Dennis, was dying of cancer, his mother had heartlessly continued her relationship with Hughes-Webb. Although his father died in 1974 and his mother twenty years later, it wasn't until his mother's twin sister, Gina, died in 2012 that Grant felt free to investigate.

# 3

## PRESENT DAY

'That's the place. That's the hotel where it happened.' Brigit followed Grant's gaze across the bay to an imposing white building on the horizon, slowly emerging from the cold January morning fog. Sitting upstairs at a window table in a warm harbourside brasserie on the west coast of Cornwall, he fell silent, lost in troubled reflection. So much had happened since that time he thought he would never be able to recollect those distressing events; but his mind had taken a trip in a time machine. He was back in 1972, recalling it all with absolute clarity.

Every year the families had travelled to the hotel from across the length and breadth of Britain. Some arrived early in the morning, fresh and raring to go, having put their cars on the overnight sleeper to Penzance; others turned up hot and exhausted after having driven up to ten hours in their vehicles from Leeds, Manchester and elsewhere in the days before air-conditioning. Even the London contingent would emerge from their cars aching and complaining about the narrow winding lanes in Devon and Cornwall in this era before dual carriage-ways. Thrown together for a two-week reunion in August every year, the families had come to resemble a club, a group of friends bonded together by successive summer holidays.

'It was such a different time.' Grant's face gazed into the distance as he started to reminisce. 'The 1960s changed things. There was this great feeling of freedom . . .'

'Yeah, whatever,' Brigit interrupted. 'Calling Planet Earth!'

'I'm sorry. I can't stop thinking about it all – the hotel and the events that took place. It was strange. We were in a bubble where so much seemed perfect until the incident.'

'What incident?' Brigit asked, despite herself. A petite, forceful-looking woman in her late forties, she was casually dressed in designer jeans and a warm woollen cardigan beneath a Barbour jacket and a bright checked scarf. Sitting there, she looked up at the hotel. She thought it resembled a castle, perched above sweeping lawns that stretched down to the sea way below. As it emerged from the morning fog she could discern a sharp precipice at the edge of the lawn, which gave way to red rock dropping steeply down to an expanse of sand washed by energetic waves.

'That would be telling,' Grant teased abruptly. He left the table, paid the bill and suggested it was time they visited the art gallery they had come to see. Brigit gave him a quizzical look.

Grant, tall and wiry, was a few years older than Brigit and was not usually noted for his reticence in telling yarns and stories of his past. The recipients of his tales could find themselves somewhat disconcerted when he got into his stride, as his eyes moved in separate directions. He maintained that this was great in meetings, where he could make two individuals feel they were the focus of his attention at the same time. It was a peculiarity that didn't cause him a moment's trouble or embarrassment; it was merely a party piece when the occasion demanded.

It was later that day that Grant became more forthcoming. 'Tom Youlen was an eccentric porter at the hotel and some-thing of a fixture there. On film nights he would interrupt the movie, even a James Bond, to announce, "Telephone call for Mr Hegarty" or whoever. He wasn't particularly friendly, regarding us as "grockles" – as necessary but rather decadent evils. We were to be tolerated. He used to mutter to himself, "Puffin, shag, herring gull, gannet and chough." It was a bit like a mantra to him. As teenagers we were intrigued and amused by this. It was pointed out by one of the grown-ups that they were Cornish coastland birds. On the day of the incident a few of our parents had gone to church in Zennor, where Tom lived, and on the way back in the car they encountered him staggering into a hedgerow by the road. Alarmed, they rushed to his aid. He was in a terrible way. All he could mutter was "It was him. Him from the hotel. He said he would . . . if I spoke."'

Brigit considered Grant's words in silence, allowing the impact of this to sink in. 'How dreadful. What effect did this have on everyone?'

'Our parents never went back. None of us did.'

Brigit was astounded. Grant had previously referred to his childhood holidays in Cornwall only in fleeting, superficial terms that had given the impression they were of little consequence. She turned to face him. Moving a strand of hair that had fallen across her forehead, she inquired, 'So did they catch the person Tom referred to as "him from the hotel"? Was it a member of staff or a guest?'

'That was the strange thing. The staff were all cleared of any wrong-doing. It was suggested that Tom had been poisoned. Five guests were questioned, but all had alibis. I later heard that one of them had confessed something to one of his children on his deathbed, but that's never been confirmed.' Grant sighed and wondered how much he should divulge to his wife. Should he tell her the truth as far as he knew it? And, more significantly, should he own up to what was really driving him, the fear that had been eating away at him for more than forty years? On that last holiday he had learnt of his mother's affair with the cardiologist Richard Hughes-Webb; he also knew that Tom's stroke had been induced by ingesting some poisonous substance with which Richard was experimenting at his cottage in Zennor where Tom was caretaker. Grant had never been able to forget Hughes-Webb's alibi – his own mother. What had she concealed, and how much had she known?

'Why would anyone want to harm the porter?'

Grant hesitated. 'Well, he had obviously seen or heard something, and someone had very real fears of being exposed for some reason. Don't forget, this was the early 1970s, and even homosexuality was barely legal then.' An inner voice was yelling at him, 'Leave all this alone!' But he knew he was now ready to examine the past; in fact, he needed to examine the past.

Later that night, as they lay in bed in their rented cottage further up the coast, Brigit's mind returned to the subject of the porter. The howling wind and the sound of crashing waves didn't exactly soothe the discomfort she had felt on hearing Grant's tale. 'Did anyone discover how Tom came to be in such a state in the lane?'

'Yes, he seems to have been poisoned – and this caused a stroke.'

'And did he live long after that?'

'About five years, I was told. But I'd like to confirm that by visiting the graveyard tomorrow, if that's OK with you.'

'Yes, fine, but can we do a rain check in the morning? I don't really fancy exploring a graveyard in weather like this.'

They listened to the pounding waves. The little cottage creaked and groaned under the strain of the gale-force wind. A loud thump startled them, but Grant reassured Brigit that it was likely only a piece of driftwood blown on to the roof.

She cuddled closer. 'So who do you think it was?'

Grant paused before replying. The storm raging outside seemed to reach a crescendo, rattling windows and doors as if some giant invisible hand was shaking the foundations of the cottage.

'The five suspects were all guests at the hotel and were each interviewed twice. Ted Jessops, a factory owner from the Midlands; Bob Silver, a merchant banker from the City of London; Richard Hughes-Webb, a heart specialist from Croydon; Paul Galvin, an accountant from London; and Arnie Charnley from Manchester, who claimed to be in print and publishing but whose son told us he distributed porn magazines.'

'Hardly the dirty dozen.'

'True, but it turned out they all could have had a motive.' Grant fell silent.

For a moment Brigit thought he was asleep, but she knew his breathing patterns and realized he was wide awake. 'Don't you feel it was all wrong', she whispered, 'that no one has ever been arrested and prosecuted? And why haven't you told me any of this before?'

'Of course, someone should have been brought to book, but at the time we were just teenage kids, carefree adolescents enjoying new experiences. To be frank, it ended in such an unfortunate and inconclusive way that for a long time I pretended to myself that it didn't really happen at all. Funnily enough, I remember the night one of our group, Jenny Charnley, came rushing down to the disco – near where we had lunch today in fact.'

'And?'

'She was hysterical. I remember Hawkwind's track "Silver Machine" was blasting out, and she tried to shout above it.'

'And?'

'She was screaming about the police having taken her father to the local station for questioning. We all felt for her, of course, but we had no experience of that kind of situation, had no idea what to say. It was only the following day, when Paul Galvin's son Danny drove four of us in his Mini to the beach at Sennen Cove, that the reality of it all hit us. I was in the car with Caroline Jessops, Suzie Hughes-Webb and Justyn Silver.'

'So what happened?'

'It was a glorious summer's afternoon, the sun was glistening off the sea and Danny was looking for a parking space, when he said, "Hey, all this stuff kicking off is way too heavy. What if it's one of our fathers?" I asked, "How do you know it isn't one of our mothers?" "Tom said it was a man," he replied. Danny's outburst made us pause for thought, and finally Caroline said, "Well, they shouldn't visit the sins of the fathers on the children." And, to be honest, that became our attitude. At our age, life was full of possibilities, great music and, at that moment, a fantastic beach on a sunny August afternoon. It was actually the next day, at the Office, when our mood really changed.'

'The Office?'

'Yes, that was the nickname of the local pub, the Cornish Arms. It was given by one of the odder guests, a bachelor of around fifty called Hector Wallace, who went there every morning at twelve midday and every evening after dinner. Hector's life ended tragically as well.' Grant's voice faltered.

'So what happened at the Office?'

'There was another incident late that night. It made my blood run cold,' replied Grant, quietly in a sombre voice that disconcerted Brigit. He was never this quiet. He didn't do quiet. She sought to reassure him, feeling she had pressed him too hard. Perhaps it was better to leave the past as a place of reference, not of residence, as her father liked to say. But it disturbed her that until relatively recently he had never once mentioned the strange events that had not only caused the curtailment of his cherished Cornish holidays but which would appear to have cast a cloud over him. She was also a little confused by the mention of so many people from Grant's past. What could be their relevance now, and would their past threaten the couple's future?

'I think we should leave off for tonight,' she said. 'Let's visit Tom's grave tomorrow if this wretched storm abates and try to make better sense of it all. It was a long, long time ago, and it wasn't your fault.' She kissed him softly on the cheek, and he half smiled.

Her words reverberated in the air as the waves continued to crash against the battered shoreline. She thought about those coastal birds: the puffin, shag, herring gull, gannet and chough. Were they out there tonight, she wondered, as she drifted into a fitful sleep. For several hours Grant thought he wouldn't sleep at all.

# 4

## PRESENT DAY

The car crawled up the tree-lined drive towards the sprawling castle; an expanse of turrets silhouetted against a dark but beautifully clear Cornish sky, windows aglow with light as the night drew in around them. It was late. They had arrived off the last train from London, their eyes slow-dancing with tiredness. As their car crunched across the gravel, the trees receded behind them, and ahead a wide lawn of cut grass ran away from them towards the sea. As they followed the winding drive the castle cast shadows in the moonlight, its turrets stretching skywards. The moon hung low in the sky, illuminating its crystal rays on to the vast expanse of restless ocean below. They pulled up outside the entrance. A thick layer of ivy covered the stone walls looming overhead. The great oak door opened, and there was Tom welcoming them in, while moths hovered around him, attracted by the glow from the cast-iron lantern above his head. They opened their car doors, stiff and weary from the journey, to be arrested by the smell of pine trees and fresh sea air. They could hear the sounds of voices and laughter from their friends in the dining-room filtering out through open windows, into the still night air. David Bowie's 'Starman' could be heard crackling from a transistor radio somewhere below, where busy catering staff were preparing meals for the guests upstairs.

Grant awoke from this happy dream of idyllic childhood holidays and was saddened to recall Tom's last years following his stroke. After a largely sleepless night Grant felt disturbed by the dream, which was a constantly recurring one. The setting was always Cornwall and the year always 1972; the porter was always present; and usually there was a cameo role for Richard Hughes-Webb. What really bothered Grant was the increasing frequency of the dreams, which more often than not turned into nightmares.

The next morning the storm was still raging, so the couple decided to postpone their visit to Tom's grave and instead to take a walk. They parked their car near Gurnard's Head and, wrapped in waterproofs and floppy hats, spent the day hiking westwards on the breathtaking cliff top, taking the south-west coastal path towards Cape Cornwall. They walked alone for around two hours, although Brigit was aware of a man some three hundred yards behind them who stopped every time she looked round. She dismissed him from her thoughts and refrained from telling her husband.

'So, who do you think it was?' she asked loudly, battling the wind.

'Ted Jessops was strange,' Grant shouted back, his eyes fixed on the rising and crashing Atlantic waves below. 'On the last holiday he had become a rather pathetic figure. Previously he had been an imposing presence, an engaging character who could enliven any company. He wasn't particularly tall, but he had a large face, a large stomach and a thick mop of grey-black hair with Elvis Presley sideburns. By the last holiday he had become a shell of the man he once was, and his hair – what was left of it – had turned ashen-white.

'There were rumours that he had fathered an illegitimate child who had pursued him to Cornwall to claim paternity. Some four years before this business with Tom he and his wife had been holidaying on the north coast at Constantine Bay. Apparently his unacknowledged daughter named Joanna confronted him on the beach, causing him to panic. Ted was a strong swimmer, and he just turned round, ran into the sea and started swimming away as fast as he could. He hadn't even acknowledged her existence, let alone responded to her pleas for recognition within his family. The poor girl apparently got into severe distress in the currents as she swam after Ted, and she had to be rescued by coastguards. By the time she was brought ashore, scarcely breathing, Ted had packed his wife and young daughter Caroline into his brown Rover and had started the drive back to the family home in Bromsgrove.'

'So how did the story get out?'

'One of the coastguards was Tom's nephew Ivan. He recognized Ted as the strong swimmer who had exited the scene so swiftly while the girl struggled for her life. Although this incident had occurred four years before, it had stuck in Ivan's mind as the most harrowing rescue in which he'd been involved. As Joanna was being dragged out to sea by the currents, he and the other coastguard genuinely feared a fatality. The waves were huge, and they really had to race to rescue the girl.'

'Still, it was remarkable for him to have identified Ted after four years.'

'It was, and it was an odd thing. It was partly a song that gave Ted away – as well as the presence of his brown Rover at the hotel.'

'Go on.'

'Apparently Ivan's radio was blaring out the Beach Boys' song "Do It Again" when Joanna got into difficulty in the sea. The song was still blasting out across the beach as Ted rushed his family to the Rover. Four years later, when Ivan went to the hotel to see his uncle about a private matter, he was whistling "Do It Again" when he bumped into Ted and spotted his car. Ted immediately recognized Ivan as the coastguard who had saved Joanna from drowning in 1968 while he so disgracefully fled the scene. Can you imagine the sense of guilt, shame and panic Ted must have experienced?'

'Did they talk to one another?'

'Apparently so. Ivan said, "I know you from somewhere." Ted said, "No you don't", and barged straight past him as Tom remarked, "Mr Jessops can be a very rude man." When Tom had his stroke Ivan was asked by the police if he knew whether Tom had any enemies; having been present at this exchange at the hotel just two days before, Ivan mentioned Ted Jessops. Don't forget that Ted's actions could have caused Ivan to lose his life.'

'Did anyone know why Ivan had gone to talk to Tom while he was on duty? Wasn't that odd? I mean, he could have seen Tom at his cottage, couldn't he?'

'Well, the story goes that Tom had been bailing Ivan out financially for years. When the boy was sixteen he got a local girl pregnant, and he lived with her and the child in a tiny bedsit near the coast at Newquay. He worked intermittently as a coastguard in the summertime across the north coast, but he was always short of a bob or two. His uncle, Tom, was his protector, as Ivan's parents thought their son had brought shame on the family and had rather ostracized him.'

'I don't suppose anyone suspected . . .'

'I know what you're thinking, but Ivan wasn't "him from the hotel".'

'Well, he was there two days earlier.'

'Now then, Miss Marple, there was no one more upset than Ivan after Tom's stroke. He visited him every day in his nursing home until he died, and he arranged the funeral.'

'How do you know all this?'

Grant didn't reply, thinking carefully about how much he wanted to reveal before deciding to ignore the query.

Brigit persisted. 'Bit of a coincidence, don't you think? Both

Ted Jessops and Ivan had children out of wedlock, even though they handled their paternity in totally different ways.'

'I take your point, but it's not for us to judge.'

'I still don't see why Ivan couldn't have visited his uncle when he was off duty.'

'The story goes that he caught Tom fifteen minutes before his night shift was due to start. Bill, the other porter, warned Tom that he had seen Ivan's battered Escort in the car park. Tom didn't seem too perturbed, but Ivan was heard to say, "You never return my phone calls, and you're never at the pub when I call, Uncle T." Apparently Tom replied along the lines of "You've bled me enough. Summer season's ending soon, and I need to hang on to some dough." In those days the hotel would close for the winter, not reopening till spring, and money would have been a major preoccupation. Meanwhile it seems that Ivan had become distracted by the sight of Ted Jessops heading for his car, the brown Rover, and recalled the day that he and the other coastguard had saved the seventeen-year-old girl.'

'Unlucky for Ted that he hadn't changed his car,' Brigit smiled.

'Unlucky for Ted – or lucky for the inquiry, one might say. When he was interviewed about the girl he was swimming away from he refused to acknowledge that he even knew her. Even though the sea rescue had occurred four years earlier, it didn't take the police long to spot the connection, and Joanna gave a full statement.'

'So what happened to Ted after that?'

'He died.'

Brigit and Grant had stopped for lunch at a coastal pub. As they walked in 'My Cherie Amour' was playing on the jukebox. The place seemed frozen in time.

'Stevie Wonder, 1968!' he exclaimed. 'The year of the

swimming incident. So many of these pubs are in a time warp.'
Far from being disappointed, he was delighted to scan the
surroundings, table skittles in one corner, a shove-ha'penny
board in another, signed photographs of lesser-known celeb-
rities behind a copper-topped bar. It had all the paraphernalia
of a 1960s' pub with a bonus – a stunning view of Cornwall's
dramatic coastline.

'So how did he die, and when?' Brigit was becoming
increasingly interested in Ted.

Her query snapped Grant out of his reverie. 'Later that year,
in 1972. It seems that Big Deal Ted was not doing as well as
he would have had everyone believe. His factory had burnt
down, there was a problem with the insurance, and he was
being treated for depression.'

'And how does Maigret know all this?'

'That summer I went out with his daughter Caroline, if you
must know. Shortly after we left Cornwall I stayed with the
family for a few days. Ted seemed withdrawn, saying little at
mealtimes and retreating to his study as soon as he could. What
I didn't know was that he was being treated for manic depression, what's now called bipolar disorder. He was rumoured to
be having electroshock therapy during that last holiday,
according to gossip in the hotel. He was a complex man. The
approbation of his peer group was very important to him. He
felt he had arrived at a type of top table by being able to afford
the hotel each year. It gave him a sense of status that reflected,
in his estimation, his business success. He particularly cherished
acceptance by people from the professions – doctors, account-
ants and so on – and he used to say, "And me, a humble man
from trade." To lose status with his peer group would have
been devastating, and no doubt that was a factor in his dis-
graceful treatment of Joanna. When I stayed with the Jessops,
Caroline and I spent most of the time at the nearby country

club, hanging around the bar and playing table tennis with her friends. The relationship fizzled out that autumn, but she wrote to me in November 1972 saying her father had died.'

'What was the cause?'

'He was quite overweight, had high blood pressure and was prone to sudden bouts of temper. These days, of course, he would have been treated with pills.'

'It doesn't seem as if he would have been mourned very much. What a sad end, even if he sounds rather disagreeable.'

'Actually there were over two hundred people at his funeral. They came from far and wide. Some were dodgy-looking individuals whom Caroline referred to as "the hoods", while a number of local friends and acquaintances turned up. Many of them had known Ted since childhood. I suppose at fifty-four he died before most of his contemporaries.'

'So he wasn't all bad.'

'Definitely not. He could be the life and soul of a party. He was a great raconteur and when he was on a roll he could entertain people for hours.'

'So what do you think went wrong?'

'He became tortured by the sins of his past. Clearly he was never able to acknowledge Joanna properly, and her pursuing him to Cornwall on his family's annual jaunt must have shocked him to the core.'

'So it should.'

'Well, whatever, he was apparently never the same after August 1972, and it was only three months later that he had a massive heart attack and died. Of course his decline may have started earlier, but running into Ivan that day at the hotel must have scared the hell out of him. When Ivan saw him again he evidently gave Ted a stare that said "I know what you've done, you bastard." Seeing Ivan that day might have tipped the balance of his health.'

'How did the police react to the news of his death?'

'No one really knew. There was a police constable called Stobart who attended the funeral. In fact, he had to take action as the coffin was lowered into the ground.'

'Why?'

'Joanna turned up, and while most people were paying their respects she came forward, tossed some earth on the grave and shouted, "Go to hell!" PC Stobart leapt forward and restrained her. He knew who she was, as he had taken a statement from her concerning her biological father a few months earlier.'

Brigit's thoughts were elsewhere. She was brooding on the man she thought had been following them on the coastal path. Uneasily she recalled seeing a man sitting in his car, deliberately feigning distraction as they drove away.

## 5

## 15 AUGUST 1972

Bob Silver rarely stayed the full fortnight. A sharp, dapper and very fit man, he was always on the go, seemingly unable to relax or switch into holiday mode. He would arrive after his family, invariably disappear for a few days during the vacation and then leave early. It was never explained why, other than that he led people to believe he was involved in high-powered meetings and deals back in London. His younger son Justyn was fond of remarking cryptically, 'He's important for being important.'

His wife, Margaret, a GP, was agreeable and long-suffering, and their three offspring seemed well adjusted. Henry, the eldest, in his mid-twenties, was a writer of sorts and was pursuing a career as a journalist. He had got a first in English at Oxford, an achievement that didn't attract the slightest bit of attention among the holiday fraternity. It was seen as insignificant compared with the fact that Justyn was in a rock band; that was really considered something. However, Henry's left-wing views could start an argument in an empty room – which it certainly became when he hit his political stride. His sister, Fiona, had followed in her mother's footsteps and qualified as a doctor. Justyn was expected to follow his father into the City but had got involved in a fledgling rock band in his last year at school and was planning to go on tour that autumn. He and his three fellow band members had deferred university places for a year to give their musical career a go.

Bob was furious. Justyn nearly didn't join his family on the holiday that year, but, faced with the prospect of an autumn of piling into a van and playing gigs in unglamorous locations across the length and breadth of Britain, he had decided on some last-minute vacation therapy in Cornwall.

Justyn would appear at odd times in the night and practise yoga – either in the downstairs lounge or else outside, if the dawn was breaking and the weather was reasonable. Tom and Bill used to tolerate him; they liked him and were irritated by him in equal measure, as he often woke them up. Some nights he didn't go to bed at all. On one occasion he saw his father pull up the drive in his white Jensen at one-thirty in the morning and, distracted from his yoga, went to ask him why he was coming in at that late hour. His father brushed past him, telling him to mind his own business.

Tom, who had been lurking within earshot, went to console the teenager, but Justyn said that was the way his father was. He confided in Tom that Bob wasn't much of a father, believing that money controlled everything, and he was unable to understand his youngest son not following him into the City. It was probably fair to say that the father–son relationship was at rock bottom. Justyn used to play Leonard Cohen's song 'Suzanne' while he practised yoga. His father had remarked it was the most depressing music he had ever heard, which became the trigger for his son to play the track incessantly.

Bob was an enigma. He defied stereotyping. He could be quite racy and charismatic, and yet his mood could quickly darken. He was involved with the administration of a West End theatre in some financial capacity and was a great supporter of the arts. In fact, the night of his mysterious late-night arrival back at the hotel he had been watching a play at the Minack Theatre on the west coast; it was rumoured that he was a significant benefactor. Bob's marriage appeared to be somewhat rocky, but Margaret seemed unperturbed by her husband's late return. Justyn, however, was angry with his father and told Tom he was worried that his parents might come to blows. It was around two in the morning by this time, and Tom had disappeared to get some tea. When he returned Justyn had decided to eavesdrop outside his parents' room.

All was quiet, so he returned to the lounge downstairs. He asked Tom where the Minack Theatre was, and Tom explained it was a remarkable open-air amphitheatre near Porthcurno. He said that during the summer months plays would start in daylight and finish after dusk. He described its stone seats and its breathtaking backdrop of a shimmering sunset over the sea beyond the stage, where dolphins could often be seen.

Justyn determined to take a group of friends to the theatre and bought seats for the following night. So Suzie Hughes-Webb, Caroline Jessops, Danny Galvin and Grant Morrison crammed into Justyn's Peugeot 204 and drove off to see the première of a play, a story based on the life of Sherlock Holmes and Dr Watson. Not long after it started, a terrible storm swept in. Thunder rolled as lightning struck almost directly over-head, and the principal players on the stage were soaked. The sea was several shades of black and grey, and Holmes had to ad-lib, 'What a terrible night to be out, Dr Watson.'

That night at the Minack Justyn and his friends spotted Bob with a young male companion. They appeared to be on cordial, even intimate, terms. Bob and his friend had watched *The Tempest* the previous evening, according to another hotel resident who had spotted them.

'I knew it. I knew it,' Justyn announced to the group.

Grant didn't believe he did for a moment but thought Justyn might have found the answer to a puzzle. On the way back to the hotel the five friends stopped off at a pub in St

Buryan, very much a spit-and-sawdust boozer. Justyn's father walked in a few minutes later with his escort and ordered drinks before spotting the group of teenagers at a nearby table. Startled, he began to stammer an introduction to his friend; this was highly unusual, given how self-assured and articulate Bob usually was. The younger generation viewed the scene, judgements written large on their faces, which generally glowered disapproval. Bob and his companion, Clive, downed their drinks in a hurry. Bob said they had to go, as he had to be in London the next day for an important meeting. Justyn, the eldest of the group and probably the most mature, remarked casually that it was a good job homosexuality had been legalized five years earlier. Overall, he seemed pretty relaxed about the situation, commenting it was 'just a drag', smiling, aware of his ironic use of word. The most awkward moment occurred when Herb Alpert's 'This Guy's in Love with You' started playing on the jukebox just as Bob and Clive were uttering hurried goodbyes.

Back at the hotel the teenagers dispersed around midnight after a late-night drink and some banter in the large lounge. Justyn, however, knew he was not ready for sleep and waited until he was alone before seeking out Tom. They talked for hours. Justyn confided in him the evening's events at the Minack and afterwards at the pub, asking him for advice.

Tom hesitated before replying, in the low boom of his powerful voice, 'I think you need to get him to see a doctor as soon as possible. I've heard about this condition, and I know some folk around here recommend electroshock treatment.'

Justyn regarded him quizzically and registered, with some clarity, the generational differences between them, no matter how much he liked Tom. He thanked him for his time and wise words, struggling to prevent himself from laughing at his own insincerity and resisting vocalizing his prevailing thought: Man, you are far out.

He entered the lift to go up to his third-floor bedroom, but just as the door was closing he saw his father walking into the hotel lobby, having rung the doorbell and been let in by Tom. He checked his watch – it was five-thirty in the morning.

# 6

## 17 AUGUST 1972

Richard Hughes-Webb leant across the table at dinner that evening and in a barely audible voice lambasted his wife. 'You bitch, you filthy little bitch.' With that he calmly stood up from the table, removed his white linen napkin from its position wedged above his bow tie and walked out of the restaurant. His wife, Yvie, a diminutive but striking woman who worked tirelessly on her appearance to belie her middle age, remained at the table triumphant as their children, Suzie and Tony, looked aghast.

A dramatic event earlier in the day had triggered this. Richard's first wife, Estelle, had paid an unexpected visit to the hotel. Theirs had been a short marriage, no more than five years, but the damage they did to each other would last until death parted them. While Richard had moved on, remarried and become master of his universe, both personally and professionally, Estelle very definitely had not, and she loathed Richard all the more for his apparent success and happiness.

After the divorce she had taken a young lover, a sculptor, who persuaded her to move west to Cornwall. It wasn't long before she caught him with someone closer to his own age, and her hatred for her ex-husband took centre stage in her life once more. She knew he went to Cornwall each August and at which hotel the family stayed; she had learnt this from a mutual friend. One day she hired a driver to take her from her home in St Mawes near Falmouth to the hotel, having ascertained Richard's presence there from a call to the switch-board. She arrived around six-thirty in the evening after drinking all day.

She told the driver to wait and staggered through the entrance of the hotel. She made it to the reception desk, where she immediately went on the offensive. 'Anyone seen that bastard ex-husband of mine? What's his name – Rickety Humphrey-Bumfrey.' With that she collapsed in a heap.

Richard was not best pleased to be called down to reception as he was running his pre-dinner bath. A man of routine, he always dressed formally in black tie for dinner, and he and Yvie were always in the bar at seven on the dot to place their order from the day's menu before being shown to their table at seven-forty-five. Yvie would match his elegance with her hair in a bird's-nest bun, stiff with hairspray, wearing a floor-length floral-print maxi gown with flowing sleeves that concealed her high platform shoes, chosen to buy her a few more inches. Her deep plunging neckline indicated a woman very much aware of her charms and prepared to display them. Their marriage had its tempestuous moments, but it was Estelle who seized the headlines that day.

Angered by the rude interruption to his cherished routine, the abhorrent vision of his former wife – an inebriated wreck of a human being – lying at his feet provoked an angry roar that could be heard throughout the hotel. 'What the devil are you doing here?'

'Don't be cross with me, Richie. I only want a little love and affection.'

At this point he picked his ex-wife off the floor and threw her over his shoulder, aided by Arnie Charnley, who then helped steer them out of the hotel. The two men saw the parked car in the drive, and Arnie hurried to open a back door through which Richard dumped the hapless Estelle. He gave the driver £10 and told him to take her home and never to let her darken his doors again. As she was driven away Estelle, barely conscious, her face smeared in rouge and crimson lipstick, cast a desperate glance at her former husband that was simultaneously pitiful and furious.

Richard walked calmly back inside the hotel, checked himself in the hallway mirror, adjusted his bow tie and proceeded to the bar to order a scotch on the rocks. By the time Yvie had joined him the story of Estelle's brief appearance was already well known.

His mood was not improved at dinner by Yvie goading him on another subject. 'So, Richard, what have you been doing in Zennor today?' she inquired, knowing this grenade would explode the moment it was delivered.

He decided to surprise his antagonistic spouse by ignoring the question and continuing to consume his cream of cauliflower soup, slurping louder than usual.

'Oh, come on, don't pretend to Suzie and Tony you haven't spent the day . . .'

With that he cursed angrily and left the dining-room. He wasn't prepared to enter into controversial dialogue with his second wife any more than he was with his first. He knew Yvie was intent on humiliating him about a relationship she was convinced he was conducting at his cottage in Zennor.

But he had other reasons for not wishing to discuss the subject. He knew that earlier in the day the police had made a discovery in an outhouse in the garden of the cottage. They had found parasite worm eggs containing infected larvae. Richard, upon being questioned, revealed that he had taken these from a London teaching hospital for use in experiments carried out on animals for the advancement of research into heart disease. The police had referred the discovery to their forensic team, who considered that worm eggs could be placed inconspicuously in food, as a result of which an intended victim could suffer life-threatening ascariasis infection. Richard had assured them that a human would need to eat extraordinarily large quantities for the toxin to have any serious adverse effects on his or her health. However, he was well aware that he was being monitored by the police, a thought that did not sit comfortably with him. So when Estelle made such an unwelcome intrusion back into his life and then Yvie decided to bait him he lost control.

The scene in the restaurant that night would have probably been quickly forgotten but for the fact that it was witnessed by the Vernon family at the next table. The son, Robert, wasted little time in telling his teenage friends at the hotel, 'We often see them argue, but this was really heavy.'

Richard's grey day was soon to become his black night. Upon leaving his family mid-meal he walked down the long hotel drive to the Office, which was situated a hundred yards on the right along the road leading to Carbis Bay. There he waited for an hour or so, knocking back several whiskies on his own. Eventually he was joined by a female companion, Grant's mother, Rose Morrison, who drove with him to his cottage at Zennor. The assignation went largely unnoticed except by Hector Wallace, the hotel's Olympian imbiber, who had already taken his customary place on his stool at the bar.

Later that evening, at around eleven, Richard walked unsteadily back up the drive towards the hotel, supported by Rose, who was both sober and alert. However, after twenty yards they were accosted by a shadowy figure emerging from a bush after a call of nature; they swiftly recognized him as Hector.

'Bloody hell,' bellowed Richard. 'You drunken old fool! You gave us a helluva shock.'

'Well, maybe you shouldn't be here together doing whatever you're doing.'

'Stop that nonsense,' Richard barked. 'You're so paralytic you can't even see straight.'

'I've seen enough.'

This prompted Richard to poke Hector repeatedly in the chest.

They were caught in car headlights by Tom Youlen, who was driving up the lane for his night shift and who pulled up sharply and rushed from his vehicle. 'Cut that out, sirs.'

Rose removed her high heels and hurried away. Hector calmly asked Tom for a lift up the drive, while Richard walked slowly back to the hotel, his mood now very dark indeed.

Later, at about two in the morning, Richard appeared in reception resembling a defeated boxer who couldn't sleep owing partly to injury but also to high adrenalin levels. It had been a truly grim day. He demanded that Tom get him a large scotch. The night porter refused, saying he had drunk enough and that the bar was locked anyway. He quoted from the Hotel Proprietors Act 1956.

Richard, not for the first time that night, became aggressive. 'Get me a drink, or I'll get you sacked in the morning.'

Tom called the manager, Mr Simpkins, who emerged from his flat adjoining the hotel and helped Tom bundle Richard out of the drawing-room and escort him to his bedroom.

The next day the episode seemed forgotten – but not by young Grant. He was extremely concerned by Robert Vernon's account of the scene in the dining-room and by Hector's tale of his mother joining Richard in the local pub before they then disappeared together. He persuaded his friend Danny Galvin to drive him to Zennor. As luck would have it, they spotted Richard heading for his Bentley and followed him out of the car park and down the drive. Danny tried to hold back, staying some three or four cars behind. When, ten or so minutes later, Richard pulled up at a modest cottage in Zennor, who should open the front door but Tom. As Danny and Grant parked in a nearby side street they immediately realized their cover had been blown. Marching towards them was a burly man with a red face and a huge neck. It was Bill, the other night porter from the hotel.

'He knows you've followed him, and Tom knows you saw him open the door. Now I've got news for you, young Mr Galvin. You and your friend Granted here are heading off in your motor, and you've seen nothing here today, have you, lads?'

The last remark lingered in the hinterland between statement and question, delivered in a strong West Country burr that left the recipients in no doubt of the answer that was expected.

'Oh yes we have,' replied Grant. 'You can't gag us. And the name is Grant,' he added.

Bill looked thunderously at the audacious teenager, and for a moment Grant thought the porter was going to punch him.

'Now look here, laddies. Either you head off or I make a phone call to the constabulary. Do I make myself plain?'

'OK,' said Danny. 'We'll go.'

'That be better. We don't want your folks up at the hotel hearing about sonny boys getting into trouble. And you have no idea what trouble you might find yourselves in,' concluded Bill, pleased with himself for achieving a stand-down.

On their return to the hotel the two boys bumped into Caroline Jessops as she walked through the car park, wearing a brown bikini with a hotel towel draped around her neck, fresh from a swim at the pool below.

'What have you two been up to?' she inquired, with a twinkle in her eye.

'Oh, just checking out the local golf course at Lelant,' Grant lied.

Caroline was amused at the response, not believing it but not sufficiently interested to challenge him.

'Why don't you play golf here?' she challenged, referring to the nine-hole pitch-and-putt course. 'I could caddy for you,' she added coquettishly.

Grant smiled, their eyes connecting, as if owning to a chemistry that was developing between him and this brown-eyed girl in a bikini. 'Great, let's play at four today.'

Danny put in, 'You can leave me out. Can't stand the game.' This provoked a wry smile from Grant, as he had to acknowledge defeat in their game of subterfuge, while Caroline broke into a broad involuntary grin.

As Grant and Caroline ambled around the nine-hole course later that day she probed him as to how he was feeling. 'You've been a bit weird lately.'

Grant admitted his upset at hearing of his mother's involvement with Richard Hughes-Webb. He revealed what Hector had told him, but she didn't register surprise; she already knew about the row at dinner, as Robert Vernon had been telling the world. At any rate it turned out she knew quite a lot about the Hughes-Webb family, as she and Suzie had become pretty close over the years.

'Did you know about her father and my mother?'

'Yes,' she replied, trying not to sound too wounding.

'Well, what do you know?'

Before Caroline could reply, Suzie came rushing up towards them, brandishing a five-iron and a putter. 'Can I join in?' she asked breezily.

## 7

# 18 AUGUST 1972

'I'll challenge the winner!'

Paul Galvin shouted at Grant Morrison and Justyn Silver, the folds of his belly falling over the top of his shorts as he watched them battle it out on the squash court. The two combatants needed no extra incentive, but eventually Grant emerged victorious and went straight into battle with Paul, who very quickly became incredibly sweaty. Galvin Senior was a smallish, stocky man with greasy, grey swept-back hair, and it soon became clear to Grant that he was cheating, reinventing the score at regular intervals and claiming some dodgy line calls in his favour. As he romped to a controversial victory he let out a roar emanating deep within the pit of his overfed stomach. Shaking hands heartily with his opponent and pretending to commiserate, he walked off the court with the triumphant look of a conquering Roman emperor.

'So that puts you in your place,' asserted Caroline, who had been the sole spectator on the balcony.

'I couldn't have cared less, but did you notice how brazenly he cheated?'

Caroline smiled, amused at how badly Grant was taking defeat; the validity or otherwise of the scoring was an arcane dark art to her.

Grant went on, 'And I was concerned that he'd worked up such a sweat and was wheezing so much – like a wounded elephant – he might have had a cardiac arrest at any moment.'

'Oh, come on. He beat you. Get over it,' she teased.

Grant was having none of it. 'I mean, what sort of man cheats at squash? Does he cheat in life, in business, too?' He continued his rant as they walked back into the hotel, where he promptly bumped into Danny Galvin.

'So, the old man thumped you,' Danny announced joyfully.

'Well, let's just say I didn't think the match was played on a completely level playing field.'

'Oh, that means Dad was up to his usual tricks, winning by hook or by crook,' Danny laughed.

'Well, you said it. I wouldn't like to accuse anyone.'

'No. Everyone knows Dad always cheats at games. He has to win at all costs, you see. There are people who say he cheats in business, but I'd rather not know.'

Paul Galvin's business dealings were largely mysterious, apart from the fact that he was a London-based accountant who commuted daily to his office in Holborn from his home in Chelmsford. However, later the same day Paul disappeared to visit a business venture of his own. He had used his experience and expertise advising clients in the property sector to set up some personal private speculation; in 1970 he had bought an old petrol station near Penzance and gained planning permission to knock it down and build three holiday homes.

By chance, that very day Paul's son, Danny, and Justyn Silver filled their cars with four friends each and drove off to the go-karting circuit at Penzance. *En route* Danny unexpectedly pulled his Mini off the main road. Justyn drew up behind him. Danny had spotted his father shouting and gesticulating at a group of people outside what looked like a new housing development. Unbeknown to the teenager, the buildings had been on the market for over a year. Paul had been unable to sell any of the houses and now had the bank breathing down his neck. Danny was later to discover that his father had borrowed to the hilt to build the houses. With costs spiralling and Paul failing to recoup any cash from property sales, the bank were threatening to foreclose, and the family home in Chelmsford would have to be sold to pay off the debts. There was a further twist, known only to Paul: the company contracted to undertake the building work, Sandersons of Penzance, had been recommended by Tom, the hotel porter. Tom's brother, Dickie, had worked for Sandersons for some thirty years as a plasterer. This brought the problem closer to home, as Dickie, Ivan's father, was now unlikely to receive his wages.

Danny alighted from his car to hear his father yelling 'You have done me' at someone who was obscured by the group in front. 'Come on out, you idiot. You have stitched me up, sold me down the river!'

Out of the group emerged Tom, for once looking sheepish and rather diminished. Paul used to enjoy a late-night brandy with the porters Tom and Bill, who would keep him company downing their 'rosy leas', as they called their tea in exaggerated Cockney accents.

In 1970, when Paul first told Tom about the plot of land he had bought in Penzance, Tom pointed him in the direction of Sandersons. When the houses didn't sell, Paul attributed this partly to a poor performance from the firm. With the cost overrun and the failure to find buyers, Paul was left in severe financial distress by early 1972. He deliberately collapsed his company, Galvin Properties Ltd; this triggered Sandersons' bankruptcy, as the firm was still owed 50 per cent of their fees. Tom, although blameless in the execution of the project, had wound up both his brother, Dickie, and Robin Sanderson, the owner of the company, by saying that Mr Galvin could still afford fancy hotel prices, living the life of luxury at the hotel on the hill, as he called it. Collapsing his company was Paul's way of protecting his financial well-being, as he had put all his assets into his wife's name to safeguard their home in Chelmsford.

As Tom moved forward from his position at the back of the group, Paul let rip. 'This is the fool who talked me into building in this pisspot town with your mickey-mouse company.'

At that moment Paul saw his son Danny coming towards him, while the others waited in the two cars.

'Dad,' Danny called out. 'Are you OK?'

'No, he's not OK. He's not OK at all,' said Robin Sanderson angrily.

Fortunately Danny's unexpected appearance had a calming effect on Paul, who returned to his car exclaiming that he had had enough for one day.

Danny saw the looks of thunder on the faces of Robin Sanderson and Dickie Youlen, but he addressed Tom. 'What's going on?'

The porter was speechless, but his brother was more forthcoming. 'Your father has cheated us – left me and my mates unpaid. And Mr Sanderson here tells us it's the end. He and his family have had this business for eighty bloody years, and now it's the bloody end!' Dickie roared.

Danny hastily withdrew from the scene and told his friends what he had just heard.

'Wow, that's heavy, man.' They fell silent for a few minutes before Caroline exclaimed that the scene with parents was becoming a real drag. Ten minutes later the teenagers were happily bashing into each other on the go-karting track, laughing their heads off.

Back at the hotel that evening the mood at the Galvins' table was even more muted than at that of the Hughes-Webbs. Danny obtained permission to leave after the main course. His father hadn't uttered a word since they sat down other than to bark his order from the *table d'hôte* menu at an unfortunate waitress.

Around eleven that night 'Puffin, shag, herring gull, gannet and chough' was heard in a deep Cornish baritone, floating into reception as Tom came on duty. Paul took a break from pacing around outside the hotel, dragging angrily on a cigarette, to utter in ominous tones, 'I'll sort him out.'

# 8

## PRESENT DAY

'Arnie Charnley always paid his bills in cash. When other guests were checking out with their credit cards he would wait at the back of the queue before producing what he called his "holding folding". He was a very popular figure who would entertain people with his risqué jokes and anecdotes.'

Grant was ploughing on relentlessly, regaling Brigit with further tales of the 1972 holiday as they trekked back towards the car after their walk from Cape Cornwall. 'The arrival of the Charnley family was a bit of a ritual. Arnie's Jaguar, his pride and joy, would pull up in front of the hotel, and he would commandeer the porter to assist. His wife, Lucy, whom he referred to as "the Duchess", would wait in the car until the luggage had been brought in, preparing for her grand entrance – powdering her nose, applying eyeliner, lipstick and so on. It was generally believed that he was terrified of her. They arrived off the night train, which transported the Jaguar. Tom always made sure he was on duty for the Charnleys' arrival, as he and Arnie had a special arrangement. Arnie's main obsession in life was the horses; betting, that is. He had long since promised the Duchess that he had given up, claiming he hadn't been inside a bookies' for five years. Indeed, he didn't need to visit bookmakers in Cornwall, as Tom placed his bets for him. In fact, Tom even looked after Arnie's stockpile of readies, as he didn't dare risk keeping cash in the bedroom or the car in case the Duchess made a discovery.'

Brigit listened patiently before speculating, 'Don't tell me, Tom lost all Arnie's money and got the blame for placing bets on the wrong horses.'

'Not exactly. In fact, that last summer Arnie was very successful. The day he arrived he told Tom to put £50 on Vivaque, at thirty-to-one, running in the four-forty at Newton Abbott. When it won, Arnie found it very hard to conceal his joy from the Duchess but wasted no time in regaling the rest of us, so much so that I still remember the horse's name.

'Each morning Arnie used to set off for an early jog, usually with Richard Hughes-Webb, Bob Silver and Paul Galvin. Tom would see them trot off at seven, enjoying some good-natured banter. They would run down through the woods, next to the cascades, before crossing the road to the beach where they would run for about one and a half miles until they hit the nudist part, which was normally the cue for some rather more vulgar banter. "Did you see her? She was about a hundred and nine!" They would usually reappear at the hotel still amusing themselves with their puerile humour but would then snap out of it pretty sharpish.'

'Are we still focusing on potential murder suspects or have we moved on to "Carry On" film territory?' Brigit did not see the relevance of all this.

'Actually this is relevant, because one morning as they came back through reception panting and sweating Tom was quick to ask Arnie for a private word. At this time I'd decided to stalk Hughes-Webb after hearing about the incident with my mother in the drive, and I happened to be loitering in reception and witnessed a bit of a scene. The others, who all had their own secrets known to Tom, moved away and returned swiftly to their rooms, eager to shower after their morning exertions. Tom seemed fraught, pacing around in an uncharacteristically anxious manner. He informed Arnie that he'd had a burglary at his cottage and that all Arnie's cash, so carefully secreted with him, had been stolen.

'"What?" exclaimed Arnie. "All my dosh? You can't do this to me. What if it's gone for ever? How will I pay the bill here? And, more importantly, what will I tell the Duchess?" By this stage his face was puce, and he was jumping up and down as he sprayed angry words at Tom, who quickly outlined an impromptu plan. The Duchess loved the gardens of Cornwall, and Tom knew Arnie was bored stiff by them, so Tom suggested that he drive her to Caerhays Castle on the south coast – at least a ninety-minute journey. "And while she's there you can go and see my nephew Ivan, who I think may be responsible, as only he knew where I kept the suitcase with the cash." Arnie was stunned. First he had been advised that several hundred pounds of his money – a fortune in those days – had been stolen, and now he had to turn sleuth to interrogate Ivan. He considered the proposal. At this stage he would have considered anything. He exhaled deep breaths saying "Calm, calm, calm" to himself while clutching his left arm with his right hand.'

'So did he go along with the plan?'

'With some of it. He thought the Duchess would love being driven by Tom acting as chauffeur, and he had heard his wife mention that Caerhays possessed over two hundred different types of rhododendrons. She had often badgered him to take her there, and Arnie couldn't think of anything he wanted to do less. He quickly got the Jag insured for Tom to drive, which would enable him to stay behind and watch his beloved Lancashire playing a Gillette Cup semi-final cricket match on television. Arnie instructed Tom to inform the police about the cash, but the porter was insistent that he couldn't let the police near his cottage, saying, "Don't let daylight in on magic." In the end they compromised, with Tom saying he would tackle Ivan himself.'

'I should think Arnie was pretty anxious, wasn't he?'

'Yes but he couldn't show it in case the Duchess noticed. The following day we all witnessed the hilarious scene of Tom wearing a peaked cap and dark suit collecting the Duchess and chaperoning her into the back seat of the Jag. He was given instructions as to where to park the car, when to speak to her and even to address her as "My Lady".'

'That woman clearly had no idea of what a ridiculous figure she must have cut.'

'Too true. We were suppressing fits of laughter at the Royal Progress as Tom slowly drove his VIP passenger down the drive.'

'So what was achieved by this diversion?'

'Two-thirds of diddly-squat. The Duchess enjoyed her day out enormously, convincing everyone she met that she was some sort of minor royal but that protocol prevented her from saying any more. Tom later revealed they all thought she was most strange. Meanwhile Arnie, free of the worry of upsetting his wife for the time being, settled down in the TV room to watch several hours of cricket. He bore a striking resemblance to Lancashire's highly successful captain at that time, Jackie Bond; he was actually seen on the hotel lawn one day enjoying a clotted-cream tea while signing autographs as Jackie Bond for a group of senior citizens who had disembarked from a coach. Apparently he tried to charge for this. Sadly for Arnie, Ted came along and spoilt his game by asking, "What's he been telling you?" Arnie's new-found admirers soon abandoned him. No one found this more amusing than Arnie himself who delighted in telling the story.'

'But what happened to the cash?' asked Brigit.

'Well, Tom went to see Ivan, who, predictably, said he didn't know what he was talking about, which Tom had no option but to accept. Arnie was devastated. He had pinned his hopes on Ivan being the culprit and returning the cash.

'Arnie's attitude to Tom changed overnight. There was no more banter, just hostility. He told Tom he had better find his money pretty damn quick or he'd call the police. Tom, feeling cornered, countered that he would tell the Duchess everything. Arnie couldn't face that, as he feared his wife's wrath like nothing else, so he vowed untold trouble for Tom if he didn't return the cash by the following Wednesday. He added that he might have to get some funny people he knew up north involved.

'The following Thursday we were all scheduled to leave the hotel, and Arnie was very exercised about checking out with his family, fearing he would be unable to settle the bill. His two children, Nick and Jenny, were made aware of his predicament but were ordered not to tell their mother. Both adored their father, for all his faults, and, knowing only too well the grief he would receive from their mother, they needed no persuading.

'Meanwhile, fearing the worst, Arnie approached his friends for a loan to pay the bill. First refusal came from Ted Jessops, who said it was a bad time for him to loan money as his factory had recently burnt down and the insurance company was being sticky. Second refusal came from Paul Galvin, who revealed the problem of the failed building project in Penzance and his worries of being wiped out. Next up Bob Silver said he would see him right but disappeared on the Thursday for some high-powered meeting in London and didn't return for the rest of the holiday. In desperation Arnie finally turned to Richard Hughes-Webb, who said, "I am a heart surgeon, not a loan shark", and left Arnie in no doubt that he did not approve of anyone being unable to pay their bill. Arnie promised that he would drive to Croydon the weekend following the holiday and repay the loan in cash, but Richard observed him disapprovingly before exclaiming, "No chance."'

## 9

# 20 AUGUST 1972

The police swarmed into the hotel on Sunday lunchtime, alighting at breakneck speed from three panda cars with blaring sirens, tyres screeching to a halt outside the front entrance. This followed a call from the ambulance services after the Sunday-morning churchgoers had discovered Tom collapsed in the lane near Zennor. The senior paramedic at the scene had been alarmed by the state Tom was in and by the comments made by the group in the car who found him. The police promptly took statements from all four: the GP Margaret Silver, Anne Jessops, Yvie Hughes-Webb and Robert's father Mark Vernon. The words uttered by Tom electrified the investigation: 'It was him. Him from the hotel. He said he would . . . if I spoke.'

The police had real fears that a murderer was at large, but the scene that greeted them at the hotel was highly incongruous. The residents were tucking into roast beef with huge Yorkshire puddings as the hotel manager, James Simpkins, was alerted to the police's arrival by his receptionist. Simpkins had been reading the Sunday papers in his flat adjoining the hotel but, as the duty manager for the day, was on call if required. He was attired in a morning suit with striped black-and-grey trousers. He donned his black jacket over his grey waistcoat, straightened his cream tie and wasted no time in marching to the hotel lobby, looking every bit the archetypal hotel manager.

'What's going on?' he asked, determined to take a firm grip on whatever was occurring. The police officers, who by this stage numbered eight or nine, got straight to the point.

'We need to interview your staff and guests immediately. This is an inquiry into an attempted murder.'

Simpkins was aghast at the chaotic scene unfurling in front of him and started to feel faint. The last words he heard were along the lines of, 'Your night porter has been poisoned and has alleged that someone at the hotel is responsible.'

As the words sank into his consciousness, he collapsed, chipping his two front teeth on the reception desk as he fell heavily to the ground. His wife Jean emerged from their flat and screamed as she saw him unconscious with a pool of blood seeping from his mouth. She soon regained control, and an ambulance was summoned. It wasn't long before Simpkins was being transported to the Royal Cornwall Hospital in Truro.

Guests came running out of the dining-room. One clumsily bumped into a large silver trolley used for gueridon service, lost his footing and tripped over the waiter who was pushing the trolley towards a table. An atmosphere of chaos ensued. There was a dearth of senior staff on hand. Simpkins had rostered himself as the duty manager for the whole weekend, giving his two assistants – a deputy who was principally in charge of hotel bedrooms and a food and beverage manager – the weekend off. The barman, Sidney, tried to take control, but it was soon clear he was out of his depth. The head waiter, Luigi, came running out of the restaurant shouting and complaining that his customers were upset; he considered this a very bad state of affairs, as upset customers were, in his experience, bad tippers. At this point Richard Hughes-Webb took control, suggesting that everyone should calm down.

'Who are you?' inquired Inspector Roy Higham, a lanky,

earnest-looking man with a pencil-thin moustache and wiry black hair parted in the middle. His stooping gait gave an appearance of awkwardness, but he was the senior police officer at the scene, and he wanted people to know it.

'My name's Richard Hughes-Webb. I'm a surgeon, and I'm trying to enjoy a fortnight's holiday here with my family, as are a great number of other people. Now I suggest you do what you need to do, Inspector, in an orderly fashion and come into this room through here.' His manner was authoritative and his presence almost overbearing, and the police, momentarily nonplussed, allowed themselves to be ushered into the empty flat of the now-absent Simpkins and his wife. Once ensconced there Arnie, by now aware of the commotion, started liberally dispensing sherry in an attempt to lighten the mood. Richard persuaded Inspector Higham to reduce his numbers, as he felt it was highly unlikely there was a murderer on the loose. Six of the police left the scene, initially to check around the premises for suspicious persons and were soon seen departing down the drive.

The scene in the flat's living-room became somewhat farcical, as Hector Wallace, returned from his late-morning foray to the Office, joined the throng, eagerly accepting Arnie's offer of a sherry. 'A free tipple is never to be declined. That would be most rude.'

At that moment Ted Jessops entered, looking whiter than a newly starched hotel bedsheet, asking what all the fuss was about.

'Fuss from the fuzz,' announced Hector, chortling loudly as he downed the sherry with alacrity.

Paul Galvin was haranguing the young unfortunate receptionist at the desk, threatening to seek compensation for the disturbance his family was suffering. Spotting the door open to the flat on the opposite side of the main corridor from the reception desk, he joined the assembled throng inside.

'What in the name of Adam and Eve . . . ?' he said, seeing Hughes–Webb, Charnley and Wallace drinking sherry while chatting to the three remaining policemen.

'Pretty random stuff, Paul,' responded Hughes–Webb, still attempting to control events. 'Poor old Tom, the porter, has suffered a stroke in the lane near his home in Zennor. He was discovered by our morning churchgoers. The inspector here and his good team are trying to put two and two together and, I rather fear, have made five.'

Inspector Higham looked stunned at this, but before he could attempt to wrestle the initiative back the group was confronted by the arrival of the head receptionist.

'I came as soon as I could,' she announced. She was a strident, rather matronly woman of advancing years. Her face looked as if it had been created from fine bone china and her voice was a little on the shrill side. She introduced herself. 'I'm the head receptionist, Thora Fabian, and I've been called on my day off by Sally on the front desk. She's new, you know, so I thought I'd better get here fast. Obviously I wouldn't be dressed like this if I were on duty. Heavens, no.'

As she joined the group in the flat's living-room she seemed more concerned with her attire than with the scene she encountered. She plainly felt self-conscious standing in front of four of the hotel guests while wearing mufti. The presence of the police didn't seem to faze her at all; what concerned her was not having the time to get herself appropriately dressed for her position with her customary layers of thick make-up. 'So, please tell me, what's the problem?' she inquired, trying desperately to establish authority.

On being told about Tom she asked if she could speak to the police in private. She related the episode on the beach in

1968. Tom had shared the story with senior staff at a Heads of Department meeting and had mentioned the angry encounter between Ted and Ivan just a few days earlier. She also suggested that the police contact Bill Treverney, the other night porter, before jumping to any conclusions. PC Gary Stobart thanked her for her information and asked for her contact details.

The porter Bill was unavailable that afternoon. He and Tom worked out the week's rota between them; both liked working six days, or rather nights, with just the one day off. They overlapped on five days, with Bill taking Sundays off and Tom absenting himself on Mondays. Bill, a creature of habit, would hit his local pub on Sunday lunchtimes and could often be seen singing his way home at about five in the afternoon. He would get back, collapse in a chair in his front room, put on the television and wake up freezing cold some hours later with his bladder close to bursting and the test card on the television. After relieving himself he would stagger up the stairs to his bed and awake around eleven the next morning. However, on this particular day Bill had managed to climb the stairs and go to bed in a more conventional way. Some years earlier his wife, Sarah, had despaired of his unusual life-style and had left him for a coalman from Redruth. Popular legend had it that she had departed on a Sunday afternoon knowing that Bill wouldn't notice that she was missing until at least Monday lunchtime.

On this Sunday the police hammered on the door but, getting no reply, resolved to interview Bill the next day. They switched their attention to the hospital in Truro where they found Tom Youlen in a stable condition. However, they made no progress, as he was now completely mute. James Simpkins, meanwhile, was in casualty awaiting treatment for his facial injuries, and the police were forbidden access to him.

Gossip in the hotel had turned to the disappearance of Bob Silver, who had last been seen three days earlier. His wife told all and sundry that she didn't have a clue where he was. However, she was being economical with the truth. She had discovered him on the Saturday afternoon in one of the art galleries in St Ives enjoying the company of a young male friend. She had decided to keep this information to herself while she thought things through, although unbeknown to her she was not the only person to know about her errant husband's connection to the gallery.

# 10

## 21 AUGUST 1972

Ted Jessops couldn't get out of bed on that last Monday morning; he was severely depressed, so heavy-headed that the rest of his body had become inert. He had no energy and felt in a sort of neutral state, like a car that couldn't move forwards or go into reverse; he had no means of achieving motion. Anne, his good-natured wife, whose patience had become increasingly tested, was at her wits' end. Ted had stopped talking and was haunted by the Philip Larkin poem 'This Be the Verse'. He was facing up to his sins and now knew that you reap what you sow. He kept thinking he should admit Joanna's existence, apologize and make it up to all concerned. He was not the first man to father a child out of wedlock, for goodness' sake, he kept repeating to himself. But he was like a politician issuing statements of innocence while in a downward spiral. He had denied paternity with regard to Joanna so many times that to admit it now would leave his credibility in tatters. He suspected that Tom, through Ivan's evidence, might incriminate him and felt that ultimately he had let all three of his children down.

Anne watched as Ted lay in bed staring at the ceiling. She noticed he had a sheet of paper next to him, picked it up and read the Larkin poem. It made little sense to her, but she was distressed at its effect on her husband. He had added his own line underneath: 'I have reaped what I have sown.'

Anne, who by her own admission had little interest in

poetry, was completely disoriented by this. She placed the piece of paper back on the bed and took another uncomprehending look at her husband, whose eyes resembled clear glass. Then she left the room, placing a 'Do not disturb' sign on the outside of the door. She went down in the lift and in the lobby bumped into Bob Silver's wife, Margaret. She asked to speak to her in private. The two women withdrew to a small lounge where they found themselves alone. Anne poured her heart out about Ted over a coffee. Margaret then suggested they should invite Richard Hughes-Webb, of whom she was rather in awe, to join them. As if on cue he walked into the lounge carrying a copy of *The Lancet*, looking for a quiet place to read. He listened to Anne's anxieties about Ted and suggested they summon a local GP as soon as possible and offered to brief the GP. Anne, who was very distressed, readily agreed to this. It didn't take Richard long to take charge and, on ascertaining from reception the name of the local doctor on call, arranged to meet him on his own. For this Anne was extremely grateful.

Meanwhile the police had been busy. Bill Treverney received a visit at eight on the Monday morning, just as he was rejoining the human race after his Sunday excess. Initially he was grumpy and told the police to bugger off, which didn't go down too well. Inspector Higham, PC Stobart and a small team of officers got heavy; doors were slammed, officers shouted and Bill found himself being knocked about a bit. He soon revealed all. Apart from incriminating Ted Jessops, whose story was beginning to become familiar to the police, he revealed details of Paul Galvin's failed property development in Penzance, Richard Hughes-Webb's activities at his cottage in Zennor, Arnie Charnley's stockpile of cash taken from Tom's cottage in Zennor and Justyn Silver's angst at discovering his father's presumed homosexuality. Tom had clearly breached Justyn's confidence by telling all to his colleague Bill.

The police interviewed Tom's nephew, Ivan, that afternoon and took Arnie Charnley into custody that evening. It was at this point that his daughter, Jenny, had rushed into the disco in a panic. It was the following afternoon, on the Tuesday, while Danny Galvin was driving his friends to the beach at Sennen Cove, that warrants were made for the arrests of Richard Hughes-Webb, Ted Jessops, Bob Silver and Paul Galvin. Arnie Charnley was released on bail, paid for by his wife, who declared it most odd that he claimed not to have any money. This was to precipitate the collapse of the marriage of Arnie and Lucy 'the Duchess' Charnley; it was to prove a permanent marital breakdown.

The police started reviewing staff records at the hotel and, following a detailed conversation with Simpkins, set up some interviews: one with a sous chef with an attitude problem and another with a former linen porter, an itinerant Kiwi who had started a fire in one of the outbuildings and been sacked. He was tracked down living rough in St Ives. These were routine interviews with a few people with whom Tom had crossed swords and didn't produce any strong lines of inquiry. Tom never minced his words but was generally a popular figure with the other staff, even though he wouldn't talk to any new members of staff until they had been there for three months, dismissing newcomers as 'just passing through' until they proved worthy of his consideration.

'Motive and opportunity, Police Constable. Motive and opportunity,' Inspector Higham impressed on his subordinate PC Stobart. The police concluded that there were five suspects staying in the hotel, all of whom had secrets – some darker than others – known to Tom. They had established that he had consumed the toxic substance at around ten on Sunday morning, some two and a half hours after he had returned home from his night shift. Any one of the five suspects could have visited his cottage at that time. Not one was in church at that precise time, and as the Sunday papers hadn't arrived that day several guests had gone into town to buy their own. So, on the face of it, none of the five suspects had an alibi and all of them had the opportunity. Furthermore they all had reasons to want Tom to keep his mouth shut.

# 11

# PRESENT DAY

'Bob Silver's young friend Clive Holford had endured a harsh childhood in a village near Tintagel.' Grant was continuing to talk about the past to Brigit as they drove back to their cottage. 'He was the only child of Ken and Mary Holford, and he had grown up in a dysfunctional family where Ken's short temper had been the prevailing force. His mother was a gentle soul who helped make pottery for a local trader and lived in fear of her husband, who was in and out of jobs, mainly as a farm labourer but sometimes part-time bar work. Ken soon degenerated into a life of wife-beating and son-terrorizing – followed by bouts of remorse and self-loathing.

'By the age of fifteen Clive had seen and heard enough, and he ran away. His life became one of itinerant squatting, including a couple of years in a disused manor house near St Austell. This was one of many buildings in Cornwall that had once belonged to a prominent aristocratic family but which had fallen into disrepair after the family had moved elsewhere. One day in 1971 Bob Silver visited this house with clients from the building trade interested in acquiring it and converting it into a hotel and leisure resort. While inspecting the decaying rooms Bob and his associates heard an unexpected noise coming from one of them. At first they thought it might be a trapped bird but on entering discovered the unfortunate Clive cowering in a corner surrounded by a few meagre belongings and items of food. On the floor, quite out of place, they saw several rather fine drawings. "Don't hit me," whimpered the boy, and they were quick to reassure him that he was in no physical danger. Bob found himself overwhelmed by a sense of tenderness for the terrified teenager and tried to ascertain why he was living in this fashion.'

'With three children of his own, did he really need any further responsibility? His relationship with Justyn didn't sound particularly good,' said Brigit.

'That was the point. His three children were, to all intents and purposes, grown up and had all hugely benefited from Bob's patronage, as he saw it, by being sent to private schools. They had enjoyed a privileged background very different from his own.'

'Which was?'

'He was an orphan, growing up in Plymouth in a home established by a merchant seamen's charity. Through hard work, intelligence, energy and opportunism he had risen in life to a position he could not have dreamt of as a child. So when he saw Clive Holford crouching in the corner of a derelict building, terrified of being hit and appearing all alone in the world, it plainly touched a nerve. And so began Bob's patronage of the boy, helping him get his life together and encouraging his talent as an artist. That Saturday afternoon in St Ives was the launch day for Clive's studio. It must have been a significant moment for both of them.'

'All of which would be fine and very heart-warming had Bob maintained a purely platonic relationship with Clive, but you said they were caught in an intimate situation at the Minack Theatre.'

'But he did keep things platonic. He took Clive under his wing and demonstrated a paternal love and guidance missing in his relationship with his own children, the youngest of whom he deemed deeply ungrateful. Their being together at the theatre was a perfectly innocent father–son relationship – hardly untoward behaviour.'

'It would be seen as strange these days.'

'Oh, piffle! Forming a platonic, paternalistic relationship hardly makes Bob a paedophile.'

'So why couldn't he come clean with his family and friends?'

'He wanted to, but he didn't know how. It seems that he always remained insecure about his childhood and had an irrational fear of returning to the abandoned and penniless world of his past. He didn't understand why his relationships with his own children were not better. He simply felt a stronger bond with Clive, who adored him as the father he had never had. Several times Bob wanted to tell Margaret, when she suspected a gay relationship had developed, but she didn't want to discuss the subject of Clive. She was burying her head in the sand for the sake of her career and her family. Of course, it would have been far better if he had told the truth. As it was, the rumour mill was in full flow, particularly when it was reported that Bob didn't return to the hotel until five-thirty the following morning after we spotted him with Clive at the Minack and subsequently in the pub.'

'So why did Bob return so late then?'

'There is a particularly unfortunate aspect to that episode. Do you remember me saying that on the way back from the open-air theatre Bob and Clive stopped off at a pub in St Buryan where Justyn, myself, Suzie Hughes-Webb, Caroline Jessops and Danny Galvin were having a drink?'

'Yes – and Bob was highly embarrassed.'

'Very much so, yes. But whereas Bob was embarrassed Clive was mortified for a different reason. He had spotted his father serving behind the bar. They had exchanged glances, and Clive was very relieved to get out of the pub before Ken could speak to him. The lad had started to feel faint and was literally shaking as they left. When Bob dropped Clive back at his bedsit in Hayle, which Bob paid for, Clive revealed the horror of seeing his father again and the terror he felt that he might follow him home. Bob agreed to stay in his car outside until dawn broke to keep watch as Clive went into his bedsit to sleep.'

'So there's no motive there, and Bob should have been eliminated from suspicion.'

'Not necessarily,' said Grant mysteriously.

## 12

## 22 AUGUST 1972

Richard Hughes-Webb was a man with an intimidating presence. On entering a room people would often stop in mid-conversation to acknowledge him. It wasn't so much his impressive height but, rather, his head, which was dispro-portionately large. He had a distinctive Roman nose and thick eyebrows below a largely bald pate flecked by a few strands of white hair on each side. On close observation of others Richard's eyes would drill through theirs, causing the impres-sion that he knew whatever sins they had committed. It was quite unnerving, but his confidence didn't stop with his appearance; he was mentally very alert and dominating. He was also prone to making speeches at every opportunity. It could be another family's celebration, such as an eighteenth birthday, and before the appropriate parent or sibling could speak Richard would be on his feet announcing the toast.

On Tuesday 22 August it was Inspector Higham's and PC Stobart's task to arrest Richard and bring him in for question-ing. As they approached the hotel Stobart revealed more than a little apprehension at their forthcoming morning's work and awkwardly slowed his step. 'This isn't going to be easy, guv. This Hughes-Webb bloke has quite . . . an aura about him.'

'An aura? I'd call it a nuclear-free zone, protecting him from what ordinary mortals have to contend with,' Higham remarked, also clearly daunted by the task ahead of them. 'But villains come in many shapes and sizes, from ragamuffins to

Lord Haughty-Haughtys. And don't forget we're the ones with the blue uniforms and badges.' At this Higham allowed himself a little chuckle, which Stobart knew was his cue to join in, laughing heartily but knowing his place in the pecking order.

On arrival at the hotel they asked for Richard at the reception desk. Miss Fabian looked initially alarmed and soon her face assumed a look of utter indignation as she protested shrilly, 'Are you absolutely sure, Inspector?' A determined look on the Inspector's face ensured common sense got the better of her, and she swiftly located Richard at breakfast.

After initially resisting Miss Fabian's entreaty Richard emerged from the dining-room with a face like a volcano on the point of eruption. His left cheek had the unusual characteristic of twitching just before he lost his temper. He remarked loudly and imperiously that he was awaiting his kippers, before demanding, 'What in the name of earth's creation is all this about?'

The Inspector's nerve appeared to desert him. 'I . . . I . . . I . . . I . . . er . . . er . . . am . . .' he stuttered as he recalled how he had been intimidated by this man on Sunday. He knew he had to assert himself now, and he pulled himself together. 'I am asking you to accompany us to the local police station, sir.'

'The man's completely insane,' barked Richard so loudly that all in earshot were transfixed by the live theatre.

Yvie rushed out of the restaurant, saw the look on her husband's face and pointed out in a firm voice that even Richard had learnt not to challenge, 'You had better go. Resisting arrest is not an option – for anyone.'

Her husband continued to share his opinion of the local constabulary with the assembled throng at the top of his voice, as he reluctantly accompanied the officers. 'This is a scandal. Heads will roll, you know.'

Higham's face was crimson. He could not recall ever arresting a suspect as imposing and authoritative as Richard Hughes-Webb. In the Inspector's experience, criminals simply weren't like this, whatever he had asserted to his assistant on the way to the hotel.

The police, although intimidated by their suspect, had been purposeful elsewhere. On the Thursday before making this arrest, they had found parasite worm eggs in an outhouse at Richard's cottage in Zennor and had tested them at their forensic laboratory. Results not only confirmed the toxic nature of the larvae but established that the substance ingested by the porter on Sunday morning was the same.

Under interrogation Richard reluctantly admitted that they were being cultivated for use in a local animal science park with which he was involved, adding in a rather patronizing manner that this fact was already known to the local constabulary. He went on to say more bombastically that he was at the cutting edge of research into heart disease and that this involved testing the effects of such toxins on the cardiovascular systems of mammals. 'And if you and future generations of Highams and Stobarts would like to enjoy longer, healthier lives you should damn well support such activities.'

Richard's condescending and arrogant manner finally caused Inspector Higham to snap. 'I am placing you under arrest for the poisoning of Tom Youlen,' he thundered, taking control, his face red, his cheeks pinched in anger. 'But first you are going to take us to this animal science place and stop treating us like Mr Plods from the village farm.'

'I know where it is, sir,' interrupted PC Stobart, hurriedly trying to placate his superior, who he had begun to fear might suffer a coronary and require his suspect's specialist skills. The veins on Inspector Higham's face looked fit to burst, so the

Constable suggested they left for the science park immediately.

On the way Richard regained some of the initiative, addressing his two captors as if he was holding forth at some major medical conference. 'Look, I understand you are rattled at the discovery of poor Tom having eaten some of these worm eggs and having suffered a terrible stroke. It's an awful tragedy, a terrible thing, but I can assure you I never encouraged him to do so. He was a charming fellow. I liked him.' Richard sought to calm the situation while feeling smug at getting under the Inspector's skin. 'Moreover I have an alibi who can confirm where I was at the time of Tom's ingestion of the eggs. I would also like the name of the Chief Superintendent of your force.' The last remark was delivered in an especially crisp and deliberate tone.

The police remained silent, once again unsure how to handle their prime suspect. Inspector Higham regained some composure, and by the time they had finished their investigation at the science park he had decided to let the surgeon off with a caution. He had by then received information from one of his officers that Richard's alibi was watertight. Grant Morrison's mother, Rose, had accompanied him to get the Sunday-morning papers when the delivery failed at the hotel; she had further added in her witness statement that she and Richard had then gone for a drive, returning to the hotel at around midday.

The police returned the vindicated and overbearing Richard Hughes-Webb to the hotel shortly before lunch and headed back to their station feeling frustrated. It was some time after they left the hotel car park before their gloomy silence was broken.

'The problem with people like him', remarked Inspector Higham, 'is they play the game from the top. If we don't get everything right, they do us; they do us every time, these nobs. They have the money and the power, and their lawyers do the rest – and we get done.'

'Done like the kipper he didn't have for breakfast,' rejoined PC Stobart, warming to his theme, successfully lightening the mood and regarding his joke as superior to anything the Inspector could offer.

'Oh, very good, Police Constable,' Higham chuckled. 'Very good indeed.'

'And who does he think he is anyway?' continued Stobart, sensing he was on a roll. 'Carrying out experiments down here in Zennor like he's Dr bleeding Frankenstein. Come to think of it, he looks like the monster.'

As they pulled up at the police station car park the men's mild amusement at the first joke gave way to proper laughter at the second, and for a while they couldn't talk. They remained in their seats until some of their composure returned. Alighting from the car they were spotted by the Chief Superintendent, who shouted loftily across at them, 'You both look happy today.'

Inspector Higham felt something sharp prick his spine.

# 13

## PRESENT DAY

'Paul Galvin had one of those irritating faces that seemed to be smiling at you all the time. Even when meeting people for the first time he had an inane, welcoming sort of grin that made you think it was an agreeable meeting of old friends, when actually you often felt like punching him in the face.'

'So, he smiles at you, and you want to punch him. That's nice.'

'Well, not really,' continued Grant. 'He was always immaculately turned out, even on the squash court, until he started sweating profusely. He appeared to radiate joy all around unless a financial issue arose, which would affect his mood dramatically. The police had heard all about his failed property development in Penzance and had taken a statement from Tom's brother, Dickie, who worked for Sandersons. The local constabulary had formed an opinion that Paul's conduct was beyond the pale and had accordingly already cast him as a villain, particularly on hearing that he blamed Tom for the whole disaster. There was, naturally, a suspicion that Paul had a motive for hurting Tom, but the position became considerably worse for him when Bill, the other night porter, revealed that he had seen Paul in earnest conversation with Ivan Youlen the morning after Tom's collapse. Remember, Ivan was not just Tom's nephew but also Dickie's son, and Dickie was seriously out of pocket thanks to Paul.'

'The son that Dickie was sort of estranged from because

Ivan fathered a child out of wedlock?' asked Brigit. 'So when and where did this earnest chinwag occur?'

'At about ten in the morning they were seen having an animated conversation outside the newsagent in Zennor. Paul had gone to get his Sunday paper.'

'And who saw them?'

'Arnie Charnley. It seemed the non-delivery of the Sunday papers had given several people reason to visit the newsagent in Zennor at around the same time, since no one had offered to get them for anyone else. When Arnie joined the scene he realized this was Tom's nephew who had been suspected of stealing his cash from the cottage.'

'So how did the police know about the row, and how did they deal with it?

'They received a tip-off at about midday from an anonymous caller about the scene outside the newsagent.'

'Who from?'

'Ted Jessops,' announced Grant triumphantly.

'I thought you said Ted was lying comatose in bed, staring at the wall glassy-eyed and unable to communicate.'

'That was on the Monday. On Sunday Ted had been very active. Don't forget he knew exactly who Ivan was and had his own reason for reporting what was going on. So the police returned to the hotel at midday on Tuesday afternoon and arrested Paul Galvin and Ted Jessops. We were on the beach at Sennen Cove at the time and didn't hear of the excitement until we got back at about six.'

'And what about the scene in Zennor? Did you find out what Paul and Ivan were discussing?' asked Brigit.

'Well, it wasn't the Test Match. Ivan was close to assaulting Paul, apparently accusing him of ruining his family. Ivan was particularly foul-mouthed and abusive.'

'Unsurprising, given Ivan's precarious financial position and the fact that his father was left unpaid by a collapsed company which was probably his only source of regular employment. I reckon that would seriously unhinge most people.'

'Yes,' continued Grant. 'The problem now was there were too many suspects for the Old Bill to get their heads around. Richard had been released thanks to his alibi. Paul and Ted had been rounded up like cattle on the Tuesday afternoon. And, don't forget, Ivan was in Zennor at ten on Sunday morning. Furthermore, Arnie had been arrested the previous day and released on bail.'

'Sunday morning papers didn't come,' Brigit sang quietly.

Grant interrupted. 'It was Wednesday morning papers didn't come. Sunday morning was creeping like a nun.' He immediately apologized, but the Beatles had always been his favourite band.

'Whatever. If Ted Jessops grassed up the others, who grassed up Ted?'

'Ivan,' said Grant emphatically, now quite pleased at how Brigit was getting up to speed. 'Ivan spotted the Jessops' brown Rover as Ted tried to leave the scene outside the newsagent in a hurry.'

'That man really should have changed his car!' exclaimed Brigit.

Grant grinned. 'Yes. Ivan reported it straight away to the police, and it was very much a case of "People in glass houses shouldn't throw stones." It didn't take the police long to trace the phone call to a box near by, although Ted always denied he'd made the call. I think making that call, grassing on a mate, triggered Ted's slide into depression. He was trying to finger Ivan, but it backfired.'

'What about Bob Silver? Where was he by this point?'

'He had left the hotel the previous Thursday saying he had important meetings in London. In reality he had stayed down in Cornwall. He booked into a B&B so that he could help Clive with his art gallery opening on the Saturday, but his wife Margaret spotted him. He couldn't believe his bad luck when she walked into the gallery, as there were several dozen of them in St Ives.'

'So how did Margaret Silver stumble on this one?'

'It wasn't an accident. She had known about her husband's friendship with Clive for a long time, and she suspected it was rather more than it seemed. While Margaret had been curious to know what was going on, she was also worried at what she might discover. She had noticed earlier in the week a sign indicating the opening of Clive's new gallery on Saturday and made a beeline for it.'

'How did Bob react?'

'By this stage he had become quite accomplished at handling chance encounters. The story went that when she turned up he said, "Oh, hello, Margaret. This is the artist Clive Holford. Welcome to his new gallery. Would you like a guided tour?" She apparently replied, "We need to talk", to which he said, "Not now, dear. I'll give you the full story when we're back in London next week." She tried one more time. "What's wrong with here and now?" This caused him to become more assertive, saying something along the lines of "Look, I've invested a great deal of money in this venture. Now's not the time, and I need to return to London to the office for important meetings on Monday." Margaret knew this tone all too well and retreated angry but knowing there was no mileage in pursuing matters there and then.

'On her return to the hotel she decided to confide in her two close friends, Anne Jessops and Lucy Charnley, the Duchess. It didn't take long for Justyn to hear the details, and, being at loggerheads with his father at the time, he tried to persuade several of us to join him in seeking out the gallery.

This was one adventure we declined. We later heard that Bob was arrested at his desk in his office on Cheapside on Tuesday afternoon.'

'That must have caused quite a shock. The thin blue line stretched to London pretty quickly.'

'Yes, the information originally gathered from Bill and corroborated by Ivan was sufficient to require interviews with all five suspects *tout de suite*. Don't forget, the police were worried that a poisoner was at large and might strike again. Some might say the policing was a bit clumsy or random. The problem was there was just too much going on. It was a very unusual type of inquiry. All five suspects had motives, but, more significantly, the police were now more convinced than ever that all five had the opportunity.'

# 14

## 23 AUGUST 1972

Richard Hughes-Webb, Paul Galvin and Arnie Charnley met outside the hotel at seven a.m. for their regular morning run on the beach. Bob Silver had disappeared the previous week, and Ted Jessops, who occasionally joined them, was yet again confined to barracks. There was a muted atmosphere between the three, and instead of being sent on their way as usual by Tom's banter they saw only a sleeping youth at the sentry post – probably a kid on a work-experience year from college – who had been allocated the night shift as Tom's replacement. If they suspected one another of foul play it certainly wasn't evident in their manner. Richard looked as imperious as ever, although Paul's usual lock-jaw grin was reduced to little more than the relaxing of muscles around his mouth. Arnie appeared pale and wan from too many interrupted nights, worrying not about the police investigation but his missing cash.

As they ran down through the woods below the hotel, the scent from the escallonia, which the rain had refreshed, enriched the early morning air and accompanied them to the road they crossed before the beach.

Their initial conversation concerned Ted Jessops, and Richard was quick to inform the others. 'Still in a bad way, I'm afraid. Had electroshock treatment yesterday in Truro. However, I heard he was seen thumbing through magazines in the large lounge yesterday afternoon, so that's progress of sorts, although I can't imagine the warrant for his arrest later on would have done much for his state of mind.'

They pounded softly along the beach, leaving three perfect sets of footprints on the otherwise unblemished golden sand. Each man was wrapped in his own thoughts.

It was Arnie who broke the spell. 'Strange thing, this depression lark. Does anyone understand it?' he asked in his thick Mancunian accent.

'Oh yes. We do,' Richard announced, in such a way as to brook no further discussion.

The three joggers continued further than usual along the beach. There was no disputing that this had now become a car crash of a holiday and thoughts were turning to departure the next day. The men defied their usual thresholds of pain and distance, running as if they were never going to stop, determined to forget the traumas of recent days.

After putting some extra miles on top of their usual, all three were desperate for a break and slowed down as if to order.

It was Richard who opened the conversation. 'So, do either of you believe any of this nonsense that the three of us, along with Bob and Jessops, are under suspicion for attempted murder?' He spat out the name Jessops in such a way that it looked like he was trying to dislodge a very hot pepper from under his tongue as quickly as possible. Ted had greatly lowered his standing in the eyes of his former friends by being thought to be the Sunday-morning telephone-box hoax caller. Paul was the first to respond to Richard, opining it was inconceivable that any of them would want to harm Tom but suggesting that the police should prioritize interviewing the porter's nephew Ivan. Arnie, his mood already fairly dark, listened but decided to keep his own counsel. He observed Paul with a knowing side glance so piercing that if Paul had spotted it he would have stopped in his tracks. Arnie's face was contorted in a frown that suggested complete mistrust. He regarded Paul as somewhat schizophrenic, prone to change from an affable, relaxed Dr Jekyll into a rather mean and unpleasant Mr Hyde whenever financial matters were involved. He frowned at Richard as well, still angry with him for being so unpleasant when he requested what he deemed would be a very short-term loan.

They had been running, walking and discussing matters for some two hours when they realized they had lost all grasp of time. They would now be too late for breakfast at the hotel, and the weather was deteriorating rapidly. A jagged bolt of lightning ripped across the sky, and the heavens opened to unleash a storm of terrible proportions. It seemed some latent elemental force had been set loose. The sky, an expanse of clear, azure blue when they had set off, had been set alight and was spewing rain that would have challenged Noah's flood. Richard urged his two friends to run to the National Trust café at the end of the headland, which he calculated would now be open, it being past nine.

As they arrived, panting and wet through, their state of miserable discomfort was forgotten in sudden amazement. Standing before them, with his hands behind his back in his Humphrey Bogart raincoat, looking as if he hadn't slept in ten years, was a haggard Bob Silver.

'We thought you left Cornwall last week,' yelled Richard as they approached.

'I did, but I had a little local difficulty yesterday in the square mile with a visit from the boys in blue. I paid bail and decided to get down to Cornwall pronto. I thought you fellows would be jogging. I tried to contact you at the hotel when I came off the night sleeper at Penzance, and I guessed where you'd be. Old habits die hard. Incidentally, Yvie,

Alison and the Duchess were not best pleased to hear my voice at that hour, so sorry about that.'

The three were incredulous. Paul spoke first. 'Bob, you were never famed for your diplomatic skills, were you? You turn up out of the blue, and now we're all going to cop it from the trouble and strifes! Henry Kissinger you are not.'

'Sorry, Paul, and of course you two as well, but I tracked your movements from the coast road,' Bob continued. 'I saw you heading for the Trust café, and I knew, with this belter of a storm, you would go straight here. The thing is, gentlemen, we need to talk.'

They received this information without demur and took four seats at a large wooden table on decrepit white plastic chairs. The three strained like dogs on leashes to hear what Bob had to say.

Richard, as usual, was the first to speak. 'We're all ears.'

'I know we all seem to have been implicated in this most unfortunate business of Tom's stroke,' Bob commenced, 'and, as ridiculous as the whole thing seems, it would appear we have all had secrets to keep, and now we are all under considerable pressure –'

'Oh 'eck, funny thing pressure,' Arnie interrupted. 'Take a good batsman, technically brilliant, got all the shots, gets a couple of noughts and next match is scratching around like rooster in the backyard.'

'Yes, thanks, Arnie,' continued Bob. 'By the way, I have settled your account with old Simpkins on my Diners Club card. You can deliver the readies to my house by the month end.'

'Cheers, mate,' beamed Arnie, his face creased in a very broad smile. 'But why didn't you tell me? I've had Rickety Humphrey-Bumfrey blasting me for being some sort of low life.'

'Apologies, Chutney,' he fired back in a good-natured way. (They had now regressed to the familiar nicknames they had for one another, and Richard had long ago dubbed Arnie Charnley 'Mango Chutney'.)

'Look, I said I would pay, and my word is my bond.' Bob sounded aggrieved that he could have been doubted.

Richard was keen that the four of them should get to the point. Despite some misgivings about each other, a strong kinship had developed between them over many years. In a typical male-fellowship kind of way they shared a feeling of injustice that they were the providers and that the world was an ungrateful place. They knew they had to stick together, that the heat was on and that they were unsure of the direction of the next line of fire.

'I think one or all three of you, in fact, may know about my pioneering work into human heart disease, using animals for research and experimentation here at Zennor,' Richard commenced in his authoritative manner. 'I have already dealt with the police's rather cack-handed inquiry in this regard.'

'You probably all know about my financial disaster with the house-building project in Penzance,' Paul put in.

'And you know I lost my loot at Tom's cottage,' added Arnie.

Bob was next. 'With me it's more complicated. Tom was one of the few people to know about my relationship with Clive Holford, and – before any of you put two and two together and get the wrong number – I should tell you I am probably going to adopt him legally as my son.' He went on to explain the circumstances in which he had first found Clive and how his patronage had turned the unfortunate boy's life around so he now had a promising future as an artist.

When Bob had finished, all the men admitted they knew some of each other's circumstances and were pleased to set the record straight with one another. Bob inquired about James Simpkins, saying he had sounded most strange when he phoned to settle Arnie's bill.

'Well, he's had a ripe old time,' responded Arnie. 'He collapsed when the rozzers were all over the place Sunday lunchtime. Anyone would've thought Jack the Ripper was at large. Simpkins blacked out at reception, chipped two front teeth and was rushed in an ambulance to the hospital at Truro.'

'Good grief! How's he now?' asked Bob.

'Well, you spoke to him,' said Richard, taking control as usual. 'He's back at the hotel. They stitched him up, checked his heart, pulse and blood pressure and wanted to keep him in overnight for observation, but I gather he more or less discharged himself.'

'True,' continued Arnie, 'and good old Jean, the wife, drove him home and told the Duchess next day. They must have made him high as a kite. He was yelling the lyrics to songs on the radio, rocking all the way back to the hotel.'

'So, what happened when he got back?'

'Well, a rock has to roll.' Arnie was now getting into his stride. 'He retreated to his flat and would only answer questions from the other side of the locked door or on the phone.'

'Yes, a hotel manager with a mashed-up boat race is not a good advert for his gaff,' said Paul.

It was at this moment that Bob spotted Ken Holford, father of Clive, whom he immediately recognized from the pub in St Buryan. The four fell silent when Bob told them who Ken was, and they saw that the man was in earnest conversation with someone they all recognized: Ivan Youlen. None of them was keen to enter into conversation with the pair, so the men paid their bill and, slipping away, headed back to the hotel.

On his return to his room Richard summoned his daughter

on the hotel's internal phone. 'Suzie, I need your attention. That old tape-recorder of yours. Fetch it. I need to set out the events of this morning's run. Be quick, girl, and bring it to my room.'

'Certainly, Father. Is everything all right?'

'Don't you worry your young head about that. We need everything properly recorded, all our ducks in a row. There are dark forces at play.'

'Certainly, Father.'

Suzie dutifully recorded Richard's recollections of the morning's discussion before extracting the tape and handing it to her father, as obediently as a slave to a master.

# 15

## 24 AUGUST 1972

The following day, Thursday the 24th, was the last day of the holiday. All guests had to adhere to the strict check-out time of twelve. Some of the group remained; those scheduled for the overnight train from Penzance were allowed to put luggage in storage until it suited them to depart. Danny Galvin's small transistor radio was blazing away in the large lounge, the Partridge Family's version of 'Breaking Up Is Hard to Do' bringing down the curtain on the two-week vacation.

Richard Hughes-Webb was first off, marshalling his family into position and formally saying goodbye to what he saw as both his supporting cast and his audience for the past fortnight. A sort of guard of honour surrounded his Bentley outside the main entrance. Suzie lost control of her emotions and sobbed uncontrollably, having been prised free of an amorous Danny Galvin. Rose Morrison was quick to put a consoling arm around her, saying, 'We'll remind you of this when you are older.' Yvie Hughes-Webb glared at Rose, looking as though she could have happily carried out one of her husband's operations on the spot, preferably a badly botched one.

Soon Richard's impressive motor was purring its way down the long drive, and several onlookers might have wondered if that would be the last they would see of the Hughes-Webbs. He had made his unflattering views of the police inquiry well known and for good measure had added a tirade against the hotel's handling of events. He had indicated that he would holiday with his family abroad the following year; it was unlikely that his family would have any say in the matter.

Next up were the Silvers, minus Bob; his reappearance at the art gallery in St Ives the previous Saturday and his rendezvous with the joggers on Wednesday morning had not developed into a family reunion at the hotel. He had taken the sleeper to Paddington the previous night and was back at work on Cheapside. Margaret Silver was being driven by her older son, Henry, while her daughter, Fiona, was waiting for Justyn to finish his goodbyes before driving them off in his Peugeot 204. Justyn, whose usual attire featured extensive cheesecloth and plenty of tie-dyed T-shirts, was now dwarfed by a huge Afghan coat as he appeared from around the corner with an emotional Jenny Charnley. He sped off down the drive blasting the Doors classic 'LA Woman' at full volume, shouting, 'Goodbye, Grant. Hello, Jim!'

The Galvins set about their departure next; Paul with his grey hair carefully greased back, Alison looking strained. She had a rather pale, heavy face, but behind her horn-rimmed spectacles lurked a pair of remarkably alert, inquisitive eyes that darted from left to right with quick precision and could unnerve people. Physically the Galvins couldn't have contrasted more. Paul was short, rotund and immaculate while Alison was taller and somewhat unkempt. In her mid-forties, she displayed a sagging fleshiness around her chin and neck. Her Mary Quant overcoat was buttoned up high, and her overall demeanour gave the impression that she was nobody's pushover. When the assembled crowd realized that Danny wasn't with his parents they immediately dispersed, leaving only Alison's close friends Anne Jessops and the Duchess to say their goodbyes. Danny, having his own wheels, had decided to stay to the end of the day and enjoy things to the very last. Paul, the unpopular father, was keeping Alison waiting while he harangued the receptionist over his bill one last time, claiming the discount for Sunday's interrupted lunch hadn't been credited.

The disturbance at the front desk drew the luckless Simpkins out of his office for the first time since the accident. His upper lip was still badly swollen from the removal of fourteen stitches and gave an unsettling view of his two chipped front teeth. This didn't prevent him from doing his managerial best to placate Paul. After several minutes of deadlocked negotiations Simpkins offered to refer the matter to Head Office if Paul settled the bill in full there and then. This agitated drama undoubtedly affected the number of holiday-makers who stayed to attend Mr and Mrs Paul Galvin's departure.

Anne Jessops revealed to the waiting gallery that her family would not depart until later that day; it was widely suspected that this was down to Ted being unable to climb out of bed again. Anne had managed to get a late booking on the sleeper train, so at least the problem of driving back to the Midlands was averted. This enabled further teenage playtime, so Caroline and Grant disappeared into town to buy some silk fabric to sew into their jeans; she enjoyed inserting colourful triangles into trouser legs below the knee to create massive flares. They were later tracked down by a breathless Nick Charnley in a sound booth inside a music shop, where they were listening to pop records.

'Have you heard the news?' he blurted out, barely able to contain himself.

'What?' asked the pair in unison, rapidly removing their headphones and emerging from the booth.

'A naked man's body has been found washed up on Carbis Bay Beach. They think he's from the hotel.' Grant and Caroline stood frozen to the spot, uncomprehending.

'What?' Grant was alarmed. Tom's collapse had destabilized things enough, but he had an overwhelming sensation that this dramatic news could be totally disastrous.

'Who is it? Anyone we know?'

'They say it's Hector Wallace,' replied Nick, uneasy at imparting such awful information.

'Who found him?'

'Trevor. You know, Trevor Mullings, the fisherman. He's part of the crowd that drinks with Hector. I'm afraid the word is that Hector drowned, probably under the influence of booze. He was completely smashed, apparently. The police are all over the hotel again. They swarmed in like the Keystone Cops.'

The three made their way back up through the woods and the water cascades to the hotel on the hill in a very sombre mood. Caroline mused that the holiday now resembled a game of Cluedo, but instead of Professor Plum, Reverend Green, Colonel Mustard and so on it was 'Mr Richard Hughes-Webb, Mr Bob Silver, Mr Arnie Charnley, Mr Ted Jessops and Mr Paul Galvin'.

When in due course Simpkins, the beleaguered manager, received a request from the police to interview the guests, he finally asserted himself. 'Look, you're not disturbing my guests a second time. Besides, many of them have already left.'

'What, run away, have they?' queried PC Stobart, at which point the rather battered Simpkins gained renewed strength.

'Certainly not. They have finished their holidays, left the hotel and returned to places where they don't get arrested every few days for crimes they haven't committed. They have been here as holiday-makers, not serial killers . . .' His voice rose to a crescendo that could have graced a key speech in a Shakespearian tragedy. Winston Churchill in full flow could not have been more convincing in his oratory.

'All right, all right,' replied Inspector Higham, looking

somewhat embarrassed, even a little astonished. 'Keep your hair on. But there's something very odd about all this, very odd indeed.' At that moment the police decided to withdraw, just as Danny Galvin and Jenny Charnley returned to the hotel, laughing and singing along raucously to 'Chirpy Chirpy Cheep Cheep' blasting out from their transistor radio, blissfully unaware of the latest drama being played out at the hotel. The police, by now confused by the departure of key suspects, needed time to assess how to conduct this new inquiry.

As they returned to their car Inspector Higham gave vent to his feelings. 'This place gives me the creeps. Where do we go with this one now? I know the Chief has been briefed from someone on what's been going on; he's asked to see me tomorrow at ten. We've got to be careful, Mr Police Constable. I suspect Haughty-Haughty's arrogant sleight of hand at work, and I don't like it. I don't like it at all!'

## 16

## PRESENT DAY

'Had they not suffered enough?' asked Brigit.

'Who, the residents?'

'No, the police. First, they had the unsolved case of a hospitalized night porter and then a naked corpse on a beach, and, to cap it all, they ended up being browbeaten by an aggressive and wounded hotel manager. The appearance of Hector Wallace's naked body must have been quite a shock for them. And what were they to think so soon after Tom? The hotel does rather take centre stage here. Being a rural constabulary they must have thought they had landed in an Agatha Christie novel, wondering where the next corpse would turn up!'

'Hector died of natural causes, and it was fairly clear he had wandered off after a particularly heavy night's drinking. Even his drinking companions, Trevor Mullings among them, said he had drunk them all under the table. Hector hated the end of the holiday. It was the happiest two weeks of his year, and his Aunt Agatha – his "Aunty Aunt" as he liked to call her – gave him a pretty free hand and then paid the bills at the end, including a very big tab at the Office.

'You mean he didn't stay alone?'

'Well, he had his own room, but Aunt Agatha paid, and he had all his meals with her. She was in her eighties, and both were driven from Torquay by her chauffeur Hinton, who apparently never went faster than thirty miles an hour. Hector was frightened that this might be the last holiday, as Agatha had been complaining that her shares had taken a terrible tumble, and, like a lot of old people, she was worried the government had lost its grip with rampant inflation and constant strikes. She had been suggesting she should batten down the hatches and didn't think she could afford to stay at the hotel again. Apart from this, she was very arthritic, and her health had become a source of concern for Hector. She had more or less brought him up; his parents had been tea planters in India and died in a plane crash while Hector was at boarding-school in England.'

'How old was he at the time?'

'He was about eight years old and at a strict Roman Catholic school somewhere in the West Country. Rumour had it that he was abused there and never developed much sense of self-worth. After that he lived virtually all his life in his aunt's house. He had a great interest in horticulture, and he loved the gardens of Cornwall where everything grows so well. He had been a talented landscape gardener, but alcohol had long since rendered any permanent employment impossible. However, he showed his aunt respect by never drinking in her house. So, you see, there were good reasons why at the end of the holiday Hector Wallace should decide to end it all.'

'So you believe it was an open-and-shut case of suicide then? I think you're missing something.'

'Don't think so.' Grant's dismissive tone riled Brigit. 'A drunken loser found naked and frozen dead on a beach after an excessive drinking binge didn't require too much police investigation.'

Brigit stood up, glared at her husband and raised her eyes to the ceiling. 'Right, I've had enough of all this. For the last two days all I've heard from you is this monologue of events from over forty years ago, according to the Great Grant, the

Oracle. So why hasn't anyone ever worked out what happened here? Why have you waited forty years to reveal all this? If there was a deathbed confession, why was it never investigated? There seems to be an absence of truth and certainly an absence of justice for Tom Youlen and possibly for Hector Wallace – "Oh, he was just a hopeless drunk –"' Brigit mimicked her husband's pompous, dismissive tone.

'OK, OK!' interrupted Grant, raising his voice. 'I'm going to do something about it. I'm still concerned about it all, more than you could ever know. I'm going to take a three-month sabbatical from the firm. I qualify for the short-term sabbatical option.'

'Woah! Calm down, tiger!'

'No, Brigit, you're right; you're absolutely right. It's time to find out the truth and to put the past to bed. Suzie Hughes-Webb, Danny Galvin, Caroline Jessops, Justyn Silver and Nick and Jenny Charnley. I'm going to see them all.'

Grant loathed himself for continuing to hide from her the real reasons for his obsession with the past. The truth was that he knew he was far less interested in securing justice for Tom than in discovering whether his mother had been in any way involved, but he knew this was not the right time to tell Brigit.

'Well, you see Nick every summer anyway on your golf tours, but I guess you've never asked him the question?' Brigit decided it was time to cool things down a bit.

'No. We've never talked about it, so it will be interesting to see what he has to say now. I'll cross-refer his version of events with his sister, Jenny, as Nick can be known to wing it a bit.'

'If you don't mind I'll leave it to you. I have my business to run, and we're seeing an upturn in the market. Things are really motoring again, in case you're interested.'

'Of course I'm interested, but I'm a bit distracted by all this, and now I need to track down all concerned and spend time with them.'

'Distracted? You don't say,' muttered Brigit to herself.

# 17

# PRESENT DAY

Nick Charnley was easy to get hold of, as over the years since their holidays in Cornwall he and Grant had kept in regular touch and had, for the past twenty-five years, enjoyed an annual golf trip with six other friends to various resorts in Europe. Nick was a born organizer. The eight had become a band of brothers. The banter on the tours would never descend to analysing dark events of the past, which remained as a place of neither reference nor residence.

Grant had now decided to interrogate his old friend. Nick had long enjoyed an entrepreneurial career; his latest business venture was called Sobbers for Rent, which supplied professional grievers to simulate bereavement at funerals. The grievers were ordered by mourners who wanted to increase the numbers present to create a bigger show for their departed. The brochure featured on the cover a full church with the entire congregation in tears – doubtless prompted to cry at an appropriate moment. 'I give them notes on the life of the departed and underline when and where to blub,' Nick would brag. He also ran a funeral service for families to pay their respects to deceased pets. He really has no shame, thought Grant, chuckling to himself.

Nick's previous business had been an outfitters for funeral directors, and he had spotted a gap in the market. Clearly the son had inherited some of the father's cheeky-chappie and entrepreneurial genes. Nick suggested they meet outside the

Grace Gates at Lord's Cricket Ground, as he had also inherited his father's love of cricket; he had two tickets for the first day of the first Test Match of the summer, on a cold day in mid-May.

As the start of play at eleven approached, there was a constant buzz of conversation and loud hellos as friends reunited for a day at the Test. Grant was sure the volume would diminish markedly when play commenced; in the event it did, for about the first three balls of the day's play. Then the chattering and popping of champagne corks continued unabated for some twenty minutes, with batsmen shouldering arms or nicking the odd single off a thick edge, together with the occasional 'play and miss'. All of a sudden the stumps were severely shattered, and the unfortunate batsman, who was employed to play professional cricket at the highest level, walked disconsolately back to the pavilion. This came as a shock to the chattering classes, and the sudden silence stunned the crowd into a numbed state for all of about forty seconds. But soon the new batsman was indulging in the same shouldering of arms and the occasional 'play and miss', nicking the odd single, even a two, as the crowd cheered a misfield that provided the trigger for everyone to recharge their drinks – and away they went again. Against this backdrop Grant and Nick finally got down to the subject of the mysterious poisoning of the porter in 1972.

'Nick, I have never asked you this before, but were you aware that the father of one of us kids confessed something about Tom Youlen's poisoning on his deathbed?'

Nick was initially silent and then distracted by the sight of a ball swung hard and high towards where they were sitting, bouncing once before clearing the ropes. 'What have you heard?'

'Only that one of them passed on some pertinent information.'

'I know my dad used to think it was nothing to do with anyone at the hotel, and he thought Tom's nephew was dodgy. But there was also that strange business with Clive Holford and his father Ken. When we learnt the truth that Bob Silver had been misjudged and had helped Clive get on in life, he was no longer suspected of being implicated. Anyway, what do you think happened?'

Grant chose his words carefully. 'As I understand it, they all had a motive: Ted Jessops with his past uncovered, Bob Silver suspected of a gay affair, Richard Hughes-Webb with his experiments with toxic substances in the Zennor cottage that Tom looked after, Paul Galvin with his failed property business in Penzance and – to be frank – your father with his cash being stolen at Tom's cottage. I gather all of them are no longer with us.'

'Would you like an asparagus roll?' Nick asked, as he started attacking the picnic basket he had brought along. At this time, thirty minutes before the lunch break, the batsmen were finally taking command and the spectators' attention was, at last, firmly on the cricket.

In the forty-minute interval that followed, Grant returned to the subject. 'And another thing, that strange business of Hector Wallace being washed up on the shore. Some people might think the events are connected.'

'No chance. Hector was a hopeless case, and I gather he was very depressed at the end of the holiday, thinking he wouldn't be back.'

'OK, so who poisoned Tom?' Having polished off a bottle of champagne and now having got two-thirds of the way through a bottle of Chablis, Grant was growing bolder, his cheeks reddened by the alcohol. 'Someone must have heard something.'

His direct approach finally drew a clear response. 'All my

dad said about it was that Ivan Youlen was a bad lot – and something about a message in a bottle he found when jogging on Carbis Bay.'

'What did it say?'

'Dunno. I think Jenny knew something about it.'

Grant concluded he would get no further with Nick on this matter, and he resolved to see Jenny in Manchester. He had always found Nick a loquacious and gregarious character, but for some reason he was rather closed up on this occasion. He was probably intent on trying to forget a holiday that had disastrous consequences for his parents and family life in general. Grant could relate to this, as the events that summer had fairly dire consequences for his own family. None the less, he wondered whether Nick had something to hide.

The following day Grant took the train from Euston to Manchester Piccadilly, where a smiling Jenny Poskett (née Charnley) met him at the station. Forty years had failed to dim her looks and bright smile, her age only slightly betrayed by the grey roots of her hair. She drove them to a city-centre hotel where Grant had booked lunch. Grant discovered that life had been stable and seemingly happy after Jenny had married Nigel Poskett, an estate agent who was both popular and well respected for the considerable amount of charity auctioneering in which he was involved locally. Their two children were now through university and embarking on their own careers. However, over the course of lunch Grant detected some emptiness in Jenny's life. After exchanges about families and events since they had last met, some of which Grant had heard from Nick over the years, they moved through the gears before discussing the holiday of 1972.

'You know, I used to envy you, Grant.' This took him by surprise. 'Not just you but all the others, all the other families who went to Cornwall with us each year.' He was dumbfounded. Surely she remembered the upset of Hughes-Webb's affair with his mother? Even if she hadn't known of the fall-out that resulted he thought the affair itself was common knowledge. 'Most people seemed so stable. I know there was the odd scene and Danny's dad was a moody so-and-so and Justyn's old man kept disappearing, but everyone else remained together.'

Funny sort of happy families, thought Grant, but he refrained from comment; he saw little point and wondered where this was all heading.

'You see, it was only my folks who split up, from what I remember, and it was really shit, Grant.'

Now he got it. Her parents' divorce was at the core of all this.

'Mum never forgave Dad for losing the cash at Tom's cottage and lying to her about it.'

Grant had a vision of a herd of cattle charging at the unfortunate Arnie when the Duchess finally discovered his duplicity.

'It all came to a head one night when they came back from the village cricket club's annual do. Dad was half cut and nagging Mum for once, accusing her of being frigid and ignoring his needs.'

Grant shifted uneasily in his chair. Playing agony aunt wasn't really in his nature, but he was keen to show sympathy and was genuinely sorry for Jenny and her brother.

'Then it all kicked off, and Dad, partly to emphasize his unhappiness in the marriage, confessed to losing the cash in Zennor, and Mum went ballistic. She turfed him out on to the street, almost kicking him down the stairs. I heard him stumble, and I saw him from out of my bedroom window. I'll never forget the look on his face as he stood on the pavement.'

Grant stood up, ready to put a comforting arm around Jenny, but she waved him away. 'It's OK, thanks. It was a long time ago.' She regained some composure, blowing her nose repeatedly on a solitary paper tissue.

'I'm so sorry, Jenny. It must have been very upsetting for you, what happened and also actually witnessing it.'

'Thanks, it wasn't a wagonload of laughs, that's for sure. And it got worse. Dad shacked up with a local barmaid – "Big Tits Wendy", as Nick so delicately called her.'

Grant struggled to resist laughing, biting his lower lip hard. He had heard his friend Nick on this subject before. Clearly the brother had coped rather better than the sister. 'What happened next?'

'Pretty sad and squalid. Dad had a massive heart attack, which occurred – according to our very discreet GP – while he was on the job, as you chaps would say. I so didn't want to know that detail.'

Grant was quick to express further sympathy, struggling again to suppress laughter as he recalled Nick once saying, 'Dad always had a smile on his face, even when he snuffed it – wey-hey!' Clearly the siblings had very different takes on Arnie's unusual demise. However, Grant was genuinely very sorry about Arnie's premature death, and he quickly got a grip. After a polite pause, he asked the question that most pre-occupied him. 'You know Tom's poisoning was never fully explained, and rumour has it that someone heard something from their father on his deathbed. Was that you?'

'For God's sake, you dickhead. It was me who told you this, after Nick's twenty-first birthday party back in 1975! I'm hardly likely to keep that news to myself.'

'Oh yes, sorry. I'd forgotten. I was probably drunk at the time, and I just had this vague memory that someone had said it.'

'Nice you could remember, Grant. We were in bed together at the time. It shows how much I meant to you!'

'I'm so sorry . . .'

'No, you're not. You were fickle as hell . . .' Jenny was outraged.

'And you weren't?' countered Grant, raising his own voice. He recalled his hurt at her promiscuousness at that time. 'You had slept with Robert Vernon and Justyn Silver, too . . .'

She stood up to go. Grant was furious with himself for the clumsy attack he'd mounted, bringing up stuff he knew should have been left well alone, particularly so soon after she had poured her heart out. Realizing his mission in Manchester was fast unravelling, he hurried to placate her and persuade her to return to the table. 'I apologize. I really do. Please let bygones be bygones. It was all a long time ago, and life has worked out pretty well for you with Nigel.'

Jenny still looked wounded but shrugged as if to say 'Whatever.'

Grant was now desperate to avoid any of their personal business, which he greatly regretted getting dragged into. He returned to the purpose of their meeting, as far as he was concerned. 'So who do you think heard something? One of the Galvins, Hughes-Webbs, Jessops or Silvers?'

'Try them all,' she replied without much enthusiasm.

'So who told you someone had said something to one of our group?'

'My father, on his deathbed,' she said slowly and very deliberately, with a trace of triumph in her voice.

Grant was taken aback, shaken by this information, but a glance at his watch alerted him that he needed to conclude the conversation and head for his train.

After they had said their goodbyes at the station he realized he hadn't inquired about the message in the bottle. He looked hurriedly for Jenny and saw her car fast disappearing out of view. He cursed himself for missing so obvious a line of inquiry and resolved to ask her about it another time. However, his mind was now made up that the deathbed story could only have come from Ted Jessops, as he predeceased Arnie Charnley by three years and the other three, Galvin, Silver and Hughes-Webb, were all fit and well at the time.

In a moment of self-reflection Grant wondered if he was simply chasing shadows. He doubted whether any of the contemporaries he was tracking down cared much about it at all. He consoled himself that at least he would find out from Caroline Jessops the truth of the deathbed story. However, he would much rather find out the whole truth as quickly as possible so that he could move on. But the feeling persisted that there were dark secrets to unearth. He already felt some unease at the responses he had got from Nick and Jenny, although the marriage breakdown and subsequent divorce of the Charnley parents didn't shock him especially. Sad as it had been for the family, it was just a sideshow in the greater scheme of things.

# 18

## PRESENT DAY

'You burnt your own town. You burnt your own town, you stupid bastards. You burnt your own town.' Such was the greeting for Grant as he met up with Danny Galvin at a football match at Tottenham Hotspur's stadium at White Hart Lane. Their opponents from the north of England were taunting the home fans about the Tottenham riots of August 2011. The Spurs fans took a while to respond before chanting in response, 'We pay your benefits.'

For some reason Danny had decided that the best way for the two of them to catch up was at a football match in London, accompanied by some 35,000 others. Over the past forty years Grant had been to a few matches with Danny, but he didn't share the latter's passion for Spurs and went more to enjoy the quality of the football. He would have preferred to be at Twickenham, but on this occasion he had an ulterior motive and hoped to have the chance of a proper chat after the game. He was therefore taken aback when Danny brought the subject up at half-time.

'So you're digging around about the Tom Youlen business.'

'Er, yes. Who told you?' Grant was surprised by the directness of the question and spilt boiling coffee from the top of his polystyrene cup. 'Dammit!'

'Never mind that,' continued Danny, oblivious to Grant's discomfort. 'So why are you?'

'Tom never got any justice, and some say neither did Hector Wallace.'

'That old soak. I don't think his demise was − or is − relevant.'

'But Tom was definitely poisoned. The coroner's report was conclusive, and nobody ever carried the can. Tom took some of the poison that Richard Hughes-Webb was using on animals. Why he did that has never been properly explained.'

'Good old Grant. Always interested in justice, always after the truth. You even thought my old man got away with cheating at squash. Well, maybe you shouldn't poke your nose in here.'

'Well, if you must know, it's become a matter of some importance to me to prove to myself and to Brigit that I can resolve this case once and for all and remove the stain of suspicion from everyone implicated at the time. Our August holidays came to a sudden end because the truth was never uncovered.' Grant had no intention of revealing the real motive for his investigation to his now seemingly confrontational former friend.

'Brigit,' spat Danny, his chewing gum performing cartwheels. 'Still under the thumb, are we?'

'Now steady on.'

'No, you steady on. You've no business delving into the case after all this time. Who are you? Tom's trustee? His next of kin? Come on, Grant, this case went dead in 1972, even if Tom didn't join it till 1977.'

'You seem to know a lot about it all.' Grant was becoming suspicious.

Danny ignored him. The second half started, and he redirected his conversation to questioning the parentage of the referee and most of the opposing team. Grant concluded that thirty years or so as a dealer in the Essex motor trade had hardened his old friend, who now seemed to lack empathy and any residual signs of his childhood charm.

After the game, travelling on the train from Tottenham Hale, Grant hoped to get back to the subject. Instead, Danny busied himself in conversation with a man well into his eighties who revealed that he had hardly missed a home game since the end of the Second World War. By the time they alighted in the West End Danny and his new best mate had selected the best Spurs team of the post-war years. Grant despaired when Danny said he would talk more about the incident but at another time. He suggested they meet in Brentwood for a drink after work the following month when Grant would be back from Cornwall.

Grant reflected on the three meetings. The Charnleys had been fairly helpful and there were clear leads to follow, primarily Jenny's father's deathbed assertion, although he needed to find out more about the message in a bottle. Danny Galvin, who had not been a particularly close friend in the intervening years, seemed downright hostile. But it surprised Grant to learn that Danny knew when Tom had died. Why should he have known that?

The following Monday Grant took the train from Waterloo to Winchester. There to greet him was a vivacious Caroline Jessops, who shrieked a greeting as he descended from the train to the platform.

'My, my, Grant Morrison,' she purred approvingly, making him feel like Robert Redford being greeted by Barbara Streisand in *The Way We Were*. 'Still gorgeous, Grant, but where is old Mr Wavy Hair?'

Caroline's trim and fetching teenage figure had given way to sedate middle age; she was now built for 'comfort rather than speed', as she had told Grant on the phone.

'Hair today, gone tomorrow,' replied Grant lamely, before

adding, 'but don't worry, it's still me. One eye can still watch you while the other watches out for satellites,' he joked, referring to his unmatched eyes.

'No matter,' continued Caroline, fixing her stare on her old flame. 'I've booked lunch at a lovely little French bistro near the cathedral.'

Once seated, and before reviewing the menu, Caroline recommended the linguine with a side salad and pesto dressing, which she insisted should be washed down with a bottle of Sancerre. The ambience of the bistro evoked Paris in the 1930s, with monochrome images of Edith Piaf adorning the walls as her songs played quietly throughout the meal. It was not exactly the setting he'd had in mind; his purpose was to extract as much information as quickly as possible, but if wine helped the conversation flow so much the better. Sensing an advantage, he suggested that two bottles might prove even better. Caroline's father, the late Ted Jessops, had, after all, been the early runner as principal suspect, and if he had revealed anything significant on his deathbed Caroline was much more likely to blurt it out after a few drinks.

'So, Caroline, have the years been kind?'

'Oh, not too bad. Stuart's insurance business bores the knickers off me, but it keeps him busy. And I have the upper hand now, ever since I caught him out with the chalet girl in Les Gets some years back.'

'Oh, I'm sorry.'

'Don't be. We get along fine now. He has his hobbies – primarily sailing on the Solent – and I have my horse. I get involved at the local stables, and I have a great circle of friends round here. I guess it's developed into more of a brother–sister type of marriage, but he won't dare misbehave again. He didn't like being sinbinned. So, how's your wife?' Caroline continued rather icily. She never could bring herself to say Brigit's name. It was precisely because of these personal tensions that he had been slightly dreading meeting Caroline again.

'Good, thanks. The girls are now at university, and Brigit' – he intoned the name carefully to give her due status – 'is working full time again, running a rather successful recruitment business in the IT sector.'

'Oh, good,' said Caroline in a voice that implied it was anything but.

Grant set about bringing her up to speed with his investigation.

'I know everyone thought Daddy did it,' said Caroline, 'all because Tom knew about that incident on the beach four years earlier. Funny thing, after Daddy died Mummy started building bridges with Joanna, and we became proper sisters. She married a stockbroker and now lives in Sydney, which is a bit of a drag as it's so far away. But they have an adorable family, and it's a wonderful place to live.'

'Quite so. Anyway, my burning question, to be brutal, is did your father say anything about a confession on his deathbed?'

'About what?'

'About – you know – Tom.'

'Why should he?'

'Because, according to Jenny Charnley, somebody told their offspring something about Tom's poisoning on their death-bed.'

'Well, I don't think it was Daddy. You see, he didn't speak at all after his heart attack, and he was dead within days. He did draw something, though.'

'Draw?'

'Yes, he could still use his hands. He drew a mermaid,' Caroline announced cheerfully.

'Do you know why?'

'No idea. But it was a beautiful mermaid. Mummy said it was the Mermaid of Zennor.'

Grant straightened in his chair. This was now getting intriguing, what with the mermaid and the message in the bottle, both associated with the sea – the sea in which Hector drowned. He told Caroline what Jenny had said about the bottle being found on the beach, and she smiled. 'You've been listening to too many Police records.'

'It's police records I'm interested in, but of the rozzer rather than the Sting variety. After I've caught up with Suzie Hughes-Webb and Justyn Silver I'm planning to go back to Cornwall and dig around a bit.'

'Catch up with Suzie? You'll be lucky. She's in Cape Town.'

'Oh. Does she ever come back?' asked Grant, slightly crest-fallen. 'She must still have family in this country.'

'She hasn't returned in five years, to my knowledge. Her father passed away just before the millennium. Her mother had a terrible time with Alzheimer's and died about six years ago. Suzie and Frank had taken her into their home in Beaconsfield, and it was a terrible strain for them towards the end.'

'What about her brother Tony? Doesn't he see her?'

'He's in New York. I suppose they may rendezvous in London. I really think you should see Suzie, Grant. There was something she once said to me . . .'

'And that was?'

'Sorry, no can say. It was in strictest confidence,' she smiled.

Grant remembered how infuriatingly obtuse Caroline could be. She loved intrigue, and he couldn't be sure if she was bluffing. He decided not to push it, settled the bill, kissed Caroline on the cheek and parted with her amicably. He decided to walk back to the station to collect his thoughts and recover some sobriety. He wanted to see Suzie, but a trip to Cape Town had not been part of the equation. He was concerned at the cost of such a trip adding to the spiralling overall expense of his investigations. When he had embarked on his sabbatical he had thought it would cost a few thousand pounds, at most, over a few months; a journey to South Africa was a different matter. Perhaps I could persuade Brigit to join me, he thought. We could make a holiday of it. But he didn't want to be distracted too much from his prime purpose. In any event, he decided to leave any plans to see Suzie until after he had met Justyn in London and had returned to Cornwall.

# 19

## PRESENT DAY

Justyn Silver had suggested meeting at his trendy private members' club in Mayfair. Grant had not seen him since Robert Vernon's wedding over twenty-five years earlier, but he recognized him instantly. The old-rocker look still prevailed, although the long hair was now whitish as was the beard, and he was thinning at the temples. He had retained all his warmth and charm, greeting Grant as if they had met only recently.

'How's old Grantie boy? Still the backbone of the establishment, maintaining the fine traditions of the legal world?'

'Yeah, yeah, all of that, thanks, Justyn, but I do live my life trying not to be too pompous or stereotypical – as you would view it.' Grant recalled how Justyn had previously labelled him as a future defender of the Empire, implying he was that dreadful sort of individual to be in the early seventies – a square.

'Good on yer, mate,' continued Justyn, ordering herbal tea for himself and coffee for his guest. 'So what's this all about, Grantie boy?' (Grant squirmed at this appellation, which he always put down to Justyn being a year older than him and feeling a need to emphasize this.)

'Before I go into that, how's life been with you?' inquired Grant.

Over the years Justyn had abandoned the music industry, although he still played guitar, and was now a highly successful interior designer of hotels. 'Well, pretty A-OK, as it happens.

I have two big projects on at the moment: doing up a Russian oligarch's new pad on the Bishops Avenue, and next month I'm off to Hong Kong to refurbish a hotel I designed in the early 1990s. There's a budget of some 60 million dollars, and I'm going to have a lot of fun. My scheme for the lobby alone will be the biggest revolution to hit the island since the handover in 1997.'

Grant shifted his gaze to the elegant surroundings, a sea of empty brown leather chairs and dark mahogany Queen-Anne-style side tables. He was flanked by two walls of deep-red flock wallpaper and watched over by a rather vulgar lead-crystal chandelier. A man and his wife – or more likely his mistress – were the only other human life in the room, locked in intimate conversation in the opposite corner. The sight of them prompted Grant's next question. 'And how's your personal life?'

'Chaotic!' said Justyn with a wry smile. 'Clare and I finally split after the biggest on–off relationship since the Burtons. I don't seem to do commitment too well. In the end we became like that couple in Noel Coward's *Private Lives*: couldn't live together but couldn't bear to think of the other being with anyone else. We've both had therapy now and agreed to leave each other alone for six months, then it will no doubt start all over again.'

'Seeing anyone at present?'

'Yeah, I'm seeing to a few people at the moment,' replied Justyn rather crudely, making Grant blanch. 'Sorry – I'm beginning to move into the ranks of dirty old man. You see, to be truthful, Grantie, my old mate, I'm rather lonely. I adored Clare, but I'm impossible to live with, what with my job and my constant infidelity. How's your life?'

'You'll think it very tame. Married Brigit, who was my articled clerk some twenty-five years ago. I've got two wonderful girls, now at university, have been a partner with Gilks and Silkin for fifteen years, specializing in corporate law. At the moment I'm taking a three-month sabbatical, which is probably the most radical thing I've ever done.'

'Why are you doing that?'

'To find out' – Grant hesitated, then went for it – 'who poisoned Tom Youlen in 1972.'

'Bloody hell!' Justyn spluttered. 'Why don't you find out who murdered poor old Hector "the Office" Wallace at the same time?' His voice had risen inadvertently, and the two men glanced anxiously at the couple in the opposite corner. They needn't have worried. The couple were embracing and kissing so fervently they were almost eating one another.

'You don't think Hector was murdered and that the two fatalities were connected, do you?'

'Who's to say? Bit odd just to walk into the sea, don't you think? And didn't they find some sort of message in a bottle on the coast somewhere?'

This was the second time Grant had heard about a message in a bottle in a matter of days, having spent over forty years completely unaware of it. 'But Hector was seven sheets to the wind that night, completely off his head, as I understand it. And wasn't he very depressed about returning to Torquay the following day with his aunt, thinking he would never return to his west Cornwall paradise?'

'Who says, Grant?'

'Well, the perceived wisdom was –'

'Perceived wisdom, piss off!' This time the couple did look across, their intimate canoodling suddenly arrested, their faces projecting disgust in the direction of Grant and Justyn. The latter now lowered his voice. 'A poisoning and then a fatality on the beach a few days later – and you think they weren't connected. Who are you? Inspector Clouseau?'

'How do you know about the message in a bottle?' asked Grant, bridling a little.

'Jenny Charnley told me.'

'When?'

'Last week, as it happens. I phoned her to ask why you wanted to meet me after all these years and what was going on. Besides, it's never a good idea to lose touch with the old back catalogue – even if some of the entries are in yours, too.'

Grant refrained from showing any reaction to this rather off-colour remark and told Justyn he was heading down to Cornwall the following week to try to find justice for Tom Youlen.

'Well, don't forget Hector. I don't think he was particularly depressed. His Aunt Agatha – "Aunty Aunt" as he called her – gave him *carte blanche*, and who do you think was going to be the beneficiary of her estate?'

'You really don't think it was an accident, do you?'

'No, and I'll tell you why. The week after Hector drowned, Robert Vernon and I returned to Cornwall – just about making it in my clapped-out old Peugeot 204 – and we headed to the Office. My pub band were playing an August bank holiday gig, and I persuaded Robert to come down and help us out on drums, as our regular guy had overdosed the previous weekend. I told the guys it would be my last performance, which I don't think devastated them too much! Trevor Mullings, the fisherman who reported Hector's death, was in the pub that night. I asked him if Hector had left on his own after his very long final session in the Office. Trevor told me that he himself was under the table by then – as the publican had closed the pub and allowed drinking to continue into the early hours. However, Trevor did recall that Hec, as he called him, had left with someone he didn't recognize.'

'How odd,' said Grant. 'Why didn't you say something at the time?'

'Robert told his old man, Mark, who contacted the police only to be told that it was an open-and-shut case, that the coroner had released the body, there were no fingerprints on him and the incident room had been closed down within days with a verdict of "accidental death by drowning" recorded. Mark was told that the CPS had no interest in the case as there were no suspects. Looking back, perhaps we should have gone to the Old Bill directly, but Mark's dad seemed so respectable – owning that private bank off Trafalgar Square that had been in the family for centuries – whereas we thought we'd be dismissed as unreliable, long-haired juvenile hippies.'

'Well, it sounds like a botched job all round – and Hector Wallace never got justice either.'

'I couldn't agree more. I had a soft spot for old Hector. I know everyone thought I was some sort of druggie flying with the teapots, but it has really bothered me all these years that Hector left the pub with someone who was never identified and who has never come forward.'

Grant saw that Justyn was genuinely upset about Hector, and the years had diminished neither his anger nor his sense of injustice. 'Then come with me to Cornwall next week,' he suggested hopefully. 'I've booked into a B&B near Zennor to try to establish what really happened, to set the record straight for Tom – but now also for Hector.' Prior to this conversation Grant had always thought of Hector as the hopeless drunk he had described to Brigit, but Justyn had provoked in him a radical reappraisal.

'I can't, old mate. My schedules with clients are tight, and I am very focused and structured these days,' Justyn replied with a slightly self-conscious smile.

'Fair enough, but I will try to find Trevor Mullings –

although it may not be easy. There are too many unanswered questions.'

Such had been the intensity of their conversation that neither had noticed that the lounge had filled up around them.

As they parted they high-fived, agreeing to speak soon, both pleased to have rekindled an old friendship. Grant now shared Justyn's view that Hector Wallace's drowning forty years ago was no accident. He was encouraged, even uplifted, by Justyn being the first of the younger generation of former holiday-makers to show any enthusiasm for his belated sleuthing. Grant hailed a cab and jumped in, feeling sprightly and thinking for the first time that he was not alone in his mission to seek out the truth.

## 20

## PRESENT DAY

The following week Grant took the train from Paddington to Plymouth. He was greeted at the station by Robert Vernon who had suggested that Grant should stay with him and his wife Jackie *en route* to Cornwall. This he was more than happy to do, as Robert was a friend with whom he had kept in touch. Moreover Grant was intrigued by Justyn's mention of Robert the previous week. He was pleased – and in some ways relieved – that the Vernons had never been dragged into the 1972 police inquiry or implicated in any way. Furthermore, Grant was keen to speak to Mark, Robert's father, who had been a witness to Tom's distress in the lane near Zennor and who had spoken to the police about Hector's exit from the pub with the unidentified stranger.

'He died last month,' Robert revealed, when Grant asked how his father was. Grant was visibly crestfallen, and, on seeing his expression, Robert added, 'I didn't think you would be so shocked. He was eighty-seven.'

'Yes, yes, I mean, I'm so sorry. His death must be a great loss, with you being an only child.'

'It's OK, Grant. We all go through it at some point, but thanks all the same.'

Grant realized Robert had no idea how sorry he was or why. However, over dinner in a nearby pub – Jackie was out at her bridge club – he homed straight in on the topic of Hector Wallace.

'Justyn told me that you and he went to the Office the week after Hector died. Wasn't that a bit macabre?'

'Possibly, but Justyn was distraught about Hector, and he had a hunch that someone at the pub would know something about his drowning.

'And that someone was Trevor Mullings?' Robert nodded. 'Pity the police weren't more interested in what you told your father about Hector's mystery companion.'

'I know, but he told them, and they closed him down very promptly. All he got back was the usual stuff about coroners accepting accidental death by drowning, the CPS not being interested and so on, so there was nowhere for him to go. Justyn was incandescent when he heard, as he knew Hector really quite well. They used to refer to one another as "the far-out men". It started with Hector mocking Justyn's use of the expression "Far out, man." I think they both saw themselves as outsiders from the rest of us and the world in general. They were both a touch eccentric, let's face it, and that created a bond between them. They used to chat into the early hours when Justyn couldn't sleep and sat strumming his acoustic guitar. Hector would often be there, asking Tom for another drink.'

'Justyn's playing wasn't that bad,' interrupted Grant.

'Ha-ha. He used to strum "Father and Son". Poignant at the time, although later he and Bob got on rather well, after they legally adopted Clive Holford and became one much happier family. By the way, did Justyn tell you that we went back to Cornwall a week after we'd all left to play a gig?'

'Yes, and you were the new Charlie Watts. But who do you think Hector left the pub with?'

'Who knows? It could have just been someone trying to usher him outside so old Keith could get some sleep. Let's face it, Hector getting legless was a regular occurrence – every night and most lunchtimes. It was just that he went a bit further than usual that night and decided to get completely wasted.'

'I think he was encouraged down to the beach, Robert, and coerced into the water. Even a drunk doesn't want to drown.'

'Why? Who would want to harm him?'

'Lord only knows, but I need to find Trevor Mullings. I'm beginning to think Tom's poisoning and Hector's drowning are related. Justyn thinks so. We have two horrendous events within a few days of each other, in a fairly remote location. How on earth were we all allowed to leave Cornwall when we chose to?'

'Fair point, but your family and mine were never implicated,' Robert replied, sounding ever more the stereotypical schoolmaster he had become, having eschewed the family banking tradition. Grant didn't want to hold on to this thought. In his own mind his mother remained implicated, deeply so, and he felt nauseous at his memory of the time that Richard Hughes-Webb and his mother were caught in the porter's car headlights. The image remained in Grant's mind, as did the fact that it was Hughes-Webb who had berated the hapless Hector Wallace.

The following day Grant rented a four-by-four, mastered its satnav system and set off on the two-hour drive to Zennor. By the time he stopped for fuel near Redruth he had grown tired of the radio's musical offerings and bought a Peter Cook and Dudley Moore recording, which made him chuckle to himself for the rest of the journey.

His first port of call on arrival was the church of St Senara. Soon after, he pulled up in a makeshift car park between the pub and the museum. Before checking the graveyard he decided to enter the church, where his attention was taken by a carving of a mermaid on one of the ancient pew ends. Ted Jessops drawing the picture of a mermaid after his heart attack sprang to his mind. What the hell was that about? Grant kept thinking there must be a connection, but he couldn't join the dots. At that moment he heard the church door shutting behind him. He swiftly left the church in time to see a shadowy figure in an old coat hurrying down the lane. Deciding not to give chase he walked over to the graveyard. After inspecting several rows of moss-covered decaying head-stones, he found what he was looking for: a simple com-memorative plaque.

HERE LIES THE BODY OF THOMAS YOULEN
*Born 25th January 1919. Died 5th June 1977*

The plaque carried no other inscription, no personal reference to the man's life whatsoever, but some roses had been planted in front in a little stone rockery. It looked as if someone tended the grave.

Grant was filled with a sense of injustice for Tom, both in life and death; a sentiment heightened by the lack of any kind of commemorative message. There was not even a 'Rest in Peace'. However, he reflected that it appeared as if the rose rockery was tended regularly; he hoped that it was by a relative or friend rather than simply by churchyard main-tenance. He found himself a little overwrought. He had never previously owned up to any personal involvement in any of this, but he now felt it by association. His feelings of guilt at Tom's poisoning elicited a quiet but determined vow that surprised even himself. 'I'll find out what happened, Tom.'

Later that day Grant checked into his B&B, a pub with accommodation. The bright-yellow building stuck out at the end of a cul-de-sac, just in front of the headland that looked down on a churning, unsettled sea. He checked into an upstairs room facing towards the barren moorland and wasn't best pleased to discover that it was right above the bar. That evening, after fish and chips, a couple of pints of the local brew in the bar and some banter with the locals, he turned in for the night and assessed his mission thus far. Mark Vernon's death the month before was a blow, and several questions preoccupied him as he lay in bed. Who closed the church door and hurried away? Why did Ted Jessops draw a mermaid? Was there a connection to the legend of the mermaid at Zennor, where Tom was poisoned and subsequently buried? Finally, just before drifting into sleep, Grant resolved he would drive further west the next day and visit the Porthcurno Telegraph Museum, which apparently had a display dedicated to messages in bottles found in the sea near by.

Grant's deep but troubled sleep was interrupted a few hours later by a quiet tap-tapping on the door. He listened intently; the noise was barely louder than a woodpecker. His watch told him that it was three-thirty in the morning. He jumped out of bed, looking for a non-existent peephole in the door. His heart thumped louder than the noisy clock on the wall that ceaselessly confirmed the time. Again came the tap-tap on the door. Hastily grabbing the key to unlock the double-locked door, he fumbled and dropped it. He eventually turned the key only to hear footsteps rushing down the stairs. Charging down the corridor he was accosted by an angry fellow guest who opened his door to demand, 'What the hell's going on?' Grant tried to explain about the tapping at his door. The other guest had heard someone running down the corridor and stairs but hadn't heard any knocking. The two men returned to their rooms, and Grant lay awake for the rest of the night trying to make the jigsaw fit together.

Despite feeling tired the next morning, Grant followed

through with his plan to visit Porthcurno, near the Minack Theatre where he and his friends had spotted Bob Silver with Clive Holford all those years ago. For over 140 years Porthcurno had been at the centre of global communications. The first undersea telegraph cable had arrived there in 1870, linking Britain to India, and it had a pivotal role in the Second World War as the largest and busiest telegraph station in the world. Of most interest to Grant was the town's museum, which celebrated the world of telecommunications long before mobile phones and the internet. He was delighted to discover a glass cabinet with various old bottles that had been washed up on Porthcurno Beach. He studied the reference book that contained the messages from each bottle, reading them in chronological order. When he found the entry for Exhibit 51 his eyes nearly popped out of his head. He felt the blood drain from his face and had to sit down.

'Are you OK?' someone inquired.

'Water. I need a glass of water.'

The entry for Exhibit 51 read, 'Dear Aunt Agatha. I will love you always. Tonight I am not alone.'

The message bore a date that was almost illegible but which he could just about decipher as 23 August 1972. Grant tried to compose his thoughts. He had not expected this. Was someone playing a trick? This had to be the message in a bottle of which Arnie Charnley had spoken to Jenny. If so, it must have washed up the day after Hector died, so why didn't Arnie report it? The Charnleys, together with everyone else, had departed on 24 August 1972 at the end of the holiday, and Hector's corpse had been found on the beach on 24 August. Grant tried, unsuccessfully, to find out how the bottle had found its way into the museum and how long it had been there.

The curator was not especially helpful. 'Nothing to do with

us, sir. We hire the bottle exhibition from a local trader, who moves it from place to place around the county. In fact, you're lucky it's here. It's off to St Ives tomorrow.'

How strange, thought Grant. 'And who's this local trader?' he inquired.

'Just a moment. I'll check.' The man reappeared, having asked a colleague. 'His name's Trevor Mullings.'

'Thank you,' said Grant. It was the fisherman who had reported Hector's death all those years ago. He was someone Grant was now even more keen to meet. For the second time in the space of five minutes he experienced a sudden light-headedness and had to sit down again. He concentrated on taking deep breaths to increase the quantity of oxygen reaching his brain. Once he had recovered, something about the message bothered him. The first part was in faded red ink, but the words 'Tonight I am not alone' were in black. He asked the curator how the ink colour could be so different after forty years or so.

'The first part is not written in ink at all, I'd suggest,' replied the curator in a voice that managed to be simultaneously officious and menacing. 'It may have ink reinforcing it, perhaps, but it's primarily written in blood.'

## 21

## PRESENT DAY

Grant was both euphoric and unnerved at his discovery that Trevor Mullings possessed the bottle in which Hector had placed his note. Euphoric, because he had specifically set out to find Trevor; unnerved, because he now had to add him to his list of circumstantially suspicious people, alongside Ivan Youlen and Ken Holford. As he headed back to his accommodation he looked forward to meeting an old friend for dinner: Ian Fothergill, who was driving over from a village near Truro. Ian had been a partner in Grant's law firm but had decided to 'go west' for a better quality of life and had joined a small regional legal practice in the town. Grant looked forward to hearing about Ian's changed circumstances and sharing with him what he was up to in Cornwall.

He was somewhat dismayed on arriving back at the pub to be greeted by an unenthusiastic receptionist-cum-general assistant who seemed to work all hours; her offhand manner was accentuated by her spiky yellow-and-pink hair and over-sized thighs that protruded from a 1960s-style miniskirt.

'Oh, there was a phone call for you, if I remembers right.'

'Oh yes?'

'I made a note here. A Mr Fothergills.'

'Fothergill,' corrected Grant.

'Yes, that be he. Anyways he says he's not coming for dinner with you tonight.'

'Really?' asked Grant, knowing this to be unusual behaviour

from his old friend and colleague, who would normally have made contact directly and would have offered a full explanation.

'Yes. I'm not a liar.' The punky young woman was affronted.

'Oh, I'm sorry. I do apologize. I mean, of course you are telling the truth. It's just not like him, my friend Ian, to cry off and not leave a message, you see.'

'Well, don't shoot the messenger, guv'nor.'

'No, of course.'

Apologizing again, Grant withdrew to his room. Seriously disappointed, denied his need for friendship and a familiar face with whom to share revelations, he decided against calling Ian and lay on his bed. Clasping his hands behind his head, he reflected on how isolated he felt; there was no signal on his mobile and no internet access. He resolved to go to the bar early that evening and order a simple ploughman's with a half of bitter, after which he would withdraw to catch up on his sleep.

As he climbed on to a high stool he noticed an elderly woman in a white raincoat and headscarf sitting alone in the corner. She seemed to be fixing her gaze on him in a most disconcerting manner. He was cheered by the 1960s' jukebox playing Richard Harris's 'Macarthur Park'. Just as the song reached its crescendo – 'Someone left the cake out in the rain' – the lights fused and the bar was pitched into darkness. The landlord called for calm, saying he would get a torch and fix it.

At that moment Grant felt a hand stroke his face. He recoiled from his bar stool and held his hands in front of his face in fear of further intrusion. Had it been a hand? If so, whose was it? While the saloon bar was still in darkness, he heard a female voice sing softly, only just audibly, 'Half a pound of tuppenny rice, half a pound of treacle'. The sound seemed close to him, but it stopped abruptly as the lights came back on.

He scoured the room for the phantom face-stroker and the mystery nursery-rhyme singer but couldn't identify any likely suspects. Was it one and the same person? He looked for the old woman who had been sitting in the corner, but she was no longer there. He was sure she had been staring at him. The hand he felt could well have been a woman's, but why on earth would anyone stroke his face? The next time he looked at the space there was an old man sitting in the spot, who also stared at him.

Grant hurriedly finished his meal and decided to retire early. His room being directly above the bar, he didn't expect to get to sleep very easily. By good fortune the jukebox turned up a number of his favourite songs, and he found himself nodding off more easily than expected to the soothing music played at pleasingly low volume. His good fortune ran out when he woke with a start about five minutes later as the jukebox roared, 'I am the god of hellfire and I bring you . . .' Arthur Brown and his Crazy World were in full flow. Grant was convinced that someone had turned the volume up to maximum. Silence suddenly descended before the song had finished. He rather hoped that someone had complained. There were five rooms along his corridor, and he was sure that all must have been affected by the noise from the bar. He was just starting to feel drowsy again when the telephone rang, giving him a bit of a shock as he hadn't even noticed there was a telephone in the room. He quickly located the handset and lifted the receiver, only for the line to go dead. Now he was beginning to feel distinctly uneasy. He momentarily thought of checking out and driving to St Ives to find alternative accommodation. At this point he heard a rustling noise as an envelope was pushed under his door. It was addressed to 'Mr Grant Morrison' in large childish letters. Just before he picked it up the phone rang again.

'Hello!' he bellowed.

'Hello, darling. That's a bit of a bark, isn't it?'

'Oh, it's you.' He had rarely been so pleased to hear Brigit's voice. 'Thank God it's you. I'm in quite a state. How are you?' They hadn't spoken since he left Plymouth, and as he never seemed to get a signal on his mobile he had decided he would have to drive inland the following day to have a proper conversation.

'What the hell's going on?'

'To tell the truth, I haven't a clue. I think I am being hunted and haunted.'

''Struth. Who the hell by?'

'I've no idea. I've had a church door slammed shut behind me by a shadowy figure that ran away, a tap on my door at some unearthly hour and a weird elderly couple staring at me in the bar downstairs, though not at the same time. Oh, and a strange hand stroked my face when the lights fused. To cap it all, I had a phantom telephone call just before you rang.' He refrained from mentioning the nursery rhyme, fearing ridicule.

'Would it be better to check in somewhere else? And what do you mean by a weird elderly couple staring at you but not at the same time?'

'They took it in turns.'

Brigit's concern turned to amusement. 'What? They had a rota, did they? I'm sorry, but this is pretty far-fetched, Grant – two old biddies taking turns to outstare you.'

'I know.' He relaxed a little and even permitted himself a small chuckle despite his anxiety. 'It is absurd.'

However, as his eyes fell again on the unopened envelope his anxiety returned, and he stiffened. He asked Brigit to wait on the line and hurriedly tore it open, only to discover it was his bill from the pub. It was clearly the management's custom to place it under residents' doors the night before departure.

Brigit waited.

'Well, at least it's not an invitation from the Loch Ness Monster.'

She was trying to suppress her giggles. 'I think you will find . . .' But Grant heard no more, as the line went dead. Further spooked by this, Grant thought of going back downstairs to inquire about the phone problem, as he found he couldn't dial out. He also considered paying his bill in advance but resisted the notion as he could no longer hear any noise from the bar. No songs were playing on the jukebox, and he couldn't hear any banter.

He decided to double-lock the door, leaving the key in the lock, and to wedge furniture up against the door. He put classical music on low on the radio – there was no television – and he resolved to stiffen his sinews and tough out the night. Finally he drifted into a deep sleep. But what happened next was to terrify him far more than anything that had gone before.

## 22

## PRESENT DAY

He woke with a start. 'Good Morning, Starshine' was blasting out at high volume from the bar below. He saw his wall clock turn four a.m. He felt his face go cold, as if walking out into an early-morning winter frost. But it wasn't the music that shocked him. That soon stopped. It was a voice.

'Half a pound of tuppenny rice, half a pound of treacle . . .'

Grant experienced a full-body shiver, for what really disturbed him was the impression that it was a child's voice, echoing as if sung in a cathedral. As he reached for the door he stopped, abruptly aware that danger could lurk on the other side. He didn't return to sleep. He was sure what had happened on his first night in the pub had infected his subconscious, leaving him in a vulnerable place. Had he really heard the nursery rhyme? Had a child really sung it?

He tried to ignore the questions pounding in his head, but while the previous night had undoubtedly disturbed him what really bothered him now was the message he had discovered in the bottle at Porthcurno. Why had Hector added the sentence 'Tonight I am not alone'? Grant suspected that Hector and another person had both written notes in blood as some sort of weird pact and that Hector had added his last bit in ink as a message to his aunt. The mystery made it all the more vital to meet Trevor Mullings, who he now thought might know rather more than he had revealed to the police in 1972.

'Tonight I am not alone.' He asked himself once more why Hector might have written this. Could it mean that he was going to the beach with a friend and wanted his aunt to know, possibly sensing that he was in some kind of danger? Or did it imply that he was going to be sleeping with someone that night. It was well known at the hotel that Hector's Aunt Agatha wanted more than anything in the world for her nephew to find a partner. She knew her time on earth was limited and that she would leave behind a sad and lonely man. So if he was 'on a promise', who was the mystery girl or boy? Grant decided the first option was the more likely, given Hector's normally lustful language where women were concerned.

His desire to meet Trevor was granted more swiftly than he could have imagined. He returned to Porthcurno and saw an elderly man removing the bottle exhibition from the museum and carefully placing it in a large white van. Grant moved slowly towards him, unsure what his reception might be and wondering how to introduce himself.

'Trevor Mullings?' he inquired.

The man turned to face him. He had receding hair, severely thinning and almost ghostly white, with a mouth rather short of teeth. He snarled, 'What's it to you?'

'I'm sorry to bother you, but I would very much appreciate a chat. You won't remember me. We last met some forty years ago. Perhaps I can buy you a coffee in the museum café?'

'I can give you five minutes but no more.' Reluctantly Trevor moved to join Grant walking towards the café.

'It's about Hector Wallace,' began Grant after they had sat down and been served their drinks.

His guest spat out his tea. 'Oh, piss off. I told the police all I knew back in 1972. What more can I say now?'

'Do you remember a conversation you had with Justyn

Silver and Robert Vernon the week after Hector drowned?'

Trevor looked vague. 'How the hell am I supposed to remember a pair of poncy Hooray Henrys from a night forty years ago?'

'You told them that Hector had left with someone else,' said Grant, ignoring the intended insult to his friends.

'Maybe I did. The devil may take me, but I don't remember who it was.'

His manner, Grant thought, now appeared rather less certain. 'Do you recall anyone in the pub that night or any of the conversations?'

'What, from forty bloody years ago? All I remember was that they went out with bottles and they put messages in them.'

'And you have one of those bottles. It's been on display here.'

'Yes, so what? There's no significance in that.'

'But why have you kept it? Why is that bottle a special one?'

Trevor didn't reply. He just stared vacantly in front of him. Grant felt he was losing Trevor's goodwill – which had been in pretty short supply in the first place. He tried another tack. 'Do you know where I can find Ivan Youlen?'

'You won't find him round here. Someone said he lives around St Austell way, on the south coast.' Trevor spat out the information in such a way as to imply it was of no consequence and seemed confident the distance would put Grant off. Trevor was keen to end the interrogation as quickly as possible, but he underestimated his companion. Just as the two men were going their separate ways Trevor called after Grant, 'I remember you now. You were that boy with the funny eyes.'

Grant decided to leave it at that, giving Trevor £5 to buy himself a beer. He handed over his business card, pointing out his mobile number. They parted cordially, but Grant lingered out of view just long enough to see Trevor make a call on his mobile.

There were now too many unanswered questions for Grant to depart from Cornwall, even though he was unhappy about not getting a signal on his phone and was still concerned about who had been spooking him in Zennor. One thing was for sure. He was not going back to the pub where he had suffered his worst-ever nightmare.

He drove inland, towards St Austell, in search of Ivan Youlen. He got a signal on his mobile, but his joy was short-lived as his battery had run down. Driving on the B3273 from St Austell towards Mevagissey, he noticed an imposing hotel, a white Edwardian-style building set back some two hundred yards from the road. As if by reflex, he turned right through its imposing gates and navigated the long drive. Out of the blue he experienced a strange sensation of curiosity as the converted manor house came more clearly into view, flanked by huge pine trees. He saw a cultivated and resplendent hotel with assorted woodland homes in the grounds. His mood improved considerably on being told there was one room left, down a corridor in a tasteful purpose-built block behind the main building. He checked in, placed his phone on charge and went to sit on the private balcony outside his room.

Having mastered the tea-maker there, he relaxed with an afternoon cup, taking in the calming view of the valley below and the glorious hills on the other side. This new-found tranquillity engendered in him a huge sense of relief and enabled him to think clearly for the first time in days. He knew his card had been marked in Zennor, but it disturbed him that he had no idea by whom. Who had slammed the church door? Who had tapped on his bedroom door? What was the significance of the elderly couple? Who had stroked his face, and who had serenaded him in low child-like tones? And was it really a child the second time round and at such an unearthly hour?

He relaxed for an hour or so and then resolved to make four phone calls: to Brigit, Danny Galvin, Nick Charnley and Justyn Silver.

Brigit's mobile was switched off, and he tried the office.

'You are through to the offices of Morrison Recruitment. All our lines are busy right now, so if you wouldn't mind leaving your ...' Grant smiled to himself. His wife's ruse always amused him. There were just three of them in the company, but she always managed to make it sound like an international conglomerate. Furthermore, he knew it meant the entire staff at HQ had finished for the day and were travelling home or were gathered in a local watering hole, but it was better that the punters thought they were still at their desks.

His next call to Danny Galvin was no more fruitful, but this time he was sure that Danny briefly answered before seeing who the caller was and hanging up, which disconcerted him. He felt more detached from Danny than ever. He called Nick Charnley and received another answerphone message, so he moved on to Justyn Silver.

'Hi, M'Lord. What goes?' replied Justyn. Grant felt elated to talk to a friendly, familiar voice. He related his experiences of the past forty-eight hours and asked him what the hell he thought was going on.

Justyn fell silent as he digested all this before suggesting, 'Someone doesn't want you pursuing this. That much is obvious. Have you spoken to Suzie?'

'No, not yet. She's in Cape Town, and I thought I would leave her till last. Why do you ask?'

'She and Danny had quite a serious relationship in their twenties. I heard she broke off their engagement after some problems with the Galvins in general and Paul in particular.'

'Why?' Grant was genuinely surprised, having never heard any of this before.

'Paul's influence over Danny and Sharon became very dominant, and there was all the fuss and upset when he was sent down.'

'What?' Grant was incredulous.

'Yes. White-collar crime. VAT fraud, so I heard. I believe he may have had two custodial sentences, but Suzie would know.'

'That would explain Caroline's cryptic remark that Suzie might know something.'

'I think you have a long-haul flight to Cape Town to consider if you want to make progress, Grantie my old mucker.'

Justyn was on good form, and Grant was grateful to receive his banter after a traumatic twenty-four hours. In no mood to end the call, he described the beautiful setting of the hotel he had discovered with its breathtaking views.

'Hang on a minute. Did you say it's near St Austell and the main building was a converted manor house?'

'Yes.'

'I know exactly where you are. Dad took Mum there some six or seven years ago, shortly before he died. He was very keen to show her where he first discovered Clive. The building was derelict for a long time before it was converted into a hotel. Actually we all became very fond of Clive. In fact, I'm meeting him for a drink in around half an hour. We legally adopted him after a search revealed he didn't have a birth certificate. As you know, he had run away from his terrible home after his parents split up, but there was all sorts of other stuff that came out.'

'Go on.'

'Well, it turned out that Ken Holford, the wife-beater, was

not his biological father. Mary, who had taken his name, was never legally married to him. She was rescued one day by her sister and now lives happily in Australia, they say. Obviously she couldn't wait to get as far away from Ken as possible.'

'Does Clive still live in fear of him?'

'He's moved on and is much stronger these days, both mentally and physically.'

'That's good to hear. Does Clive have any contact with either of them?'

'He corresponds with his biological mother occasionally. They have an OK relationship, and she has no problem with the Silver family's adoption of her son. They Skyped one another a few weeks back, but they both found it rather too emotional. Clive has done well as an artist and makes a decent living from a Marylebone studio he shares with two others. His mother is very proud of him, and he's going to visit her in Brisbane soon. He's settled in a happy marriage, and Duncan, his son, is going to university this autumn. So it's all worked out well,' Justyn concluded with a tone of some satisfaction.

'And the father?'

'Well, Clive and Dad once hired a private detective to try to get him brought to book for his sins, but the file they handed to the police didn't particularly interest them, as it was really just a character assassination – with some circumstantial evidence of what a prize turd he was. There was no hard evidence of criminality.'

'Is there any chance I could have a copy of that file?'

'Sure. I'll dig it out, get it scanned and email it to you.'

'Many thanks. I think I'll chill out here for a day or two and book a flight to Cape Town once I have established that Suzie can see me. I also need to connect with Messrs Youlen and Holford.'

'Good luck. I am with you all the way on all this, Grantie. There are just too many unanswered questions.'

They hung up, leaving Grant excited and impatient for the arrival of the private investigator's report, which he hoped would provide some strong leads.

## 23

## PRESENT DAY

Grant knew he couldn't leave Cornwall without finding Ivan Youlen and Ken Holford. He thought he had left the horrors of Zennor behind until parked below his balcony he spotted a car, an old Austin, that he was sure he had seen on the previous two nights. He made a note of its number plate, and a swift internet search revealed the car was registered in Essex. This confounded him. However, if the car belonged to the elderly couple who had been staring at him unnervingly there might just be someone he knew behind all this – his former friend Danny who he was sure had tried to put him off pursuing the matter further. But why would he want to frighten him? What could he be hiding? He resolved to locate Ivan Youlen, but he couldn't get back online at the hotel. He asked reception for a copy of the Yellow Pages. On receipt of this he was delighted to discover an Ivan Youlen living near by at Mevagissey.

He hurriedly dialled the number and heard the message, 'Neither Ivan or Julie are here at present, so please leave a message.'

He left a short, succinct one. 'Hi, Ivan. You won't remember me, but my name is Grant Morrison, and I used to stay at the hotel where your Uncle Tom worked. Can you please call me on . . .' He didn't have high hopes of a returned call. He reasoned that Ivan must be well over sixty years of age, as it was over forty-four years since he and another coastguard had rescued Joanna Jessops from drowning off Constantine Bay Beach. He now turned his attention to tracking down Ken Holford, who he guessed must be in his mid to late seventies if he was still alive. He looked at his iPad for Justyn's emailed report, but it hadn't arrived.

That evening Grant drove to a nearby pub on the road to Mevagissey to seek out some local gossip. He sat at the bar, making out that he had lived in Cornwall most of his life and was now looking to settle in this particular area, even bluffing that he had friends near by called Ivan Youlen and Ken Holford. No one identified either as being acquaintances, but one of the locals, a hairy, thickly tattooed man with forearms that could have belonged to a professional wrestler, raised his eyes heavenwards at the mention of Ken Holford.

'Do you know him?' asked Grant eagerly.

'No I don't,' came the clipped reply. 'But if hanging was still allowed, that man would have swung from the old gallows in Truro.'

'Wow, strong stuff. What's he done?' Grant had overplayed his hand, sounding a bit too London toff, and the landlord interrupted the opinionated Cornishman.

'Now then, Ernie. That be dangerous talk.'

Much to Grant's chagrin, there would be no further discussion on the subject. The barman turned up the music to such a volume that conversation became almost impossible, which was plainly his intention. As Grant had consumed four pints of bitter – in addition to buying pretty much everyone in the pub a drink while claiming he was celebrating his birthday – he ordered a taxi back to the hotel. This was a deliberate ploy. He knew taxi drivers were a rich source of local information, and he would order another in the morning to help him retrieve his car. Just as he was about to leave, the publican and a coterie of others appeared with a dessert, a small slice of Black Forest gâteau with a solitary candle burning on it, and delivered a hearty rendition of 'Happy Birthday to You'. Startled and a little hazy as a result of his hop-fuelled evening he thanked them, saying it had all been very enjoyable. He climbed in the cab, dessert in hand.

'What a prat,' the landlord said to the assembled drinkers, as the taxi pulled away. Grant didn't catch the words but saw their laughter all too clearly.

'What a jolly bunch,' he remarked to the driver, before asking, 'Do you know a man by the name of Ivan Youlen?'

Grant's fortunes were on the rise. As luck would have it, his driver lived in the fishing village of Mevagissey, on the same street as Ivan Youlen.

'Ivan the greenfingers,' announced the cabbie in a proper West Country burr.

'Why is he called that?'

'Well, he works at the gardens.'

'Which gardens?'

'You know, the ones that were lost and are now found.'

'The Lost Gardens of Heligan,' Grant announced triumphantly. 'Will I find him there?'

'Expect so. And Julie works in the shop.'

'Has Julie been there long? I mean she and Ivan have been together a long time, haven't they?' he bluffed.

'Don't think so. Julie's only forty-odd, more than twenty years younger than that old rascal Ivan. He trades in his women for younger models more often than rockin' Rod Stewart,' the cabbie chortled.

'Lucky Ivan if they look like Rod's women.'

'Well, whatever,' said the cabbie. 'That'll be £6.'

Grant gave a tip of another £2, delighted that he now knew where to find green-fingered Ivan, the ladies' man. Heading back to his hotel room, he was sober enough to look for the old Austin with the Essex number plate. He didn't know whether to be relieved or not that it wasn't there. On closing his bedroom door he moved swiftly to fill a bath and then he called Brigit.

'Well, hello,' she replied. 'I've been worried about you.'

'Yeah, sorry. Phone got cut off last night. Don't know why. I tried the office around six, but I guess you were on your way home.'

'Anyway, no more being haunted by old biddies?'

'No, but it's creepy. There was a car at Zennor I saw in the car park here.'

'Are you sure?'

'Yes, and it's an Essex number plate. You don't think Danny is trying to freak me out?'

'Unlikely. But lock your door anyway.'

Grant decided not to mention the second of his interrupted nights and ended the call with dutiful amorous declarations. He couldn't wait to get back home, but he wasn't going to quit now.

The following day he set out to find Ivan at the Lost Gardens of Heligan. The tourist attraction was well signposted, instructing Grant to turn right off the B3273 heading to Mevagissey and following the brown signs. On arrival in the car park he surveyed all the shops and tea rooms and wondered if he had arrived at a run-of-the-mill garden centre. He was soon to be educated, however, marvelling as he read the potted history that explained how the gardens had been hidden for seventy-odd years. He noted the motto, 'Don't come here to sleep or slumber.' He asked for Ivan at reception, and it so happened he had just clocked on for his shift.

'Ivan,' he announced when they came face to face, 'I'm Grant Morrison. I left a message on your answerphone last night.'

Ivan studied him carefully but made no reply.

'Can we talk?' He followed Ivan outside.

'What the fuck about?' Ivan marched away to start his work, with Grant following hurriedly in his wake, noticing that Ivan walked with a pronounced limp. As he rushed to catch up, he wondered whether Ivan had acquired the infirmity by being battered by waves in his coastguard days or, more likely, by getting involved in a skirmish or two over the years. In other respects the man appeared much as he would have anticipated. His ambling gait seemed to diminish his height to around six feet; Grant was sure he used to be taller. His jet-black hair, now silver grey, was still worn long. The only other notable change was a couple of rather grainy chipped teeth.

'Look, I know it was a long time ago, but there was never any justice for your Uncle Tom and neither, it would seem, for Hector Wallace.'

Ivan studied Grant again, disapprovingly. 'And who are you? Inspector fucking Morse?'

Grant became bolder. 'Look, you can swear at me as much as you like, but I'm not going away, and I would much rather we had a cordial conversation.'

'What about?' Ivan repeated again, this time without the expletive.

Grant felt this was progress of sorts. 'Someone has got away with these events, these crimes, for a long, long time, and there is some evidence as to who the killer might be.'

'And who might he be?'

Grant pursued Ivan around the Italian section of the gardens, figuring that as long as Ivan didn't make a citizen's arrest he would continue, as it was his only hope of speaking to Ivan the Irascible.

'Three questions. First, were you in the pub that night with Trevor Mullings and Hector Wallace when messages were written in bottles and Hector was found washed up dead the next day? Second, did you go to the beach with Hector? And, third, did Ken Holford go?'

For one glorious moment Grant hoped his direct approach had paid off, as Ivan studied him again before instructing him to 'Go play with yourself', at which point he disappeared into a shed and slammed the door.

'And what happened to the cash Uncle Tom was looking after, Ivan? The truth will come out. You can't ignore it, and you can't ignore me,' shouted Grant, getting angrier than he could ever remember being before.

'Oh, can't I?' shouted Ivan through the closed glass window.

'No. I will find Ken Holford next, and I'll find out from him.'

'I don't think so,' countered Ivan, breaking into a deep spine-chilling laugh.

'And why's that?'

'Because he's – as you Cockneys would have it – brown bread! Yes. Would you Adam and Eve it? Ken's brown bread. 'E don't go down the rub-a-dub-dub no more. 'E don't even go up the apples and pears no more. 'E's brown bread!' Ivan's belly laugh from inside the hut seemed to rock the wooden foundations and rendered Grant speechless. As he walked away disconsolately he looked back and could just about make out Ivan mouthing every expletive invented in his direction; he was minded to report him to his employers but thought better of it.

Grant suddenly felt a fool. Hadn't the man in the pub, Ernie, said about Ken Holford, 'That man should have swung from the old gallows in Truro'? And he had completely missed the comment being in the past tense. As he turned to make his way back through the gardens, he couldn't help but be struck by the incongruity of such a wondrously beautiful place bearing witness to such an ill-natured conversation. Grant lingered just long enough to turn and witness Ivan on his mobile phone. Recovering his equilibrium, Grant couldn't help smiling as he read a noticeboard saying, 'Enjoyed today? For the same price you can become a Friend of Heligan for a year.'

Great, he thought. I could be abused by Ivan every day of the year for no extra charge.

## 24

## PRESENT DAY

The file on Ken Holford presented to Bob Silver and his adopted son, Clive, and subsequently emailed to Grant, did not make for pretty reading. Holford's story was littered with references to drunkenness and cruelty to women. One of them, an Irene Clements, had lived in a small village called Tregorrick. Grant couldn't help but suspect that Ernie, the character in the pub who maintained that Holford should have swung, was either known or related to her, as the village was in the watering hole's vicinity. There was clearly personal bitterness in the tirade at the bar. However, there was no escaping the unsettling fact that Ken had evaded prosecution for any serious criminality. Grant personally believed that wife-beating should receive automatic custodial sentencing, but each of the women questioned had been more concerned about escaping the monster's clutches than testifying against him in court – all but one, a Carol Todd who appeared to be with him at the time of the investigation in 2003.

Despite a bruised face, explained by the usual 'walking into doors' story, she was hard to interview and would say only that he was 'basically a good man and misunderstood by folk'. Grant, who did not know how or where Holford had died, resolved to find Carol Todd. Before doing so, he continued reading the private investigator's report that had tried to piece together the subject's working life. Holford had moved to the village of St Buryan in the summer of 1972, which Grant surmised was shortly before Clive and Bob would have seen him in the pub, after attending the Minack Theatre. At this time he appeared to be holding down two jobs, the other being an assistant in a National Trust café on the nearby north coast. He recalled Suzie Hughes-Webb relating the story of the four fathers' run on the beach at the end of the holiday, as told to her by her father and recorded on tape at his suggestion.

Tracking down Carol Todd was Grant's next task, and he extended his stay in the sanctuary he had found near St Austell. The usual internet searches proved useless, as did the Yellow Pages. Grant delved into the report and saw that, at the time of writing, Holford had been living in the small village of Trelill on the north coast near Pendogett. He noted in an index to the report that there were some addresses and phone listings of relevant people, but, remarkably, there was no data on Holford. He inquired at the local pub as to whether anyone knew a Carol Todd, bluffing that he was related to her by marriage. He was greeted by stony faces until one local piped up, 'Yea, she be over there', pointing out of the window.

Grant felt a sense of impending gloom and turned to see his fears confirmed; the man's finger indicated the graveyard next to the church. He thanked the informant and tried without much success to engage him in conversation. There were the usual grumbles about grockles invading their county every summer, together with more general moans about the government and how many foreigners it would let in before the people shouted 'Stop!' but Grant didn't find out anything more about Carol Todd. And no further light was shed on the infamous Ken Holford, with his well-known predilection for alcohol. As much as he loved Cornish pubs, Grant felt deflated and was even beginning to wish they could move on from jukeboxes stuck in a fifty-year time warp, particularly when the only hit by Zager and Evans, 'In the Year 2525', struck up.

He left the pub, pretending to go to his car, and crossed the road to look for a gravestone or some other form of memorial to Carol Todd. He didn't have to go far. A relatively recent headstone set against the wall of the churchyard stated 'Here lies Carol Ann Todd, beloved daughter of Jack and Marion Todd, 1955–2005.' Someone other than her parents had been responsible for the tombstone, as the graves of Jack and Marion Todd lay adjacent to Carol's; they had evidently passed away years earlier. As with Tom's memorial stone, there was evidence of someone attending the flowers there. Grant silently seethed. Someone must know something, he said to himself. He crossed the road to head back to the pub, blood rising in his head and throbbing from ear to ear. He threw open the door to the saloon bar and felt giddy as the music boomed out even louder. He took a few steps forward, staggered towards the bar, saw the lights go on and then off before crashing to the floor.

He regained consciousness in the ambulance on the way to the Royal County Hospital in Truro. He came round throwing up all over the paramedic deputed to sit in the back with him. His new companion told him what had happened and said that they needed to keep talking to ensure that he didn't lose consciousness again. In fact, Grant slipped in and out of consciousness several times, each time awakening to unleash projectile vomit in the direction of the paramedic, who found himself ducking for cover. Grant asked what he thought was wrong with him.

'Well, I'm no doctor, sir, but I would hazard that you've suffered some form of poisoning, which has caused you to have a vasovagal attack. But please don't take that as gospel. Maybe you've been under undue stress lately, perhaps much more than you would normally be.'

Grant panicked at the implications of this. In his heightened state of insecurity he suspected foul play. He wasn't too concerned about stress, as he felt that would soon pass, but he was concerned about the possibility of being poisoned. On his arrival in hospital he was left lying on a trolley awaiting medical attention, like holiday luggage abandoned at an airport, for some two hours. He recalled Mr Simpkins, the hotel manager who was rushed to the same hospital after blacking out and chipping his two front teeth when he collapsed at the reception desk some forty years earlier.

Eventually, after undergoing various tests, he was informed that it was almost certainly a severe case of salmonella poisoning and that there was no evidence of other noxious substances. In his mind he had become obsessed with the idea of poisonous worm eggs entering his system somehow. He thought of poor Tom Youlen and how, hours after ingestion, he suffered the terrible stroke that destroyed his life. In his half-conscious state Grant thought that perhaps he was receiving his comeuppance, that he had been singled out by the Almighty to level the score as far as Tom was concerned; he was taking the hit on behalf of all the holidaying families for the crime committed in 1972. After a further four hours of observation he asked if he could be discharged. Following some negotiation about this he took a taxi back to his hotel.

After a brief conversation with Brigit, during which he made no mention of his recent hospitalization, he retired early to bed without food. He knew she was annoyed with him for prolonging his stay in Cornwall, and she seemed rather weary of his investigation, but he was becoming so obsessed that he had become increasingly insensitive to her feelings. He sent an email to Justyn updating him but was dismayed to receive an 'out of office' reply, advising all callers that he would be away until the following Monday, some four days hence.

The following morning Grant awoke to a gloriously blue Cornish sky and decided to visit the beautiful coastal village of Fowey. He walked to clear his head and to allow his stomach a period of recovery before eating again. He crossed the beautiful harbour on the ferry and reflected further on events. Daphne du Maurier's house was pointed out to him, and for a moment he felt he might be in one of her novels. His mind took him back to 1972 and the incidents that had lodged in his memory as being odd: Paul Galvin spotted in heated conversation with Ivan Youlen that Sunday; the scene that included Arnie Charnley being witnessed by Ted Jessops who made an anonymous phone call to the police. Then there was the issue of Ivan Youlen conversing with Ken Holford at the National Trust café, as witnessed by the four joggers. Grant had been advised by Suzie that this had occurred on Wednesday 23 August, as she had taped the events of that morning on her father's instruction. He also reflected on Ted Jessops drawing a mermaid, 'the Mermaid of Zennor', according to Caroline's mother. But what really stumped him was the message in the bottle. Why did Hector add the line 'Tonight I am not alone' in different ink? And with whom did he leave the pub to go to the beach?

Grant mused on how all the prime suspects, as well as the victims, were now part of a world that had gone for ever, and momentarily he wondered why he had become so obsessed by it all. For the first time he asked himself whether it really mattered. Then he remembered what was really driving him on; he wanted to discover whether his mother had been an accomplice to murder. He felt frustrated at his results so far, but one person kept coming to mind as central: Ivan Youlen, whose behaviour had been so hostile when he caught up with him at the Lost Gardens. Grant felt he couldn't really trust Trevor Mullings, but he had at least given him some idea of where to find Ivan. But then why had both Trevor and Ivan gone straight on to their phones as soon as they thought Grant had departed? Was he missing something? Had they been working together all the time? Ken Holford was reportedly dead, but no one seemed to know where he was buried or even when he died. The unfortunate Carol Todd was bruised and still with Ken at the time of the private investigation in 2003 but died two years later at the age of fifty. Several locals in the two pubs had hinted at further knowledge but had closed ranks when pressed. Grant began to think he was wasting his time in Cornwall. He had his reasons for trying to unearth the truth, but he was not prepared to admit them to anyone, and that included his peer group and even Brigit.

Now was the time to see Suzie. A journey to Cape Town was both inevitable and essential, as he was merely spinning tyres in the sand at present. Hadn't Caroline given a pretty big steer that Suzie might know something? And Justyn had let slip about the relationship that was to develop between Suzie and Danny in their twenties, involving a broken engagement, possibly suggesting dark forces at work in the Galvin family emanating from Danny's financially stressed and criminally prosecuted father, Paul.

Grant returned to the hotel that had given him peace of mind amid the turmoil of the last four days. He packed and drove back to Plymouth to return the hire car and took the train back to Paddington. He refrained from contacting Robert again, as he wasn't sure what he could tell him and he didn't see him having any further relevance to his investigations.

On his return to Brigit at their home in Mill Hill, after telling her all that had happened in the West Country, he tried hard but without success to persuade her to join his planned visit to South Africa. Brigit, while sympathetic, was growing tired of his pursuit and was alarmed when Grant admitted that he had allocated a considerable sum of his own money to its continuation.

'Look, for some reason you have a crusade going on, and I am beginning to suspect a case of obsessive-compulsive disorder. So just go to Cape Town, see Suzie whoever-whatever and complete your cold case, because it seems to be heading from the fridge to the freezer!'

It dawned on Grant that Brigit was becoming disengaged from the whole project. 'Well, thanks ever so much! It would be nice to receive more support, but I'm not backing off now. And, for your information, I think someone tried to poison me in Cornwall.'

'What?'

'You heard. I collapsed and was rushed into hospital. My condition didn't last long, and I discharged myself as soon as I could. I recovered the next day.'

'Now listen to me. This is becoming really creepy. It's seriously dangerous territory. Why can't you leave all this once and for all? Get a grip, Grant. Someone might die – and it might just be you. Actually, I didn't mention this before, but we were followed on the walk that day from Gurnards Head to Cape Cornwall.'

Grant was not really listening. Her words floated past him. He knew the next stage of his mission loomed large, and nothing would put him off.

For a few moments the *froideur* between them was maintained until she drew him to her with a warm hug. 'Go on then. Go off to Cape Town. But please be careful. You're not a teenager any more. This isn't *Swallows and Amazons* for adolescents. There is something I don't like about this, something really quite dark, so I wish you'd leave it alone. But if you have to pursue it, just get it over with as quickly as possible.'

## 25

## PRESENT DAY

Grant arrived in Cape Town after an eleven-hour flight, Table Mountain dominating the landscape as his plane descended towards the runway. His hotel on the outskirts of the city, approached through a manned security barrier and at the end of a rose-bordered driveway, was a lovely white converted farmhouse. He arrived too early to check in and pondered what to do before his appointed lunch with Suzie on the harbour front the following day. He decided to visit the wine plantations of Constantia, an area with cool, lush sea-facing slopes flanked by granite surrounds. He enjoyed himself tasting wines and touring wineries, cellars and bistros.

He dined alone in his hotel that night, contemplating the next day's meeting with Suzie, which he now regarded as make-or-break for his investigation. After he had polished off several wines by the glass to accompany his lavish meal, he decided he would ask her what she knew of the relationship between her father and his mother. He would also press her about her on–off relationship with Danny, only too aware that this would stretch both of their powers of diplomacy and tact. Danny's father, Paul, would come in for inevitable scrutiny, although Grant's hopes of revelations were severely limited in this regard. He was, however, intrigued as to why Suzie's father had felt it so important to ask her to tape his full recollection of the conversations and people involved in the run on the beach.

The following morning he had booked a ticket on the nine a.m. ferry to Robben Island to see the cell in which Nelson Mandela had been incarcerated for eighteen of his twenty-seven years of captivity. As the tourist-laden vessel set off on the forty-minute journey across a very choppy sea, he was struck by contrasts: the wonderful view towards the harbour front of Cape Town as against the forbidding, flat, barren island of low-lying buildings that they were approaching and which had taken the freedom of those interned there in such a horrific fashion. Grant toured the island by coach, with a well-informed guide relating the history and geography of the old prison and leper colony. A former political prisoner then took him on a tour of the buildings, stopping poignantly at the 'home' – a tiny cell – of Nelson Mandela. Quite apart from the story of the great man himself, Grant thought the guard a truly inspirational person, as he had found it possible to forgive the repressive apartheid regime and move on.

On his return journey he reflected on the injustice of what he had seen, as he watched a group of seals lying on their backs and riding the waves with flippers extended upwards, enjoying their freedom in the water under the glorious sun. As he approached the breathtaking waterfront he scrutinized the landing stage for Suzie and spotted her waving furiously from the shore.

Slightly chubbier than he remembered her, her face looked tired and gaunt, lined and wrinkled prematurely, probably as a result of too much sun. She strode towards him wearing a cream round-necked cardigan – protection against the stiff breeze – above a lemon-coloured pencil skirt, which Grant thought, uncharitably, did little for her rather shapeless figure. After the obligatory hellos and kisses she took him to an informal, trendy restaurant where they exchanged pleasantries while attempting to bridge the gap of some twenty-five years. Caroline Jessops had given Grant some of Suzie's more recent background, enabling him to be direct.

'I'm so sorry your mother had such a terrible time. It must have been awful for you and Frank.'

'Yes. Thanks,' replied Suzie. 'Alzheimer's is not a disease you would wish on your worst enemy, but at least we were able to look after her, and she had little idea what a burden she was. It was tricky because Tony was overseas, but Frank was fantastic. Anyway, how are you?'

Grant brought her up to speed with the personal details of his life, but it wasn't long before he moved things along. 'You see, Suzie, I think someone doesn't want me pursuing this matter. The Spooks in Zennor were a manifestation of this.'

'What?'

'Well, strange things happened when I went to Cornwall. I booked into a pub near Zennor and was woken by tapping on the door. Then there were anonymous phone calls, and during a power cut in the bar someone stroked my face in the dark. And someone slammed a church door shut behind me. There was also the extraordinary matter of an elderly couple taking it in turns to stare me out both before and after the power cut.'

'What! You were rattled by a pair of senior citizens outstaring you? Come on, Grant. You do take yourself a bit too seriously. You always have done.' She started to giggle, slightly patronizingly in his opinion.

He decided to avoid further humiliation by withholding any mention of the nursery-rhyme serenading. 'OK, OK. Brigit had the same reaction. Anyway, that is all just background noise. The fact is, I am no nearer to discovering who poisoned Tom and who may have helped Hector drown.'

'Is it so important?'

'What?'

'Is it so important? You've just visited Robben Island and seen for yourself one of the worst human injustices of all time and you are concerning yourself with events from over forty years ago that had nothing to do with you and with which no one has been much concerned since – apart from you, it would appear.'

'OK, I admit it has become an obsession, but why won't people talk to me? Why did Ivan Youlen close up like a clam after spewing language that would have shocked a sailor? What does Trevor Mullings know – and should Ken Holford have hanged?'

'Probably,' Suzie replied. 'And the Beatles should have got back together, and Danny always used to tell me that Brian Clough should have been the England football manager, but you can't change the past.'

Grant decided to change tack. 'I gather you and Danny became pretty close some years after we all stopped going on holiday together.'

'If by close you mean we were going to get married, had named the day and I pulled out the week before, yes, you could say we were pretty close.'

'So why did you?'

'You know, if you even consider marrying into a family like the Galvins you virtually have to sign a compromise agreement, like the sort of thing employers insist on, so that when an employee leaves there's no badmouthing or litigation.'

'Yes, I understand. I know perfectly well what a compromise agreement is, thanks,' Grant replied, a little bit aggrieved at Suzie's schoolmarmish tone. But he got the message; this was a no-go area. Their conversation was stilted. Suzie veered from dogmatic, verging on dictatorial, to putting up a brick wall whenever she didn't like a question.

Grant had always feared that this meeting – in contrast to

the ones with Jenny and Caroline – would prove somewhat awkward. He had found the others quite convivial, whereas Suzie seemed colder and more complicated. While old friendships can easily be rekindled, they had lived about half a lifetime since their holidays in Cornwall, and other relationships had intervened. He had never gone out with Suzie and was finding it much harder to re-establish a rapport. He longed to raise the subject of the potential complicity of their parents but opted for safer ground with the tape-recording of the four fathers' beach adventure.

'I have always wanted to ask you, why did your father want to record that episode of the run on the beach and the meeting with Bob Silver in the National Trust café?'

'Father was a very careful, precise man, and he had little confidence in either the police or the Crown Prosecution Service. He thought the original arrests were clumsy and badly thought through, so he started recording everything and obtaining witness statements. He was involved in some very serious pioneering work into heart disease using animals in a way that has remained highly controversial to this day. Working in the spotlight like that made him particularly cautious.'

'Fair enough.' Suzie's warming to the conversation emboldened Grant to ask a more delicate question. 'Did you know that he and my mother were quite fond of each other?'

'Yes.'

'How much did you know?'

'They were lovers,' she continued. 'Everyone thought Father got involved with one of his nurses down from London at the cottage in Zennor, but I'm afraid, Grant, that it was your mother.'

Grant went pale and ordered a beer, neglecting his usual manners by forgetting to ask whether she wanted another drink, too.

'I'm sorry to be so forthright. I thought you knew. You'd heard about the interrupted walk up the hotel's drive, I presume? Yes, of course you had. We all talked about our parents' various shenanigans that night in the pub after the Minack Theatre, didn't we?'

'Yes, that was the night Hector was abused for having spotted your father and my mother walking arm in arm and Tom arrived to break up the quarrel.'

'Whatever,' continued Suzie, with a hint of resentment. 'I think that little episode went round the hotel pretty quickly.'

'But how did you know the rest?'

Before she could reply they were interrupted by the arrival of her husband, Frank. After polite introductions Suzie asked Grant when he was leaving Cape Town.

'The day after tomorrow. I'm going up Table Mountain tomorrow morning, but I should be free later in the afternoon.'

'Perfect,' she said, as Grant took stock of Frank, a burly former policeman now working in security in Cape Town. He wore the hangdog expression of a dominated, henpecked husband who had long given up trying to be Suzie's equal, as she left him in little doubt that he was subordinate in the relationship.

'Frank, darling, you don't mind if I take Barnard for a walk with Grant tomorrow afternoon, do you? We still have some catching up to do.'

Frank acquiesced grudgingly, knowing that their beloved border terrier would welcome the exercise. Suzie arranged to meet Grant at Kirstenbosch, assuring him he would enjoy walking round one of the greatest botanical gardens in the world.

They met as arranged, but with so little time left Grant was impatient to find out how much more she knew about their parents' affair. Walking through the magnificent trees and plants, they managed to lose the border terrier Suzie referred to as a 'border terrorist', which was about as close to humour as she got. Barnard reappeared just as Grant was about to learn how she knew so much.

'OK, Grant, here's the unexploded bomb. Henry, Justyn's elder brother, was busy with his film-making most of that last holiday in 1972, and before his death Father was keen to get hold of the film. Unfortunately Danny got his hands on it first and refused to return it. When I broke off my engagement to him I grabbed the film together with a lot of other personal stuff that I had kept in our flat in Fulham. Danny was burgled the very next day, and I don't think he ever suspected I had taken it – and, no, the burglary was nothing to do with me. Anyway, years later someone took it upon themselves to convert Henry's cine films to DVDs. And let's just say there was some incriminating stuff on them. Father never saw the films. I thought they might upset him, as I knew what was on them. I thought let sleeping dogs lie, so I didn't actually tell him I had the films, but I never felt good about deceiving him.'

'I understand,' said Grant solemnly. 'Is there any chance I can see them?' He was bursting at the seams to view the footage; he felt that it might just provide important answers to some of the mysteries he was pursuing and that he might finally get somewhere.

Suzie had, of course, been expecting this query and had already decided to be helpful. 'Well, you could, but they're in storage back in England with a lot of other stuff.'

By the end of their walk she had agreed to make arrangements with her solicitor in London for Grant to have access to the DVDs.

He asked her one final question. 'Why did Paul Galvin go to gaol – twice?'

Suzie, who had been a qualified nurse and who knew when to leave questions unanswered, stared so coldly at him that he was sure he felt a drop in temperature. 'Look, I support you finding out the truth, but I am not going to talk about the Galvins. I know Father would have advised against it.'

Grant was struck by her total obsession with her father even from beyond the grave. He reflected silently: if only Richard Hughes-Webb had been worthy of such idolatry.

He flew back to London later the same night, feeling he was at last making some sort of progress. He was happy that Suzie now seemed involved in his quest to establish the truth from so long ago; this was a significant change from her attitude when they were first reunited on the harbour front. However, something about her troubled him. He had felt, at times, that he wasn't so much talking to a brick wall as a brick wall was talking to him.

On the flight home, after his meal he sipped a Cognac. It induced a soporific haze, and he found himself humming 'Half a pound of tuppenny rice, half a pound of treacle' as he fell asleep, the glass still precariously in his hand. He continued to doze intermittently during the eleven-hour flight but woke after dreaming about the burglary at the Fulham flat Suzie had shared with Danny. Was there any connection with the burglary at Tom Youlen's cottage in Zennor where Arnie Charnley's cash had disappeared? Two unsolved burglaries, where only selected items had been targeted. He had no doubt that Danny's burglary had been solely about the film footage, as Suzie had told him that no other items apart from these had been taken.

On one score, though, Suzie had definitely put him right. He had seen for himself the appalling circumstances of Nelson Mandela's captivity – and that of so many others – and Grant shifted uncomfortably in his seat, knowing he had lived through the years since that time to witness the incredible power of the human spirit to overcome adversity and forgive injustice. His own quest for truth and justice suddenly seemed rather inconsequential. He felt like a pygmy on the shoulders of a giant.

## 26

## PRESENT DAY

Grant returned from Cape Town to Mill Hill and found relations between himself and Brigit somewhat strained. On his arrival she had been frosty, almost indifferent, and there was a lack of engagement in her conversation. After he had unpacked, showered and changed, he started telling her his news, which she half-heartedly tried to take in. However, she seemed distracted, as if she had no interest in his discoveries. Despite this he carried on talking about incriminating DVDs, burglaries and Suzie's failed relationship with Danny quite impervious to the atmosphere until Brigit finally yelled, 'Enough!'

'What?' he asked, stunned.

'Enough. I've had enough! This is your story, Grant – your world, your obsession – but please leave me out of it. I think you are embroiled in something I wish you would leave well alone. Don't forget you were very ill in Cornwall, very likely poisoned, but what does my opinion count for? I know you need to find out what happened and then get closure. Then I'll be here for you again.'

'So what are you suggesting?'

'I have had it with your Jessops, Charnleys, mermaids, messages in bottles, trips to Cornwall and South Africa, your obsession with all this. The fact is, Grant, I don't care. I couldn't care less about any of it, save for the rather unsettling fact that you are playing with fire and someone might actually harm *you* next. Why can't you accept that this case went dead forty years ago? The police carried out their investigations, and the CPS closed the file. Nobody was tried, nobody has died because of those events – and nobody, apart from you, gives a damn.'

'I am not going to drop it – and somebody did die . . .' Grant tried to sound defiant.

'I know,' she said, controlling her crying. 'I know you can't drop it, and that is partly why I can't go on like this. I need a break. I support you in what you're doing, but I need a break from it. We need a break from each other.'

Grant was astounded and felt as if the air was being sucked out of the room. He had only just returned from time away from Brigit. He threw on a jacket and collected up his mobile, glasses case, wallet and keys and stormed out of the house, slamming the front door behind him. Once outside he called for a cab and phoned Justyn, choosing him mainly because he had demonstrated the most interest in his investigation.

'What's up, M'Lord?' asked Justyn, in that jocular but slightly patronizing style he reserved for Grant.

'Can we meet?'

'Sure, as it happens I am at a loose end tonight. Let's meet at my club in Mayfair. I'll be there in twenty minutes. Just give my name and they'll let you in.'

'Brilliant!' said Grant in an enthusiastic tone that surprised himself. Justyn's carefree manner had lifted him off the floor – but now he wanted to fall back on to it. He felt like getting completely legless. He hadn't felt so reckless in years. All the tension of recent weeks needed to burst, and he felt powerless to stop it.

He arrived at the club before his host and settled down in the bar with a whisky sour. He was already on his second when Justyn arrived. He immediately detected a deterioration in his old friend since their last meeting a few weeks earlier.

'What gives?' asked Justyn, more seriously than usual.

'It's Brigit. She . . . she's asked for time out,' Grant blurted.

'Ah. I think it rhymes with "clucking bell",' Justyn observed, taking in Grant's surprising news.

'Yes – and all of that. It's a huge shock, a bolt from the blue.' Grant stared straight ahead.

Justyn consoled his friend as best he could, ordered a bottle of Dom Perignon and suggested that they share a dozen oysters. He outlined the agenda for the evening as it suddenly formed in his head. They would dine at his casino – 'quails' eggs, fresh lobster; they've got the lot' – have a flutter at black-jack and then they would go on to a lap-dancing club. Despite his red, swollen eyes and scrambled mind Grant compre-hended the normally forbidden path his friend was suggesting, but his usual caution had been anaesthetized.

'How do you know all these places?' he asked, warming to the prospect ahead.

'It goes with the territory. Some Chinese clients love the gambling – it's illegal in Hong Kong – and the Russians love pretty young girls. Communist thinking and doctrine are a pre-Stone-Age concept now. And, of course, they all have the wedge.'

'The what?'

'The wedge, the wonga, the dosh,' continued Justyn. 'They have great big cruise liners of the stuff, aircraft-hanger quantities of it. The old order has gone, Grantie, the Empires of Europe and even the USA are being replaced by . . .'

At that moment Grant heard his phone ring and spotted that the missed call was from Brigit. He hesitated and ignored it. A few moments later he saw he had a voicemail message that he also ignored and within another few minutes a text message. 'I know you are angry but can we talk tomorrow? By the way a package has turned up for you to sign.' He shared this information with Justyn, who suggested it might be a good idea to call back, but Grant had no appetite for arbitration with Brigit there and then, and he decided to call in the morning. He knew he had rather overreacted by storming out, but he needed time to think things through.

Justyn set one rule for the evening: there would be no ranting about Brigit. Nevertheless he listened patiently to Grant's tale of woe, but by the time they had left the club and were enjoying a lavish, expensive dinner at the casino the two men had begun to analyse Grant's attempts at playing sleuth.

'I told you Suzie was important,' proclaimed Justyn, allowing himself some self-satisfaction.

'Yes, but she wouldn't open up about the Galvins. That was a complete no-go area.'

'But you did hear about the film footage.'

'That Henry took in 1972?' replied Grant. 'Did you know he was filming just about the whole of that last holiday?'

'My brother was rather quiet back then. He had his problems with Dad, too. He just went into a shell when he was with the family. Nobody took much notice of his constant filming. He was a bit nerdy really, a bit of an anorak. He was also quite left wing, had been involved in student marches at Oxford – CND and all that malarkey. Whenever he mentioned politics at home there would be a fearful row, so he just sort of shut up shop around that time and stalked around after everyone instead, spending all his time filming on that final holiday. He had done the same thing during the previous years there, so no one took much notice. Of course, in hindsight, we should have done. Those events in 1972 were radically different from all the other years. Even I didn't think to watch what he'd caught on camera, though.'

'Great,' said Grant. This was the best news he had heard all day. 'I can't wait to see the film.'

They finished their meal and went downstairs to the black-jack table. Grant had set himself a float of £200 and was not, even in his current reckless state, prepared to lose any more. Within twenty minutes and two 'shoes' he had lost it, not helped by the minimum stake being £25.

Justyn, meanwhile, appeared to be losing rather more heavily, but when Grant suggested leaving he said, 'I know this game, Grantie. I'll win it back in time. The odds are only twenty to twenty-one in favour of the dealer.' He snapped his fingers to order more whisky sours. True enough, the cards started turning in his favour, and he turned a loss of some £400 into a gain of over £1,000 as picture after picture flowed for him. He even got a double blackjack by splitting aces. 'Right. I'm out of here,' he finally announced.

In the taxi on the way to their next destination, Grant asked Justyn how he had turned his luck at blackjack around so dramatically. 'I count the cards,' he revealed. 'I know how many tens or pictures and other cards there are in a shoe, and I counted them carefully before placing my bets towards the end of each shoe. It's something a Chinese client taught me many moons ago in Macau.'

'I think you're from Planet Zog,' replied Grant, now beginning to feel much the worse for wear. 'And where are we going?'

'Stringfellows, Spearmint Rhino – who knows?' announced Justyn triumphantly.

Suddenly Grant was engulfed by a rising panic. He had no idea how much alcohol he had consumed, but he was sure he had already exceeded the weekly recommended medical intake of units of alcohol for men. In his control-freakish, precise mind such considerations were never entirely ignored, no matter what his circumstances. He became more daunted about their next destination.

'Look, I think I'd better turn in. Let's head back to your pad, Justyn. I think where we're heading is forbidden fruit in my world, .'

'Chill out, Grantie. Nobody will attack you. In fact, you are not even allowed to touch; just look.'

Grant acquiesced and alighted from the taxi with Justyn hoping that no one would recognize him. The first person they encountered walking out of the nightclub was a vicar. Wearing a dog collar, the man looked somewhat out of place. Grant then did a double-take as a procession of lookalike clergy followed behind.

'That'll be a stag night,' Justyn announced cheerfully.

## 27

## PRESENT DAY

Grant didn't know which club they were in, and he didn't much care. He was mesmerized by the dancer in front of him. Justyn had given him £200 of his winnings, and Grant kept thrusting £20 notes into whatever garments he could find on his scantily clad new lady friend. After some ten minutes of this sublime entertainment he was rudely interrupted by a call from Brigit. He excused himself, deciding to retire to the gents to call back, amid protestations of affection from Roxy 'from Rio' who was murmuring, 'I lurve you. I want you to meet my mother in Brazil.'

Wow, they move fast in the love game these days, he thought.

Once ensconced in the cubicle, he saw that Brigit had not left a message. Sobering up quickly, he decided against a trip to Latin America to make Roxy's mother's acquaintance. He thought his time would be better served going in search of Justyn, who had evaded the private dancers and who was chatting from a stool at the bar to a small entourage.

'Grantie, what gives?'

'I've a missed call from Brigit and I think I had better return it.' Despite the temporary respite of a clearer head, Grant slurred his words and looked as if he was about to keel over.

Justyn moved to prop him up. 'I think it might be better not to ring Brigit at this time, old mate. It's after midnight, and you are pretty Brahms and Liszt. She might detect some of the background noise here and realize you're not working late at the office!'

'Yeah. Guess you are right. Now where's my Roxy?' He couldn't see her through the maze of beautiful bodies confronting his rather blurred vision.

'Hi, I'm Chardonnay,' said a sparky Cockney voice, 'and I have an idea involving you, me and that booth over there. Yes?' She led Grant firmly by the hand, and before he knew it she was gyrating in front of him, smiling seductively, while shedding what little clothing she had on. Despite Chardonnay's best efforts, far from being aroused he became overwrought with emotion and started to break down in tears, which alarmed his private dancer and stopped her in her tracks.

'I'm sorry. I'm so, so sorry,' said Grant. 'I've had a very difficult day.'

'It's all right, mate. We get all sorts in 'ere,' consoled Chardonnay as she gathered up her minimal clothing and hurried out of the booth as quickly as she could.

Grant felt hugely embarrassed and sought out Justyn, who suggested a taxi back to his place in Maida Vale, where his friend could spend the night in his spare room.

The evening's events left Grant feeling foolish. It had been a long day since he came off the night flight back from Cape Town, and a roller-coaster of emotions had swirled around inside him, turning his normally well-ordered life upside down. Following his breakdown in the club, he resolved not to drop his guard again; he would get a grip. As they left the nightclub Grant was alarmed to see a doctor barge past him wearing a stethoscope around his neck. Why do they need a doctor? he thought anxiously. He soon relaxed as scores of doctors emerged from cabs chanting, 'Here we go, here we go, here we go!' As Justyn and Grant waited for their own taxi, they were not surprised to see that a great number of ersatz medics were refused entry.

'That Roxy from Rio. You know, I think she rather fancied me.'

By this stage they were back at the Maida Vale flat where Justyn was preparing two strong espressos.

'Oh, really,' Justyn teased. 'Nothing to do with those £20 notes you were placing in her G-string then?'

'Well, I suppose it could sort of be connected,' replied Grant slowly, sounding like a character lifted straight from the pages of a P.G. Wodehouse novel. 'But I think she carried a bit of a torch.'

'I didn't notice her carrying much at all, but at least Roxy from Rio cheered you up. A tart with a heart.'

Grant was distracted, looking at the text from Brigit. 'Oh my God. The second part of her message says a package arrived for me to sign. I didn't think . . . It must be the DVD.' Justyn nodded. 'I'll have to go home tomorrow, but I'm not sure whether it was delivered or not.' He decided to text his wife: 'Please advise whether package was delivered. Yours G.'

'Bit formal, isn't that?' Justyn said. 'But I don't blame you. D'you know, I never saw any of the film footage Henry took. I just assumed it was holiday-brochure-type stuff, which was how his previous years' efforts struck me. But presumably this must have had some incriminating stuff on it for the Galvins – or at least Danny – to want to get hold of it.'

'It must have also contained stuff that would have rattled Richard Hughes-Webb, or why else did Suzie protect him by not letting him see it?'

At this point, Grant was startled by Brigit's swift text response: 'Yes, arrived. Love B'. So she had not only signed for the package on his behalf but was still awake at that unearthly hour. She was also communicating in a more friendly way – a fact not lost on Grant and Justyn.

'Don't react,' urged Justyn. 'Little good can come from a conversation at this time of night, if you ask me. Just draw comfort from her more mellow tone. It gives us something to work on tomorrow.'

Grant hadn't planned on asking him but thought it sensible advice anyway. As neither seemed ready for sleep, he thought that now might be a good time to discuss the progress he had made since he had embarked on his three-month sabbatical. But this suggestion was met with a less than enthusiastic response from Justyn.

'Oh, and I hoped we were going to review our favourite albums and singer songwriters of all time,' he countered in a voice that betrayed both disappointment and lack of interest.

'Another time perhaps,' suggested Grant, now determined to pursue his agenda.

'OK, well, here goes.' Justyn seized the initiative, realizing that he had no chance of the type of conversation he felt like having. 'Let's make a list of potential suspects, starting with non-hotel folk. First, Ivan Youlen. Dead dodgy, almost certainly stole the money from his uncle Tom and could have been behind Danny's burglary – which you mentioned earlier. Also, what was he doing talking to Ken Holford in the National Trust café that Wednesday, and what was the reason behind his altercation with Paul Galvin outside the newsagent in Zennor that last Sunday?'

Grant chipped in. 'And why was he so aggressive to me in Cornwall last month, and who did he speak to on his mobile the moment I left?'

'Grade A candidate,' Justyn concluded.

'Grade A plus.'

'Second, Ken Holford,' continued Justyn. 'It's hard to talk

about him without having to hold your nose at the putrid smell of his obnoxious behaviour.'

'Yes,' continued Grant, 'and he had a habit of turning up at significant times, at the pub at St Buryan and the National Trust café at the end of the beach, both of which are a long way from Tintagel. But your dad's and Clive's report doesn't point to any criminal activity. However, he could have been in the pub the night Hector drowned. It'll be interesting to see if that's captured on Henry's film.'

'Circumstantial, Rodney, circumstantial, but I agree we need to see the cine film before deciding where we grade him precisely, so at present B plus. Also it's a bit of a drag that he's now joined the choir invisible himself, as far as we know.'

'But has he?' asked Grant. Justyn ignored the question. 'Three, Trevor Mullings,' Grant continued, 'who both reported Hector's death and was in the pub with him. No suggestion he had anything to do with Tom, and he did give me an indication of Ivan's whereabouts. Hard to see him as particularly relevant. C plus, I feel.'

Justyn looked doubtful but decided to keep further thoughts on Trevor Mullings to himself.

So two living candidates and one apparently dead one from the locals list, the two friends concluded. They then moved on to the subject of the families, the hotel guests. They started with the Hughes-Webbs, and Justyn was surprised at Grant's refusal to eliminate Richard.

'You know he was having an affair with my mother?'

'Yes,' came a quiet reply. 'I can see why that still upsets you, Grant, but affairs and the murder of innocent people are dots I can't join up. I think we should disregard him and, while we are at it, my father, too.'

'I'd certainly go with the second part, but let's park Richard H.-W. for the time being,' Grant said with more than a hint of bitterness. Justyn shrugged. 'And I think we have to look again at the message from the deathbed of Ted Jessops, as recounted by Arnie Charnley.'

'I liked those guys,' interrupted Justyn. 'Arnie always made me chuckle, and Ted could tell the most amazing stories.'

'Yes, I bet they would never have imagined we'd be sitting here, some forty years later, talking about them and that last holiday, although I guess both would have wished they had never gone to Cornwall that time.'

'Unless, of course, they really did take some dark secrets to their graves?'

'Don't think so,' said Grant, who had given considerable thought to all five of the hotel suspects. 'I've reached the end of a cul-de-sac with the message-on-the-deathbed bit. Arnie claims Ted said it, while Caroline says it's highly unlikely as her father was mute by the time he died. But we do have Arnie discovering a message in a bottle from Hector twenty-four hours after he was found drowned and Ted drawing a mermaid – surely a pointer to the church in Zennor.'

'So that just leaves Paul Galvin,' interrupted Justyn, scarcely listening to his friend.

'And Richard Hughes-Webb.'

'Whatever. Do you know why the Galvin family alarmed Suzie so much?'

'So much so that she cancelled her wedding the week before? No, any queries about the Galvins seemed to provoke a brick-wall response. She did seem very wary of the family, and Danny hasn't wanted me investigating any of this.'

'Let's hope the film reveals more. Paul definitely had a split personality, and it was financial issues that caused him to switch. I don't know what caused Danny's personality to change; in those days he was always one of the most laid-back people you could meet. Anyway, Grantie, the clock has just struck four. You're still alive, but shut-eye drives me.'

'Just one thing, Justyn. How come you didn't go to a booth with one of the young ladies?'

'It all rather bores me, to be honest. I have been there too many times with clients to find it exciting, let alone erotic any more, but I do enjoy talking to the lovelies. No, it may surprise you to hear this, but I discovered a long time ago that it's only real relationships that provide fulfilment and are worth while.' Grant arched an eyebrow in surprise but was still too inebriated and exhausted to discuss matters further. Justyn, observing his friend's haze, continued, 'And on that score, we're going to have to work out how to get you back with your old lady ...' With that he pointed out Grant's bedroom. 'Switch that mobile off. You're in mortal danger. Look at it tomorrow with a clear head.'

## 28

## THE RECENT PAST

'I was there! I was there, Glen. I saw it with my own eyes. They were walking back up the drive. I was there, I was hiding from view, well screened by trees on the edge of the golf course. I saw Mum with Richard Hughes-Webb, arm in arm like young lovers. I saw the altercation with Hector Wallace, and if Tom hadn't arrived to break it up I do believe Hughes-Webb could have . . . killed someone. His eyes were bulging like saucers. It wasn't just that he was angry. He was demonic!' Grant's voice trailed off.

This was the conversation he was going to have with his younger brother, Glen. This was the conversation he had never had. For a long time Grant had been haunted by these terrible thoughts. He had never got out of his head the memory of his mother walking arm in arm with Richard Hughes-Webb at the end of the long drive, as they went back to the hotel that night. He had never admitted to anyone he was actually there. It was like a jittery speckled old film clip ingrained in his mind. But as if that wasn't traumatic enough, what had really burnt into his memory cells was the fact that the aggravated altercation between Hughes-Webb and Hector Wallace that ensued had involved Tom the night porter. Both Tom and Hector were to suffer serious and ultimately fatal mishaps shortly afterwards.

His mother's involvement in that scene and the witness state-ment – her alibi – to the police had protected Hughes-Webb from further investigation at the time of the poisoning; she confirmed that they had gone for a drive after getting the Sunday papers from Zennor. The veracity or otherwise of his mother's statement was what he knew really drove him to try to establish what really took place. Was she an innocent bystander, or was she implicated in some way? *Was she involved in attempted murder?* He had never come close to admitting this awful fear to anyone; it was the ghost that had driven him so hard, compelling him to establish the truth. He had never even hinted to Brigit or his brother, Glen, that this had become his real *raison de faire*.

Perhaps now he should – perhaps it might save his marriage – but his feelings for Brigit were caught up in a fairground of thoughts, of emotions from the highs and lows of the big dipper to crashing in bumper cars. He didn't think he could tell her while he was on such an emotional roller-coaster, particularly with the content of the amateur film footage still unknown. He knew deep down that she was still on his side, but he also knew he needed time away to attempt 'closure', as she had put it. He also now understood why she needed some space as well, and for the first time he felt some guilt at the singlemindedness of his pursuit. He also knew she was genuinely worried about his physical safety, and he had ignored her concerns.

The discovery of the existence of the film footage gave his investigation its next dramatic focus, but viewing it was an uncertain journey he had yet to make. What would it show? Would his mother be absolved from blame? Grant felt it was all 'on the nail', impossible to predict, like a sports fixture no forecaster could call. One thing for sure was that it would include incriminating activities of one sort or another.

In truth, he was desperate to view the cine film and terrified as to what it might reveal. What further dark secrets might emerge concerning Paul Galvin, and why was Suzie so protective of her father? Grant knew he should meet the cinematographer, Henry Wilson, after he had viewed the footage. He was aching to know whether Henry had shot any scenes in the Office, and, if so, was he there that fateful last night of Hector Wallace's life? Would such footage – if it existed at all – show Trevor Mullings truly hammered and collapsed under the table, or would it show him staggering out towards the beach with Hector? Was Trevor's role far more sinister than had been previously assumed? There were many questions to which the film footage had to provide answers.

Grant kept thinking about his mother walking back up the drive with Richard Hughes-Webb. All he could picture was his mother's smiling face, her dimples embedded firmly in her cheeks; that face his father used to know and love but which had been withdrawn from view as their marriage deteriorated and Hughes-Webb replaced him in her affections.

His mother had died in 1995. He always thought she had never been quite the same after that last Cornish holiday, which had also proved to be the last holiday Grant and Glen ever had with their parents. He regretted this deeply, particularly in relation to Glen, who had been just fifteen at the time.

In her youth his mother had been a vivacious air-hostess with BOAC; she had met Grant's father, Dennis, on one of her flights. Subsequently she had devoted her life to her husband's career as he ascended the ranks to become chief executive of a FTSE 250 engineering company. Rose became an accomplished hostess at their home in Highgate. Grant would get home from school in the late afternoon to be greeted with a 'Hi, darling. Hope you've had a good day. Can you and Glen fend for yourselves this evening? Daddy's got clients in town and we need to entertain. You know, put on a show.'

The year 1971 had brought the devastating news that Grant's father had been diagnosed with cancer. It had started in his gall bladder and within a few years spread to his liver. That last holiday in 1972 had seen him in remission, but that winter another tumour was discovered. It was around a group of major blood vessels, which effectively ruled out any chance of surgical removal.

The brothers were totally distraught when he died early in 1974. By that time Grant was pretty sure his mother's affair with Richard Hughes-Webb had ended, but he remained bitter that it had been going on after his father had first been diagnosed. He shuddered as he remembered that he had challenged his mother about it shortly after his father died. He had been very accusatory and hadn't given his mother a chance to defend herself. Angry as he was at that time, he regretted his approach. Their relationship was never the same again.

Grant was snapped out of his reverie by a letter he was reading. 'She's dead.'

'What? Who?'

'Aunt Gina. Gone from this world,' Grant announced with some satisfaction as he read his mail one Saturday morning.

Brigit looked at him disapprovingly. 'Bit callous. Not very nice referring to the passing of your aunt like that.'

The fact was that after his mother's death in 1995 Grant had started thinking more and more about the incident involving Tom Youlen back in 1972. He had been reluctant to do anything about it while his mother's twin sister Gina was still alive for fear of upsetting her, but after she died in 2012 he started to become fixated with the mystery, as he finally felt free to investigate properly. His legal training had taught him to assimilate all the facts before drawing any conclusions, and this was what he now intended to do.

'Can I persuade you to take a short break with me to Cornwall, B?'

It wasn't long before he finally revealed all to Brigit, when they revisited the scene of his distress – the white hotel on the hill that resembled an imposing castle.

Grant now knew he had developed an obsession, as the events in 1972 were constantly permeating his thoughts in many of his waking hours and, as he would discover in Zennor, some of his sleeping ones as well. His hope was that Brigit would not become fed up with his preoccupation with the past. He became fretful. He started to worry that a number of their close friends had split up, often when their children had left home to go to university or start careers. They were now at this watershed stage themselves, and there was no doubt it was very different from having a vibrant, noisy household at home. He knew he had to tread carefully, but events were taking over.

## 29

## PRESENT DAY

It was the morning after Grant's night on the town with Justyn that he viewed the film footage. He had returned to his home in Mill Hill with a hangover and in a state of some anxiety. Brigit, who had left for work some hours earlier, had left the parcel in the hallway. With it she had placed a small note. 'So sorry. Let's talk. Love B.'

Such was his preoccupation that Grant hardly registered the note but ripped open the parcel with all the excitement of a starving man opening a pack of food. Inside he was somewhat startled to discover three DVDs apparently spanning six years of the holidays in Cornwall. Having anticipated viewing a single film, he had forgotten that Suzie had referred to DVDs in the plural. He made himself a large espresso and sat down to watch. He loaded the disk dated August 1972 and was disappointed to find that there was no soundtrack and that the picture quality was frequently poor. Still, at least it was in colour. The film showed a hotchpotch of holiday antics, and it took him some time before he found anything of real interest. Eureka! He could make out who all the people were, happy smiles from the hotel's tennis courts, the nine-hole golf course and swimming-pool. Tom was featured greeting all the arrivals, and the date was recorded as 10 August 1972.

The first car to arrive contained a family Grant hadn't thought about until now: the group included identical twin brothers in matching sports jackets and grey flannels who appeared from the back seat. He burst out laughing. He recalled Justyn had nicknamed them the 'Speaking Clocks'. Burgess was their family name; they had driven down from Yorkshire, and the twins, Frederick and Edward, were then aged around fifteen. They did everything together. Grant remembered them being very serious and constantly being mistaken for one another. He recalled their excitement on watching the Test Match on the hotel lounge television when their favourite player walked to the crease, 'Boycott's batting!' repeated almost immediately by the twin, 'Boycott's batting!' For the others it became their catchphrase, adopted rather cruelly behind their backs. Justyn used to inquire, 'Is there an echo in here?' Grant also remembered them asking if they could watch a game of pontoon he and some of the usual crowd were playing one evening. As it approached nine one twin remarked, 'It will soon be nine o'clock.' The grandfather clock in the hallway promptly chimed, and the other remarked in a deadpan voice, 'It is nine o'clock.' Suppressed laughter had ensued. Grant now found himself wondering what might have happened to the Speaking Clocks. He couldn't recall giving them a second's thought since that time, as they had seemed an entirely inconsequential part of his early life. Or were they?

The weather in the film was bright and sunny as Justyn pulled up in his white Peugeot 204 with his sister, Fiona. Grant was struck by his now ridiculous-looking white flared hipster trousers, held up with a belt with an oversized silver buckle and worn below his once familiar blue, pink and purple tie-dyed T-shirt. There were people hovering around the Silver family, but there was no sign of the father, Bob. Justyn greeted someone who looked like Jenny Charnley, and before long there was quite a gathering.

Grant could make out Richard Hughes-Webb with his two children, Tony and Suzie, hauling luggage from the car. Then with a powerful sensation of sadness he saw his own family arrive, his father looking drained, as they had come off the night train from Penzance and Dennis had driven the twenty miles or so to the hotel, quite an ordeal for him in his state of health. He saw his younger brother, Glen, aged fifteen, helping Tom with the baggage and carrying golf clubs.

At this moment the land line rang, and after a moment's hesitation Grant decided to answer it. Brigit's voice sounded strained and distant. 'Hi, how are you?' she asked wearily.

'Oh, hi. Thanks for calling. Look, I guess I overreacted a bit yesterday. I was knackered after the long flight . . .'

'It's OK,' Brigit said quickly. 'Look, could we meet in an hour's time at the office? We can go for a coffee round the corner.'

Grant was torn. He had turned off the DVD, but he couldn't wait to see the whole thing. He didn't think he could watch it in twenty minutes, and it would take him about forty minutes to get to Brigit's office in Cromwell Road. After some muttered prevarication he became more forthright. 'Look, Brigit. I really want to see you, but I need a bit of time. Can we meet this afternoon? I hardly slept last night.' Guiltily he refrained from revealing to her the reason why.

'You're watching those DVDs that arrived yesterday, aren't you? You just can't let up, can you? I can't meet you this afternoon. I've got back-to-back interviews and a client meeting in Watford at five.' Brigit found herself biting her upper lip, her characteristic way of revealing disappointment.

'So be it,' said Grant, and he heard the line go dead. Caught between a rock and a hard place, he nevertheless had to see the rest of the film. He returned to the living-room and pressed 'Play' again, and it didn't take long for his silent movie to provide some drama and intrigue.

He saw Tom surreptitiously hand over what looked like a

key to his mother. He felt an uneasy twinge in his lower back, cursing aloud that Richard Hughes-Webb could stoop so low as to include the porter in his subterfuge; it added further humiliation to the betrayal of his father by his mother. By this stage most of the teenagers were arriving in family cars and none of them took much notice of the adults, greeting one another enthusiastically as if it was the greatest of reunions or a close friend's wedding day.

Tom was next seen heading away down the drive; he had, after all, worked all night. Hector Wallace then came into view with his frail Aunt Agatha, emerging out of a chauffeur-driven car. At that point Grant imagined it was approaching midday, as Sidney, the barman who had tried to take control when the police swarmed in at Sunday lunchtime after Tom's collapse in the lane, was filmed loading up a mobile bar by the kidney-shaped swimming-pool.

Henry's footage next featured a shot focused on a bedroom window at the hotel. Paul Galvin was visible, appearing to shout at someone from within; it was a jarring image, made worse when he slammed the sash window shut. Grant replayed this scene a few times but couldn't make out at whom he was shouting. Henry's attention had then switched to Hector walking briskly out of the hotel and down the drive to his first midday session at the Office, wearing a three-piece checked suit with the tie pinned in place and a monocle protruding from a breast pocket attached to a small chain. Grant scrutinized his awkward but hurried walk, focusing on his pock-marked face – evidence of a life of too many sherbets, he reflected. He was now so immersed in the film he jumped half out of his seat when his mobile rang. He was surprised to see that it was Danny calling. Grant answered, and Danny got straight to the point. 'We need to talk.'

## 30

## PRESENT DAY

Danny insisted that the two meet that morning, preferably at Grant's home. The latter was surprised when Danny said he could be there in twenty minutes; clearly he wasn't phoning from Brentwood. Reluctantly Grant agreed. When he got off the phone he ejected the DVD from the television and placed it carefully in a briefcase that he locked before pocketing the key. With the key safely wrapped in a handkerchief, he felt he had control of things, but he needed to turn his concentration to his unexpected visitor, as he had decided to resume viewing the film after Danny left.

The doorbell rang on cue, and Grant wondered if his friend had been waiting round the corner. They greeted each other formally, with none of the affection and informality of their youth.

Danny got straight to the point. 'Why are you pursuing this, Grant?'

'What?'

'Why are you investigating Tom's poisoning after all these years? Who are you trying to nail?'

'Justice was never done. Besides, Hector's drowning was no accident, and I can't rest until I know my mother wasn't involved in some way.' Grant decided to go for broke and went on to reveal the affair between his mother and Suzie's father.

His explanation had the required effect. Danny fell silent

and finally said slowly, 'Your mother?' He put the stress on the first word.

The two stared at each other. Perhaps, hoped Grant, his revelation that his mother was his main concern might change things for the better with Danny.

Danny repeated, mechanically and without emotion, 'Your mother?'

'Yes. Is there something you need to tell me about your mother?'

Danny stared blankly at Grant. He couldn't decide whether to open up. He felt like a child standing at the edge of a swimming-pool, knowing he should jump in but afraid to do so. 'Where's Brigit?' he asked.

'At work,' replied Grant, who had no intention of discussing his private life.

Danny went quiet again but continued to stare at Grant, who was tempted to explode at his old friend. 'Read the tea leaves, Grant.'

A cold sensation washed over Grant. He felt his blood pressure dropping but decided not to respond in the hope that the other might feel the need to fill the silence and reveal his hand.

An acute tension descended over them as Danny took some chewing-gum out of his pocket, put a piece in his mouth and started chewing in a slow rhythmic motion, staring at his host all the while.

'Would you like a coffee?' asked Grant, finding the atmosphere hard to bear.

Danny continued staring as if he hadn't heard. Finally he spoke. 'Henry Wilson filmed that last holiday on Super 8. Nobody took much notice, of course. He had filmed pretty well all our holidays down there on his cine camera.'

Grant shifted uneasily in his seat, avoiding Danny's gaze. He unconsciously felt in his pocket for the key to the case that contained the DVDs and grasped it tightly. 'Go on,' he said.

'They got stolen. All my DVDs got stolen the day after Suzie left.'

'That's strange. So nothing else was taken? But I thought you just said the footage was on Super 8 film rather than disk,' said Grant, trying to box clever and pleased they were talking once more; the silence had created even greater tension.

'It was shot on celluloid but converted to DVD.'

'Had you seen what was on it? Did you report the theft?' Grant was beginning to jabber.

'Yes. Look, I don't want you pursuing this further.'

'I rather guessed that.'

'How?'

'Because you tried to put the frighteners on me in Zennor last month.'

'No I didn't!' Danny protested in such an incredulous tone that Grant believed him. He knew he was unlikely to lie, as awkward and unpleasant as he could be these days.

'Then who the hell did?' Grant replied. He told Danny about the 'spooks of Zennor' – as he had termed them – withholding only the matter of the nursery rhyme, as he was sure this would invite derision.

'Gordon Bennett, Grant, old son. Someone really is trying to put you off the scent.' Danny seemed perplexed – but also appeared cheered to discover that he had an ally in opposing Grant's obsession.

'I won't stop,' Grant announced defiantly, but he was cut abruptly short as all of a sudden Danny jumped up and lurched towards him. Grant feared that he was going to pull a knife or a gun. He was prepared to punch him hard in the stomach if he tried anything.

However, Danny turned his back on Grant, and when he

spoke his tone was more controlled, almost conciliatory. 'Look, it will destroy Mum if you go on with all this.'

Grant had not expected this – Danny a mummy's boy! However, he knew that Danny had never married, and received wisdom had it that he had never recovered from Suzie's rejection of him more than twenty years earlier. But before Grant responded, an uneasy feeling swept over him. Maybe Danny's mother was involved. Perhaps the DVD would reveal this. There was clearly something that he was not telling. The fear of the unknown was unwelcome and unnerving.

'OK,' replied Grant, after another awkward interlude. 'No one wants to destroy innocent people.' He watched Danny's face carefully for a reaction. But his former friend remained as inscrutable as ever. 'How is your mother?'

'Living in Majorca. She's in an apartment block in one of those built-up resorts near Palma.'

'Is she well?' asked Grant, already planning a budget airline flight to the island.

'Um, yes. Kind of. Her arthritis is bad, but she has a gentleman friend who looks after her.'

'Do you like him?' asked Grant, pushing his luck but intent on keeping Danny talking.

'Sort of. He's solid enough. He got elected president of the block where she lives. He seems to get off on that, but he's decent to Mum, and he's a good odd-job man.'

Grant was pleased at how things were going. At least now Danny was conversing in a fairly civilized way, but he needed to make more progress. 'When did your father die?'

'About twenty years ago. He did well to survive the poisoning.'

'What? Tom's?'

'No, his own.' Danny released the three words slowly, pregnant with meaning.

'I see,' gasped Grant.

'No, you don't see. No, you so don't. You meddle in affairs from forty years ago that destroyed my family long ago, that sent the only girl I ever loved spinning out of my life and left me feeling bitter for the rest of my days. You don't see, matey boy. You don't see at all. To hell with you!'

Rocked by Danny's heavy artillery, Grant considered walking out, when to his enormous relief the front door opened and in walked Brigit. For a moment they stared at one another; Brigit was in her City attire, wearing a skirt with patterned tights, high heels and heavy jewellery, with matching lipstick and nail varnish. Grant, by contrast, looked as though he had an unwelcome starring role in a horror movie.

'Hi,' Grant said, far more enthusiastically than Brigit expected. She was unaware of the tension filling the room. 'Good to see you. Do you remember Danny Galvin? You met many moons ago.' His greeting startled her.

'Er, hello, Danny. Nice to see you again,' she dissembled.

'Yeah, hi. Well, I'd better be off. Catch up with you later, Grant.'

'Yes, sure,' replied Grant. 'Good to see you. Keep in touch,' he added, as the door closed behind Danny.

Once alone, Grant kissed Brigit on both cheeks without saying a word and looked solemnly into her eyes. Some of his familiar warmth towards her started to return. Brigit sensed that she had walked in on something but, bewildered as to what, she just pulled him towards her, and as they gently embraced she started to become emotional.

'It's all OK,' he reassured her. 'You have no idea – I am so pleased to see you . . . If you only knew what you just walked in on.'

Brigit wiped her blurry, tear-filled eyes and smiled, still trying to comprehend what she had interrupted.

## 31

## PRESENT DAY

Danny left the house with a curious feeling. He hadn't registered it at first, but the thought now entered his head that
his friend hadn't seemed especially surprised at the revelation
of the existence of the Super 8 footage. He thought more
about the DVDs, but he wasn't aware that Grant had been to
see Suzie in Cape Town, although he suspected that he might
do so as Suzie was no doubt on his contacts list. Danny was
sure that Suzie would make contact if Grant had visited. At
this point he remembered that he had a missed call from a
Suzanne Barber, and he had completely forgotten that this
was Suzie's married name. He started ruminating about Ivan
Youlen and began to wonder what Ivan might divulge to
Grant. He felt a sudden urge to speak to the man and was
pretty sure that Grant would have his number. However, he
was reluctant to ask him so soon after their meeting and
decided instead to call Justyn. They had kept in touch for the
first twenty-five years since 1972, but they'd had little contact
over the past fifteen or so. He was relieved to discover that
Justyn's mobile number hadn't changed.

'Hi, this is Justyn Silver. Please leave a message unless you
are the Aga Khan, in which case tell me where I can reach
you at your earliest convenience.'

'Hello, Justyn, Danny Galvin here. Long time no speak.
Could you call me back on this mobile number, please.' He
was surprised to receive a return call almost immediately.

'Hey, Danny. How are you, man?'

'I'm all right,' replied Danny, trying to sound cool. 'And you?'

'Pretty stretched at present. Fully occupied with Russian oligarchs' houses and the tai-pans of Hong Kong. Life is one long set of schemes. Anyway, what can I do for you?'

'Can we meet?'

'Sadly not this week or next, old chap. I'm off to Morocco tomorrow for a bit of R&R.'

'Sounds good. Anywhere in particular?' asked Danny, hiding his disappointment and trying to mask his bluntness with a bit of uncharacteristic charm.

'Atlas Mountains, then a nice riad in Marrakesh.'

'Great. Switching subjects, I don't suppose you have a number for Ivan Youlen, do you?'

'Are you having a laugh? Not you as well. I thought Grant was the only obsessive trying to roll back time.'

'Well, I personally couldn't give a monkey's about the whole thing – and I think Grant should be committed to some sort of institution – but there is just one thing I need to ask Ivan.'

'And there is one thing I need to ask God, but I don't think I'll get the opportunity either . . .'

'Oh, come on. Ivan isn't as big an ask as God,' said Danny, missing the joke.

'No, but he could be the devil,' retorted Justyn, this time with a hint of feigned menace, 'and he could be just as hard to contact, from what I've heard.'

'Well, have you got his number or not?'

'No,' said Justyn matter-of-factly.

'Well, I guess I'll have to call the lunatic Grant.'

'Probably, but tread carefully. He's having a bit of local diffi-culty with the old lady.'

After Justyn had hung up Danny pondered this comment briefly. He had only just seen the couple together and had not detected any tension between them. In fact, he had thought them nauseatingly lovey-dovey.

Justyn was straight on the phone to Grant to alert him to a potential call from Desperate Dan, as he called him.

'Thanks for the heads up,' said Grant. 'I can understand Danny getting involved now. He must be feeling the pressure. I keep thinking about one particular scene – his father having that heated conversation with Ivan Youlen outside the newsagent that last Sunday morning when the papers didn't get delivered. And of course Paul told the runners on the beach that the police should interview Ivan.'

'Sunday morning papers didn't come,' Justyn sang tunefully.

'No! It was Wednesday morning papers didn't come. Sunday morning was creeping like a nun. I've had this conversation with Brigit.'

'How is she?' Justyn inquired.

'I think repairs are on the way.'

'Good.'

'Yes.' Grant sounded distracted. Now that Danny had left he was keen to get back to viewing the DVD he had paused in order to take Justyn's call. 'I think I may need to go to Majorca.'

'Why?'

'To see Danny's mother. I think she might just hold the key to the whole thing. In fact, in my mind she is now front and centre.' At that moment he became transfixed by an image on the DVD. He was astounded to see that Henry had filmed the arrival of the police at the hotel on the Sunday lunchtime after Tom had been found staggering in the lane; he had even filmed them inside the Simpkins' private accommodation. 'Can I call you back later?'

'Difficult, Grantie boy. I'm off to Morocco in the morning. I'll get on the blower when I'm back in ten days' time.'

'Yes, fine. Great,' replied Grant, now barely concentrating on their exchange as Justyn hung up. What had arrested his attention was spotting Hector Wallace talking privately first with Richard Hughes-Webb and then with Paul Galvin as the rest of the throng chatted away together. What the hell had been Henry's vantage point? Then he worked it out; he must have been outside the ground-floor window in the car park. Grant could just make out a wooden window frame around the glass. Filming stopped abruptly as Henry's last shot captured PC Stobart striding towards him.

Grant scrutinized the film, repeatedly searching for clues on the faces of Messrs Hughes-Webb and Galvin. Henry's filming had been somewhat erratic at that point as a rather battered Ford Escort pulled up the drive and out jumped Ivan Youlen. 'Sodding Ivan again,' muttered Grant. He watched carefully as the man went into the hotel only to reappear shortly afterwards. Annoyingly there was no way of knowing the time lag between the two events. It was also impossible to tell what Hector was saying in his two private conversations or what effect these had on the other two men. He thought about Ivan and replayed his cameo appearance, which seemed both arresting and significant. What had Ivan been carrying in his pocket? Was it for someone?

Grant switched off the DVD to reflect on recent events. He resolved to continue being ruthless in pursuit of the truth – at least until he had uncovered what that might be. It was not ideal, but he knew he couldn't go back to Brigit while he was so distracted. It simply wasn't fair on her. He thought some more about the suspects from 1972. Ivan was ever-present in his mind, particularly now Grant knew that he had been caught on film at the hotel on the day of his uncle's stroke. Paul Galvin remained a prime suspect. And why was his son Danny so keen to stop Grant in his tracks? Richard Hughes-Webb remained a wild card, more Grant's hunch than anything else, but that private conversation with Hector Wallace increased suspicion. And now Alison Galvin had joined the ranks. He recalled her bright, inquisitive eyes, the only redeeming feature of her otherwise very plain appearance as she walked around wrapped in a Mary Quant coat. Could she have been the secret killer?

He retired to his bedroom. He was tired after the night before. His present mental state reminded him of the unsettling nights in Zennor – and who might have been responsible for those if it wasn't D. Galvin Esquire? He fell into a deep sleep but was troubled by a vivid dream. This time his door wasn't being bashed down; he was having a cup of coffee in a roadside café with Alison Galvin in a built-up resort west of Palma in Majorca. Her face had become lined and rutted with skin as ragged as the rocks around the nearby sea shore. She was puffing on a cigarette, fiddling constantly with the packet that rested on the copy of the *Daily Mail* she had bought that morning.

'I am so sorry to bother you, Mrs Galvin,' started Grant.

'That's all right, dear. I don't get many visitors. Rory doesn't welcome them.' Rory was a large tattooed Glaswegian with a bald head and a crisp manner, and Grant couldn't understand a word he said. He thought heard him say what a great party the UK was, but he soon realized what he was actually saying was what a great party UKIP was.

'Do you remember the events from Cornwall and your last family holiday back in 1972?'

'Oh yes, dear. I could never forget them.' She smiled, and Grant remembered the strange way she screwed up her nose when she wanted to emphasize a point. 'I mean, who could forget that murder? I always felt for poor Tom. He was only testing the poison, and he only took a little; he told me it would need a lot more to finish him off . . . Oh, I am saying too much . . .'

'No, please go on. You're not saying enough.'

At that moment, predictably, he woke up. He felt extremely frustrated and more determined than ever that his next move would be a trip to Majorca.

## 32

## PRESENT DAY

At home in Mill Hill Grant checked his mobile. Missed call: Caroline Howe-Jessops. Why would she be phoning him? He played the message.

'Hi, gorgeous. You won't believe this, but Suzie née Hughes-Webb wants to come to London and see you urgently. Do call. Lots of love, Caroline.'

Grant was elated. He had not expected this turn of events. His mind started racing. The Galvins. The Galvins! Hadn't Danny revealed that his father had survived a poisoning? His latest weird dream had Danny's mother Alison admitting liability. Who else could have been responsible for these past crimes if not Paul, Alison, Danny – or even Danny's younger sister, Sharon, perhaps? He allowed himself a wry smile as he was aware he was getting carried away, partly out of frustration but also out of a sense of encroaching dread. He knew he was charging forwards dangerously, but he had to speak to Suzie; he needed to get things back in proportion. He hoped she had reflected further and now wanted to reveal more. He couldn't wait to hear. He hurriedly dialled her Cape Town number.

'Suzie Barber speaking.'

Her going by her married name threw him slightly. 'Hi, Suzie. It's Grant returning your call.'

'Er, yes, hello,' she replied somewhat formally in her clipped businesslike tone. 'There is something I need to show you, Grant.'

'Show me?' he queried. He had not expected an exhibit. 'What's that?'

'Have you watched the three DVDs?'

By this stage Grant had seen them all, and apart from a few significant moments that had grabbed his full attention he had found most of the film footage disappointing in terms of content.

'Yes. Thank you very much for sending them to me. I was about to drop you an email.'

'Grant,' Suzie whispered in an urgent, conspiratorial tone. 'There's another disk.'

'What? I mean, where?'

'I've got it. It's far more revealing than the others. I've kept it since taking it from Danny's flat, but I think you should see it so I'm going to bring it to London with me next week.'

'Thank you,' said Grant. 'Thank you very much. Can you tell me what's on it?'

'No.' She reverted to her more usual manner. 'But I can tell you . . .' She hesitated before delivering the bombshell. 'Henry filmed in the pub on Hector's last evening.'

'Really?' Grant exclaimed, exhilarated by this revelation.

They reverted to small talk to ease the tension, and she gave him her flight details. He was keen to keep her talking. He could barely wait for Wednesday week, but she wasn't pre-pared to divulge any more at this point. He offered to meet her at Heathrow Terminal 5 and said he would drive her straight to her aunt's flat in Bayswater.

'Suzie,' he continued, in a further and somewhat desperate attempt to prise more information out of her, 'Danny came to see me. He was quite aggressive, most unpleasant really. At one point I actually felt in fear of physical attack.' He felt a bit feeble revealing this and immediately wished he hadn't.

'Did he?' she asked, after a long pause, during which time

he wondered if the line had gone dead. 'Be very careful, Grant. You don't know the half of it with the Galvins.'

'And are you prepared to tell me everything when we meet this time?'

'I will show you the last film taken on the Tuesday, Wednesday and Thursday at the end of the holiday. I think that will suffice.'

'Ivan Youlen,' he continued, still trying to keep her on the line. 'Did you know he showed up that Sunday lunchtime at the hotel when the police set up shop in the Simpkins' flat?'

'Yes. I've seen it on film.'

'Why?'

'I think it'll all become clearer when you see the last film. I must go. Thanks again for agreeing to meet me at Heathrow. I'll text you the flight details and my ETA.'

'Great. Many thanks, Suzie. I really look forward to seeing you.'

She didn't respond. She was already planning her London visit, which she knew would require meticulous preparation. She didn't have much time for Grant's schoolboy excitement, as she regarded it, but she did know it was time to move everything on.

The night before, Grant and Brigit had agreed that he should move out for a short while to continue his research. He had called to ask his brother, Glen, if he could stay for three or four days, which Brigit thought a good idea.

After speaking to Suzie he packed some necessities and set off on the North Circular Road. He soon became aware that a car, although it wasn't right behind, seemed to be trailing him. He pulled up at a petrol station to see what would happen, and the vehicle sped past. In his paranoid state he fully expected to see either Danny or Ivan behind the wheel, but instead he spotted a rather heavy-looking guy, the type that might be described in the criminal fraternity as 'a bit of muscle'. This could take things in a sinister new direction. He dallied at the petrol station, buying coffee from the vending machine and drinking it slowly, watching the passing traffic keenly. Some ten minutes later he was back behind the wheel. By the time he was on the A3 he saw the same car about three vehicles behind him. His mind began to race. Should he call the police? He didn't feel inclined to do so, as he thought it would only complicate things at this stage. He resolved to tough it out. After all, the 'Spooks of Zennor' who had pursued him on the west coast and then on to St Austell had never actually carried out a physical assault, although the hand on his face in the dark had been pretty weird and not an experience he was likely to forget. He pulled up at an off-licence close to his brother's home in a picturesque village near Guildford. As an offering to Glen and his wife, Mandy, for his invasion of their space he purchased three bottles of their favourite Australian Chardonnay to accompany the flowers and the box of chocolates he had bought at the petrol station.

'Gordon Bennett, are you staying a month?' inquired Glen, partly delighted to see his big brother and partly anxious as to how things might play out with Mandy, who could be somewhat highly strung and rather temperamental. Glen shot her a swift glance, but much to his relief she had adopted her inscrutable face. Grant was slightly taken aback at Glen's greeting, as he recalled that Danny had used the same expression a few days earlier; he hadn't heard anyone say 'Gordon Bennett' for around twenty years until that week.

Mandy made sympathetic noises as her brother-in-law revealed his temporary separation from his wife over dinner that evening, although she privately felt for Brigit. She thought poor Brigit must have been driven to distraction by Grant, whom Mandy had long regarded as a self-centred individual.

(In addition, she had always been somewhat disconcerted by his eye movements, as he never seemed sure where to focus – but she was not proud of this.)

Grant didn't mention the events of summer 1972 to the pair. He waited for Mandy to retire before asking his brother if they could talk for a bit, and only then did the elder brother unburden himself, waiting for the fraternal fall-out he rather dreaded. Glen remained silent throughout, expressionless bar a few grunts, raising the odd eyebrow but taking in everything. Finally Grant asked the inevitable question: had he known or suspected anything?

'What, anything at all?' responded Glen rather glibly. While he appreciated his brother coming clean on a dark family secret and putting it in context in a lawyer's concise way, he resented the slightly patronizing tone that Grant reserved for him, although their bond was strong and he knew that he meant well.

'Well, anything at all or in particular? For instance, did you know that Mum was having an affair with Richard Hughes-Webb?'

'Yes,' replied Glen, deliberately sounding authoritative.

'How did you know?'

'She told me.'

'What?'

'It was just before I took up that golf scholarship in America, after I left school, and Dad was in a pretty poor state.' Glen looked close to tears.

'I guess that would have been about September 1974.'

'Yes that would be about right. Dad died the following spring, I remember that awful call from you when I was in Florida.' Grant nodded as his brother continued. 'She wanted me to know before I left the nest –' Once again he found himself faltering.

'Why?' Grant couldn't stop himself interrupting.

'Because,' Glen took a deep breath, 'because, because . . .' He froze like a tennis player getting a bad case of nerves as he tried to throw the ball up in the air, attempting a crucial first serve. 'Because she was going to go and live with him!' He blurted this out so loudly that the dog, a docile black Labrador, jumped up and barked.

Grant didn't twitch a muscle. He was suppressing painful memories of his father. He was imagining him lying there, his face contorted with discomfort, after being told that there wasn't any chance of surgery, any chance of recovery. He knew he must remain calm, remain the responsible older brother. Finally he spoke. 'So why didn't she?'

'Dad's condition deteriorated rapidly, and I guess I gave her a volley of abuse – my gut reaction – which really seemed to shock her to the core. I can't for the life of me think why, as I don't think anyone else would have reacted any differently in the situation.'

'No, of course not,' Grant said, showing the empathy he had always felt for his brother. 'Your reaction was entirely understandable and justified. Did you find out how this affected Hughes–Webb?'

'Yes,' came another slow reply. 'I sort of heard him give her an ultimatum, along the lines of "I've been waiting three years for you to get on with things. Sort it out by Christmas or it's all off."'

The bastard! thought Grant repeatedly in his head. 'So how did you overhear this?' he asked as calmly as he could.

'I listened to the telephone call outside her bedroom door. From her responses I could make out his side of the conversation. Dad was already in that converted room downstairs by this stage, with all his medications – deteriorating.'

'Yes. I understand.' Grant patted his brother gently on the

shoulder, thanked him once more for giving him a port in the storm and made his way to the spare room. He had much to reflect on.

Glen, meanwhile, wished Grant had lingered or had demonstrated some real emotion. He wanted a big hug from his brother; even after all this time Glen found it hard to deal with the events from their shared past. However, he knew his sibling all too well and knew he would always play the calm protector to his 'little bro'. He also knew that Grant cared deeply for him and had tried to protect him from the fall-out of their mother's affair with Richard. What his brother hadn't realized was that he had known all along.

As Grant lay in bed, unable to sleep, he knew that he had been unable to admit one of the nastiest aspects of the whole nightmare – the demonic look he had seen in Hughes-Webb's eyes that night when he accosted Hector Wallace – the full fury of the heart surgeon's face caught by Tom's car headlights. Grant wished belatedly that he had been able to give Glen a hug.

Grant's meeting with Suzie the following week now had an added complication: her father's ultimatum to his mother. However, he knew he had to suppress his personal animosity towards her father if he was to uncover the truth. Throughout his dealings with Suzie, he had managed to control his feelings fairly successfully. In a way he was relieved to have heard Glen's revelation, but he very much wished that none of this had ever happened.

## 33

## PRESENT DAY

'Hello, Grant. Danny here. Can you please phone or text me with Ivan Youlen's number? Thanks.' Grant stared at the message on his mobile phone as he lay in bed at his brother's house wondering whether it was too early to get up. It was five in the morning. He had woken with a start, his mind instantly alert. He knew himself well enough to know he had no chance of returning to sleep, and he decided to text back the number. He had been quite shaken by Danny's behaviour at his home a few days before, and he could summon neither the inclination nor the resolve to speak to him now.

Danny received Grant's reply but waited about three hours before contacting Youlen, until the world was more properly going about its business. Danny guessed, from the speed of Grant's texted response, that he must be getting right under his old friend's skin, a thought that didn't make him feel any better. He felt the whole matter was getting murkier by the day, bringing out the worst in people. How he wished it would all just go away.

'Ivan Youlen speaking.'

'Hi, Ivan, Danny Galvin here, Paul's son.'

'I've been expecting you,' replied Ivan, in a more sombre and less detached tone than he had afforded Grant.

'Er, yes. I mean why?'

'Well, let's be blunt here. Your old man ruined mine. If you care to remember, he never paid Sandersons in Penzance properly, and also I knows your mother got hold of some of my uncle's poison. Now that pompous arse Morrison has been down here digging the dirt.' Ivan stopped at this point, wondering what reaction he was getting. 'Are you still there?'

'Yes,' said Danny, who had been content to allow Ivan to make the running in the conversation he had initiated.

'Why are you calling me?'

'I think we need to meet.' Danny realized he had to take the initiative.

'Well, get down to Cornwall then. I work at the Lost Gardens of Heligan these days and live in Mevagissey.' Ivan had been very direct, while avoiding the bad language to which he had subjected Grant. Danny had hoped for a half-way meeting point and suggested Cerne Abbas. However, Ivan was never a man to compromise, and Danny soon conceded, agreeing to meet at Ivan's cottage in Mevagissey.

'Yeah, OK. Um, I'll come down soon. So what did Morrison want?'

'He threatened me a bit and said he would get the truth out of Ken Holford until I told him Ken was brown bread.'

Danny was surprised by this. 'How did he die?'

'You had better ask Trevor Mullings that.'

Danny knew who Mullings was and was anxious to learn more. 'You know someone hounded Morrison when he was at Zennor, knocking on his door at night and other stuff. Were you behind that?'

'No, but you should ask Trevor Mullings about that as well,' replied Ivan knowingly.

'I see.' Danny tried to sound casual to keep him talking but to no avail; Ivan hung up without any niceties. Danny assumed that Mullings was behind Grant's Zennor misadventure, which both pleased and perplexed him.

He decided to take a risk and phoned Grant. He got

straight to the point. 'I know who hounded you in Zennor.'

'Who?'

'Trevor Mullings.'

'What? Why?' But Grant's queries were answered by a dial tone, as Danny had hung up, much to Grant's exasperation. What was Mullings's motive? And why was Danny telling him this when it seemed he had so much to hide? Perhaps Danny had experienced a twinge of conscience after his performance in Mill Hill. Or perhaps he thought the information might cause Grant to back off. The latter, decided Grant as he paced around his borrowed bedroom. Not for the first time he started questioning himself. Am I particularly stupid? Am I missing some massive clue here? Mullings knew that someone had left the pub with Hector Wallace but was apparently too inebriated to say who, and he had deliberately tried to put Grant off the scent in Cornwall. Furthermore, Mullings knew that Ken Holford, 'the Tyrant of Tintagel', had died. Had he killed him? Could there be a motive for Mullings, the easygoing heavy-drinking fisherman, to do something like this?

Grant stopped pacing, his reflection in the mirror above a chest of drawers revealing a drawn and haggard face he barely recognized. He studied his eyes. He had never felt sorry for himself over their condition, but he was concerned now that one looked very bloodshot. It was still a week before Suzie would land with the DVD. The wait was excruciating. He realized that he needed to calm down. However, he didn't see what he could do for the next week apart from kick his heels, which he found very frustrating. His slow progress was wearing him down. He found himself humming 'Half a pound of tuppenny rice, half a pound of treacle . . .'

He was stopped in his tracks when Glen knocked on the door. 'Are you all right? Are you going to join us for breakfast?'

Grant was keen to patch things up with Brigit, who he knew was on his side, but he was concerned about the outcome of viewing the fourth film. He would no doubt become further distracted and that could cause further damage to their relationship. And he couldn't mull things over with Justyn, who was still in Morocco.

He thought of meeting up with Caroline but decided that could set hares running, particularly as she seemed less than enthralled with her marriage. He still planned to fly to Majorca to see Danny's mother, but he knew doing so would significantly raise the stakes with her son, and he wondered whether it was really such a good idea. He resolved to contact Henry Wilson, the film-maker upon whose evidence he was now pinning his hopes. Justyn had given him his brother's mobile number some time back, and it didn't take long to get Henry to return a call.

'Hello, Henry. This is Grant Morrison. I don't know if you remember me.'

'Yes, of course. Hello, Grant. I know exactly who you are. I remember you well – and Justyn has told me about your investigation. How's it going?'

'Wheels stuck in the mud at this moment, but I have made some progress, thanks, and I have seen some of your films, which are an unbelievable record. Well done.'

'Seen some? Which haven't you seen?'

'The last one, which I am led to believe is the most revealing.'

'So where is it now?' asked Henry, his voice betraying anxiety.

'Suzie Hughes-Webb, er, I mean, Barber has it. She's bringing it from South Africa on Wednesday.'

'Is she?'

'So this one is the hot ticket, Henry.'

Henry hung up after saying a hurried goodbye. This threw Grant. He couldn't fathom why the conversation should have been curtailed so suddenly. He tried Henry's mobile number again, but this time there was no response.

The reason that Henry had cut short their discussion was that he had seen Danny Galvin park his car in the road, and he was now approaching his front door. Being a person of nervous disposition, Henry hesitated before opening it and greeting his uninvited guest as calmly as he could.

'Danny Galvin, isn't it? I haven't seen you for . . .'

'Yeah, years, decades probably, whatever. May I come in?' Before Henry could consider the request Danny had moved over the threshold and was heading to a living-room chair. 'This used to be your folks' place, didn't it?' Danny asked, making an attempt at small talk.

'Yes, I bought out the other two after Mum died.'

'Yeah, thought so. I remember Justyn's twenty-first party here. Quite a night, if I remember correctly. I got lucky with Jenny Charnley.'

'Didn't everyone,' countered Henry, recalling one of his brother's former conquests and trying to lighten the atmosphere. Henry was feeling distinctly uncomfortable, and his feelings were exacerbated by the fact that it was his own territory that had been invaded. An awkward silence enveloped them, prompting Danny to reveal his agenda.

'Look, I know you shot film footage of our holidays in Cornwall, and I want to see it.'

'Why?' Henry feigned ignorance.

'Because I used to have copies. Well, Dad did, and he gave them to me.' He paused. 'I mean, Morrison is muck-raking, and those films should be destroyed.' Warming to his theme he continued, 'They won't do anyone any good. They're nothing but trouble.'

Henry had to think quickly. The films had been stolen when his home had been burgled – although he later found out that the Galvins had gained possession of them. His own family had told him to leave matters alone, not to involve the police. The Silvers and the Galvins hadn't been close in the intervening years. Bob regarded Paul as a charlatan, and Alison Galvin had never really felt she had been on the same wavelength as the GP Margaret Silver.

'So how did you lose them?' inquired Henry.

'They were stolen from my flat in Fulham years ago,' Danny replied.

Well, what goes around . . . thought Henry; yet something made him suspicious. He felt that Danny's bluster was just that and that he didn't really believe that Henry had the films at all. No, he was sure this little bit of theatre was really for someone else, someone Danny wanted Henry to warn off the whole business. He assumed that person was Grant.

Danny wanted to know whether he had made any copies, but Henry was able to dismiss that idea with a nonchalant wave of his hand. Danny continued, 'You know that madman Grant Morrison has taken it upon himself to try to dig up all that crap from 1972. I expect Justyn has told you all about it, and it won't be long before Morrison gets hold of the films, which I gather have been converted to DVD.'

'So you're in a race against time?'

'I'm not in a race against anything' replied Danny tersely. 'I simply want to keep the doors to the past firmly shut – bolted and chained, in fact. Why does Morrison have to do all this now? What's he on?'

'I've no idea. Why've you come to see me?'

'I thought you might know something – you might know if there are any unwanted copies lurking around.' Danny looked accusingly at his host.

Henry considered his response, but he shared his family's general distaste for the Galvin family, particularly as he knew they had stolen the films in the first place. By contrast, of all his brother's friends he had always rather liked Grant, and he resolved to do all in his power to help him. He began to doubt whether the films were even stolen from Danny at all and suspected that his approach was to determine whether any copies had been made.

'Look, I lost possession of that footage a long time ago, which I was very angry about at the time. After all, I shot the film in the first place. Anyway, I don't see how I can help you now. Frankly, I think we should all let bygones be bygones.'

'I couldn't agree more, but that lunatic Morrison is going on as if he's tracking a lost NASA satellite, as if this is the Holy Grail, the discovery of Tutankhamen and all that bollocks.'

'Why?'

'I don't know. I really don't know. He's even been down to Cornwall to see Ivan Youlen and Trevor the fisherman. I mean, what is he on? He tried to find Ken Holford and was seen visiting the grave of Ken's old lady.'

'You seem to know an awful lot about what he's been doing,' Henry challenged, deciding it was time he stood up to this bully who seemed totally changed from the teenager he had once known.

'Yeah, well. I want him to stop. He's making it personal. If he calls you, can you tell him you never filmed anything controversial, that you never saw anything that would be remotely significant for him to watch some forty years on.'

Henry considered this request and was half tempted to let rip, to tell Danny that he had total recall of everything on those DVDs and that Danny was in big trouble; but he knew discretion was the better part of valour, so he limited himself to 'Yes, of course. Let's all move on.'

'Yeah, right,' said Danny as he got up to leave. 'Thanks for your time. A cup of tea would have been nice,' he teased with a half-smile, and Henry was relieved at this attempt at humour.

'Oh, sorry. It's just that I have an appointment with my chiropractor and . . .'

'Don't be,' said Danny. 'I was only joking. Good to see you, old son. Give my best to Justyn, and don't forget to tell Morrison he can stick his head where the sun don't shine!'

'Yes, of course. Quite so. See you again some time. Bye,' replied Henry as he shut the door firmly. He waited until Danny's Audi had departed and then called Grant.

'Hello, good to hear from you,' said the voice at the end of the phone.

'Danny's on to you. He doesn't know that you already have some of the DVDs, but he's pretty paranoid about them – and you.'

'Good, good,' Grant announced playfully. 'This is getting to the business end of things. Thanks, Henry – and lock your doors.'

'I think it's you who'd better lock yours.'

## 34

## PRESENT DAY

It was a discovery one afternoon in September that led Brigit to reappraise her husband. There had been a phone call at their home from a Tom Youlen, who had left an answerphone message for Grant. 'I'm sorry to bother you, Mr Morrison, but I just had to tell you I've been made a partner at Foster and Moon Solicitors here in Penzance. Once again I owe you. I'm sorry to ring your home phone, but I tried your office, and they said you were taking a sabbatical. So as I'd kept this number I just had to ring and tell you.' He left a contact number, and Brigit knew that Grant would want to hear the message for himself. She thought about the name. Wasn't that what the hotel night porter was called?

That evening she and Grant met for a curry at their favourite Indian restaurant, both pleased to be getting back together.

'Tom Youlen phoned you today from Cornwall,' said Brigit. 'Look, I know the porter was called Tom Youlen, so who on earth is this?'

'What did he say?'

Brigit gave him the gist of the message. Grant seemed pleased and decided it was time to tell her the full story.

Some twenty years earlier he had got involved in his firm's pro-bono committee, which undertook mentoring and facilitation work in various locations and in schools with little access to or knowledge of the legal world in which he worked. Such had been his commitment to this activity that for the last ten years he had been committee chairman. Back in 1988 he had visited a large comprehensive school in west Cornwall. He knew in his heart that this wasn't entirely altruistic; he was drawn to the area, as he sometimes dwelt on the events of 1972, although they were yet to attack his mind as mercilessly as seal pups being assaulted by marauding sharks.

'Tom was a spotty youth sitting in the front row of a class of second-year A-level students, and he came up to speak to me after my talk there. Initially I just told him how to apply to law school, what sort of A-levels he would need, that sort of thing. He told me he came from a family with no interest in academic qualifications and that even being allowed to do A-levels was quite a struggle, as his father said they were a complete waste of time. Delving into the child's home life was strictly off-limits, so I asked him why he was interested in the law. He was reticent at first and then told me how his grandfather had suffered severe hardship upon losing his job as a plasterer when his employer went bust after a developer left everyone in the lurch. He reckoned his family never recovered from this, regarding it as a great injustice, and said that he had set his sights on becoming a lawyer so he could right wrongs, as he regarded it. I told him I thought his motivation a good one and encouraged him to aim high. Then he told me there was another reason. His grandfather's brother, also called Tom, had worked at a prestigious hotel in the area and had been poisoned in 1972. He said he had grown up hearing this story from his father Ivan. By this time I knew exactly who he was but figured that under no circumstances must I let on that I knew the boy was the child born to a sixteen-year-mother and kept in a Newquay bedsit by his father. I saw tears in his eyes as he revealed his sad family history, and I resolved to do everything I could to help him.

If ever there was a lad who really deserved a chance, I had discovered him. I sponsored him until I managed to place him in a training contract with Ian Fothergill's firm in Truro. There he took up his articles. I am so happy for him that he's been made a partner.'

'And I'm so happy you're back,' smiled Brigit. She listened as Grant told her about what he'd been up to since their rift, omitting only the tale of his wild night out with Justyn. At no stage did he show any self-pity, even when he elaborated on his meeting with young Tom's father at the Lost Gardens of Heligan. They smiled at the irony. However, he related there was one cloud still on the horizon – Suzie's arrival at Heathrow early the following day.

When he finished Brigit gripped his hand across the table, staring warmly into his eyes. 'I understand. If it helps, I'll come with you.'

'That's very sweet of you,' Grant replied, 'but I think I'm stuck with the cast of '72. We all need closure now.' He was relieved to see her eyes still looking at him with affection.

## 35

## PRESENT DAY

On her arrival at Heathrow Terminal 5 Suzie moved swiftly through customs towards baggage retrieval. For the first time she began to feel nervous about her expedition to London, arranged largely to show Grant what was on the fourth DVD. 'No time to be faint-hearted,' she admonished herself. She knew he would be waiting when she emerged in the arrivals hall. She stopped briefly, ostensibly to check where she had put the scrap of paper with the address of her aunt's flat in Bayswater but actually to buy a little time before the anticipated encounter with Grant, an event that she knew would set the hares running. She was the genie in the bottle – and then with a shiver she thought she was Dr Frankenstein about to unleash the monster. She hesitated a moment longer before reverting to being the no-nonsense, pragmatic person she had become: the practical nurse dispensing care and performing her duties with a sense of purpose and appropriate professionalism. This was merely another task that had to be undertaken, she told herself. But still she hesitated. She had been through so much with the Galvins, and even though Paul, Danny's ogre of a father, had long since passed away, the sudden breakdown of her engagement was never far from her mind. She still harboured strong feelings of affection for Danny . . . She pulled herself together, braced herself and walked purposefully into the bright lights of the arrivals hall.

Grant's broad smile – more from relief that she had arrived

than pleasure at seeing her – greeted her, but she presented a slightly frosty, businesslike countenance to which he was oblivious. 'So good to see you,' he said with an enthusiasm she knew was sincere. He kissed her formally on both cheeks and took her heavy luggage. She retained her hand luggage, which he felt sure contained the precious DVD.

After his routine inquiries about her journey she got quickly to the point. 'OK, I have the disk, and I know you are breaking bones to see it, but first I must deal with niceties at Aunt Mary's where I'm staying.'

'Yes, sure. Of course,' he replied, privately cursing her aunt. He knew that he must not be too pushy. Parking ticket in hand, he left Suzie in order to retrieve his car, having arranged where he would pick her up. What if she were mugged? What if she had a stroke? Such was his paranoia that he ran through the short-stay car park to locate his Toyota and could barely contain himself as he screeched out of his parking spot as if racing in a Grand Prix. On reaching the assigned meeting point he scanned the pavement, thronged with people awaiting collection. Where was she? Where in the name of the Almighty was she? She was nowhere to be seen, and he felt panicky. He sensed the blood rush to his head, his breathing becoming shallow. He stopped the car, controlled his breathing with deep intakes and expulsions of air from the pit of his abdomen, which immediately evoked memories of his panicky nights in Zennor.

Several agonizing minutes passed. Still no sign of her. Had she been kidnapped. Had a Galvin or a Youlen waited in the wings, watched her making her way through arrivals and pounced? To his huge relief she suddenly appeared in his rear-view mirror walking calmly, almost nonchalantly, towards him. He jumped out of the vehicle, almost in one motion, and felt a sharp twinge in his lower back. 'Damn,' he exclaimed as quietly as he could. But that was nothing compared with the pain and disbelief he experienced when he noticed with horror that she was no longer carrying her hand luggage.

'Grant, I'm so sorry. I had to go to the ladies'. It's the rush-hour. It could have been ages before . . .'

'And you've lost your hand luggage?'

'Didn't lose it. I put it down to wash my hands, and while I was using the dryer it was taken.'

'Have you reported it?'

'Yes, I tried,' she replied. 'I have to go to Lost Property at some building on the airport perimeter.'

Grant didn't know whether to cry or curse, but he had little option other than to play the gentleman. 'Don't worry. We'll drive there now. There's bound to be CCTV footage. Hopefully we can identify the thief, which might give us a breakthrough.'

'Why? What makes you think we'll be able to identify him?'

'Because people have been trying to thwart me for months now, trying to scare me and generally put me off the scent. I have a pretty good idea of who we will see on CCTV.'

Suzie looked at him, her face betraying a trace of triumph that confounded him. 'Don't worry. I have a duplicate of the DVD in my luggage. I know the contents are dynamite, and I was never going to risk coming all the way to London with just one copy.'

Her words transformed his mood, and he found himself genuinely in awe of her. 'Phew.' Grant released the word as if he was relieving all the tension that had built up since she had arrived. He could now focus his thoughts. 'But someone's followed you and in all likelihood me as well today,' he continued as they drove off towards the West End. 'They knew of your journey and your arrival time, and in all probability they will know you have the DVD. We have to be very careful now. We are probably being followed now. I've been tailed quite a lot recently.'

'Should we call the police?'

'I have thought of doing so many times, but if the truth . . . Well, we may yet have to, I suppose, if things get worse.'

She fixed her eyes on him and for the first time thought he might be quite a catch, a feeling she had never had in Cornwall on those family holidays. The chemistry had never been right between them, unlike that between her father and his mother. She knew he had been involved with Caroline and briefly with Jenny Charnley. (Who hadn't? she reflected.) Her own romantic involvement had centred on Danny. Meanwhile she had been all too aware of her father's abiding passion for Grant's mother, which had always been something of a major complication. She knew her father would have disapproved of a second liaison between the two families, and that had made any glimmerings of attraction to Grant a total no-go zone. For a brief moment she wondered how her life might have panned out if she had fallen for him. And would she have prevented the crusade that now so consumed him?

'How's Brigit?' she asked breezily, as if their previous conversation had never occurred.

'Fine,' he replied. He had no more intention of discussing his private life with her than he had had with Danny on his unexpected visit to his home in Mill Hill. 'So how long are you here for, and when can I watch *Apocalypse Now*?'

She laughed and relaxed a little. 'As soon as Aunt Mary has left the flat. She has a hairdressing appointment at eleven.'

He glanced at his watch. It was only eight, but he knew he had to be patient. He found himself reflecting on how odd the situation had become, Suzie having travelled all the way from Cape Town with the cherished DVD on which so much seemed to rest. He, too, wished there was more of a rapport between them; he had never felt very comfortable in her presence. At least as an adult she had gained some self-confidence.

'OK, so why don't I drop you off, go and get a coffee near by – which might throw off any unwanted hangers-on – and return at eleven-fifteen? But first let's go to the Lost Property place.'

'Oh, I have a number. I'll call it now.'

No sooner had she dialled than she was put through. After being asked at which terminal she had arrived, her time of arrival and place of embarkation, she was told, 'No, we've had nothing from Terminal 5 since six last night. If you call in after three today we usually have the items handed in from six p.m. last night onwards.' Suzie cast a knowing glance at Grant, which seemed to suggest she had anticipated an answer like this.

He headed into the West End, a journey made onerous by the morning rush-hour; a trip that should have taken no more than forty minutes was more than doubled.

'How on earth do people cope with this every day?' Suzie asked, staggered by the volume of traffic. As with much of their conversation in South Africa, the flow of conversation was stilted. They decided to keep off the subject of the DVD. He thought of inquiring after her family but decided not to invite any reference to her father.

After some minutes of silence he suggested putting the news on the radio; Suzie welcomed this diversion, remarking that she felt very out of touch with UK news when in Cape Town. The first item they heard could hardly have been more appropriate: a piece about advances in DNA technology and how murderers should live in perpetual fear of being convicted because even the most microscopic strand of hair could provide evidence in a new prosecution. Suzie listened in silence, glancing at Grant to see if he showed any reaction to the news story.

Meanwhile his intermittent curses about the M4 arterial route into London grew more vocal at the blockage around Hammersmith. Finally, he decided to break their own conversational traffic jam. 'Did you ever want to go back to Cornwall after 1972?'

'Danny suggested it once, but I thought there were a lot of other places to visit.'

'A pity,' replied Grant. 'We all had five or six great holidays there, our parents rebooking for the following year the moment the latest one ended.'

'Perhaps we just grew up. We were no longer characters in *Alice in Wonderland*. It wasn't even as if it was the way normal people in their late teens generally behaved back then. Normal teenagers would have spent the summer backpacking around Holland or camping out at music festivals. I remember thinking that I should have been at the Isle of Wight festival.' She said this with some vehemence, almost intentionally raining on Grant's parade, before softening slightly. 'I'm sorry, I'm not soaked in your nostalgia for it all.'

'Yeah, probably I am – but it was fun while it lasted. I guess it *was* a bit of a bubble. At least we all avoided marrying one another!' He was deliberately lightening the tone but also trying to get her to reveal more about her relationship with Danny – especially why the wedding had been cancelled at such short notice. It failed, as did all attempts to scratch beneath the surface of her past.

'Well, whatever. It was a pretty false world, being on family holidays in our late teens in an expensive hotel financed by the Bank of Mum and Dad.'

It was the Bank of Dad that Grant would have loved to

have asked about. How wealthy had her father been? Had he been trying to play God with his experiments? What risks had he taken in his professional and private life at his cottage in Zennor? But Grant knew he had neither the communication skills nor the rapport with Suzie to broach the subject.

Just after nine-thirty they arrived in Bayswater. Grant dropped Suzie off. She removed her luggage with the minimum of fuss or even acknowledgement and proceeded to ring the front doorbell, with a merely cursory backward glance towards him. He welcomed the opportunity to park several streets away and undertake some surveillance. From the time he had left his home to stay with his brother near Guildford he had been convinced that he was being followed. In his mind there was only one suspect: Danny Galvin, although he knew now that the stalker in Zennor and the driver of the car that followed him to Glen's home might not be one and the same person. Danny had, after all, alerted him that Trevor Mullings might be involved.

Grant monitored cars parking near Suzie's aunt's residence. The fact he had at least ninety minutes to kill before he could finally view the film footage was very convenient. Anyone following him would surely despair of him entering the flat after such a long wait, even if he had been spotted dropping Suzie off.

## 36

## PRESENT DAY

Shortly after eleven Suzie opened the front door to her aunt's flat to find a very impatient Grant on the doorstep. Initially she thought she would play it cool, offer him a coffee, engage in some light conversation, but his body language made plain that any conversational foreplay wasn't on the agenda as he paced the room looking for a DVD player.

'OK, it's showtime in the sitting-room,' she announced with a little more than her customary matter-of-factness. Grant sat on the edge of a large chair and watched her operate the controls until there it was at last: the fourth DVD, the converted Super 8 film, being played out before his eyes on the television screen. So absorbed was he that he didn't notice the family photographs adorning the mantelpiece and the Steinway piano that flanked the television; they all featured Mary's brother, Richard Hughes-Webb.

Henry Silver's final cinematic offering commenced on the evening of Wednesday 23 August 1972 with a scene at the hotel, a number of residents taking their seats to watch the last in-house movie of the holiday. Grant quickly identified a trio of middle-aged women: Alison Galvin, Anne Jessops and Lucy 'the Duchess' Charnley. However, Henry didn't linger on this scene. Grant remembered that the films shown at the hotel started at nine, and Hector had been seen starting his walk down the drive to the Office at around seven-thirty that evening, a fact revealed at the time in witness statements.

Henry walked down the drive himself shortly after nine. By this stage the evening was in full swing, and the next ten minutes would remain in Grant's consciousness for a very long time.

The filming at the pub started with a few people arriving from the hotel, some of whom stayed and some of whom exited fairly quickly. It wasn't so much the film's content but its vantage point that intrigued Grant; Henry was filming from *outside* the pub. But why? The answer soon came to him. Henry didn't want anyone to know he was filming. So there they were in a cluster at a table near the window: Paul Galvin, Hector Wallace, Ivan Youlen and Trevor Mullings. What a strange group to find together, thought Grant. Hector was not at his usual bar stool, and they were oblivious to Henry filming outside the window. The police inquiry had revealed that Hector didn't have dinner at the hotel that last night, so by the time Henry filmed him, at around nine-thirty, Hector would have already been fairly drunk. The conversation of the quartet at the table was animated. Paul, who earlier in the evening had claimed to be a little below par, had skipped dinner, which, in addition to being a relief to his family, gave him the opportunity to ingratiate himself with the group with which he was now drinking. He seemed to be doing most of the talking, gesticulating to emphasize his words. Was Paul trying to entice Hector into parting with his anticipated inheritance from his Aunt Agatha with some crooked investment scheme into which he had already roped Youlen and Mullings?

The benefit of hindsight greatly assisted Grant's interpretation of what he was viewing. He knew that Hector's aunt had been diagnosed with a particularly aggressive form of breast cancer, and that day Hector had apparently disclosed this fact to some of his friends, saying she was unlikely to make it to Christmas. (Agatha Wallace had died on 23 December 1972, so the doctors had got it right.) Grant's mind raced to work out what was going on.

Paul had previously engaged Youlen in heated conversation. Did he suspect Ivan was complicit in the poisoning of his uncle? And was Paul now blackmailing Ivan into endangering Hector – to suit his own purposes? Or was Paul seeking to make things up with Ivan, whose father's livelihood had been so adversely affected by the failure of the Penzance house-building project? If so, was he engineering 'a nice little earner' for Ivan to redress the balance, while cleaning out the hapless Hector for his own financial gain?

Henry's attention on the four drinkers was diverted by the arrival and set-up of the pub band, which included Justyn on lead guitar. What happened next seemed highly significant. Suzie's father, Richard, entered the premises with Grant's mother, Rose, but no sooner had they walked in than they left again.

Suzie, watching the film footage with Grant, now fixed him with a rather cold stare that he found somewhat unnerving. To alleviate the tension he asked, 'What d'you reckon is going on here?'

'Justyn is about to take the piss,' Suzie announced dismissively. 'He sees Father enter and immediately launches into "Lily the Pink".'

'Why?'

'Think about the lyrics,' she said, with a look that could ice a warm summer's day. She started singing, 'For he invented medicinal compounds . . .'

'Oh, sure, yeah, I get it,' Grant replied hastily, trying to catch up. 'But why's that so significant?'

'Justyn was trying to embarrass my father. Some stupid people thought he played God and was pushing at too many frontiers in his experimentation into heart disease. Little did they understand that Father could save them.'

'I thought it was animals he experimented with?'

'Yes,' she hesitated, unsure of saying too much. 'But there was no way Father had to listen to Justyn's judgemental rubbish. What did Justyn know about his work, for goodness' sake?'

Grant pondered this. Suzie had temporarily stopped the film but now resumed it to reveal the startling image of Grant's father, Dennis, arriving at the pub with Yvie Hughes-Webb. Grant was once again disturbed by Suzie's cold stare, fixed firmly on him. What disconcerted him particularly, however, was that her mother and his father were not shown leaving the pub before Henry's film cut to the end of the in-house movie being shown back at the hotel. Henry had caught the end of the credits to the film *Carry On Henry*, a bawdy satire on the reign of Henry VIII that he perhaps regarded as a fitting conclusion to his holiday movie that year.

Grant turned to Suzie, about to speak, as the film appeared to end.

'It's not over yet,' she informed him in her best schoolmarm manner. And so it wasn't, as more footage from the pub filled the screen. And there they were, Hector Wallace and Trevor Mullings heading across the road down towards the beach, clutching their bottles. 'So it was Mullings all the time,' exclaimed Grant. Suzie said nothing. The film ended with Paul deep in conversation with Ivan before they went their separate ways – Paul on foot, Ivan driving away in his battered Ford Anglia.

Grant decided to play down what he had just seen, to give himself time to organize the confusion of thoughts in his head. 'So there was no sign of Ted Jessops and Arnie Charnley in the film?'

'Why should there be?' asked Suzie dismissively.

'Well, wasn't Ted the number-one suspect and Arnie the first to be arrested?

'You just don't get it, do you?' Suzie admonished, now sounding quite unpleasant.

'What?'

'You don't get what was going on, do you?'

At that moment a sharp ring of the doorbell increased the tension and awkwardness of the situation. Grant was irritated by the intrusion. Then his blood pressure began to rise as he heard Danny's voice at the door. Suzie replied with a softly spoken 'Yes, he's here.' She and Danny walked into the sitting-room far too casually for Grant's liking. His first sensation was one of fear, as if he was about to be the victim of a kidnap.

'Hello, Grant.' Danny sounded almost amiable, almost like the old Danny.

'Well, what the . . .' exclaimed Grant, trying to move from his chair; he was immediately arrested by a sharp twinge in his back.

'It's OK. Don't have a coronary. Let's sit down and discuss things.' Suzie tried to sound empathetic but was wearing a smug look of contained triumph.

'Discuss things! Fucking hell! You two have stitched me up.' Grant's mind started to race. 'You knew Suzie was flying in. You followed my every move. You've been working together all the time. You've stitched me up!' His voice rose in volume and pitch.

'Calm down, Grant.' Danny tried to sound reassuring. 'We had to stop you pursuing this any further, but nothing seemed to throw you off the trail.'

Grant jumped up, feeling he might be sick. 'I need the restroom,' he announced – although he never usually called it that; it indicated his panic and disorientation. 'I need it – now!'

Once inside the bathroom his nausea subsided, and he thought quickly. He felt highly vulnerable. He needed to contact someone. Perhaps a text. Brigit? Not a good idea just then, although he knew she would try to help. Caroline, perhaps? Yes, she was a friend of Suzie's as well and had, after all, suggested that he contact Suzie in Cape Town. Despite Grant's faith in the human race being at an all-time low he needed a friend, and Caroline ticked enough boxes. Justyn was the other possibility but he would probably be unavailable, even though he was now back from Morocco. So while pretending to retch Grant texted Caroline and typed the word 'Help', followed by the postal address that he remembered inputting into his satnav on the way from the airport. He flushed the toilet unnecessarily and made a performance of washing his hands. By the time he had finished drying them he saw Caroline had texted back, 'Why?' He swiftly replied, 'Please get here ASAP.' Ignoring another spasm of pain in his back, he thrust back his shoulders and strode into the sitting-room.

Danny spoke. 'This must be a huge shock, but we had to put a stop to your inquiries once and for all.'

In a quiet but authoritative voice Grant managed to ask, 'Why?'

And so the story unfolded.

'OK, Grant. Let's put you in the picture. You see, Father's worm eggs had nearly done for Tom, who had inadvertently and very foolishly taken too much that day in 1972, after Father told him that a little would give him a surge of energy, enabling him to cope better with his night shifts. Tom had told Father that he had begun to find the shifts very tiring as the season wore on, and Father had said he'd need to take industrial quantities for the substance to do him any harm.'

Grant listened in grim silence. He felt like one of those motorists who rubberneck at an accident from the other side of a dual carriageway and then get involved in an accident themselves. At any rate he felt trapped and humiliated, even though he was now at last learning the truth.

Suzie continued, 'Father had told us that a small quantity of the stuff was harmless. It certainly wouldn't have given anyone a stroke. Tom, it turned out, had started by taking a small amount each evening, but he had been stealthily increasing the dose as the season wore on and his energy levels were increasingly sapped. He did all this on the sly – in effect stealing from Father.'

Grant was now inclined to view Suzie as a genuinely nasty piece of work. She was not only the first person he had encountered who hadn't felt sorry for Tom, she was blaming him for his own demise and making out that her parent was, in fact, a victim.

Grant struggled to avoid an expression of incredulity as she continued. 'What Father didn't know was that Tom already had a heart condition, which had first been diagnosed in his childhood but which he never mentioned, so the effect on him of even a small quantity of the infected worm eggs was bound to be devastating. I really don't see how Father could be held to blame. If anything, he was ripped off. Robbed in his own cottage because he had trusted that fool Youlen, and what made things worse – way worse –were Tom's last words. "It was him. Him from the hotel. He said he would . . . if I spoke." He made Father a suspect!' Her voice was angry.

Grant and Danny avoided making eye contact with either Suzie or one another. Instead they stared at the floor, visibly unnerved by this interpretation of events. Grant for one felt he was in the company of a very dangerous woman.

'Coffee?' inquired Suzie breezily.

'No, thanks.' Grant fumbled a reply, feeling numb.

Taking advantage of the lull, Danny took up the story. 'You see, Grant, you've been chasing ghosts we would have far preferred you had left alone.'

'I understand now why Suzie wanted me off the case, but I don't understand why you've been so hostile.'

'Because my family is caught up in all this, too.'

'Oh, you don't say,' Grant replied sarcastically.

'Steady on. Let's try and get through all this nicely,' Danny continued.

Grant, far from being offended, was struck by how Danny's disposition had changed. Even though the news unravelling in front of him was both revelatory and shocking, he could not help noticing a bit of the old Danny returning; he got a glimpse of the engaging teenager he had once known. It was time to stop antagonizing him; in fact, his animosity towards him had subsided. As for Suzie, Grant felt utterly betrayed.

Danny went on to reveal why he had tried to obstruct Grant and frighten him off the scent. Surprisingly, his reasons had nothing to do with the drowning of Hector Wallace. No, the big Galvin family secret had manifested itself years later when Danny and Suzie were engaged to be married. By then Paul had lost his position in his accountancy firm and was reduced to doing independent work, mainly completing tax returns for a few high-net-worth individuals and setting up tax-avoidance schemes for dodgy clients. His reduced status, together with the consequent financial embarrassment that befell him, contributed to his becoming an alcoholic. In his altered state, Paul became a thoroughly disagreeable man. Even worse was the effect on his family. Danny's mother became genuinely scared of her husband, and his sister ran off with a boyfriend against her father's wishes; no one in the family knew where she had gone.

At this point Suzie re-entered the room carrying coffee for Danny and herself. 'So, you see, we had to do something about Paul.'

'I see,' said Grant, half expecting this turn of events and now regarding Suzie as a potential felon, someone capable even of murder. As Danny had seemed very concerned for his mother in an earlier conversation, Grant was not surprised that he would seek to protect her – but why had Suzie got involved?

'You see, I stole some other poison from Father, something rather more lethal. He never knew anything about it.' Grant wondered why Suzie needed to add the second sentence.

'We gave Mum the chance to do the dastardly deed, or we said we would,' continued Danny. 'She couldn't bear the idea of us doing it, and . . .'

'She played Lady Macbeth,' interrupted Grant.

'Yes, but she didn't do a very good job. Dad recovered. He died about a year later; it would be convenient to say he was a broken man, but in reality he had been broken for many years before that. It started with the house-building fiasco in Penzance and reached rock bottom when his partners booted him out of the firm. He hit the bottle – and then another and then another. He would sit morosely in his chair saying, "I used to be someone. I used to matter. I had a position. I used to be asked for my opinion."' Danny stopped reminiscing about his father's decline. 'So we had to get Mum off to a new start. She had always loved Majorca . . . And then you started digging.' He fired an accusatory glance at Grant. 'And I could see you heading to Majorca next and digging deeper and upsetting her all over again.'

'I would have,' Grant confirmed.

Danny went on. 'And I also didn't want you dragging Suzie into all this. She has suffered enough. I decided to pay Henry a visit. It was clear from his demeanour he had something to hide, so that was when I decided to ring Suzie and we hatched our plan.'

Grant had been watching Danny speak, seeing his lips move but not listening properly. For some obscure reason a quotation by the American financial guru Warren Buffett came into his head. 'Only when the tide goes out do you discover who has been swimming naked.'

## 37

## PRESENT DAY

One other thought kept running through Grant's head, Suzie's statement that 'You don't know the half of it with the Galvins.' And yet here she had unveiled herself as the Princess of Darkness, a new lightning-rod for his anger. A surge of indignation welled up inside him. Why had she gone to such lengths to deceive him? There were so many questions he wanted to ask. Now that Tom's unfortunate stroke had been explained, he wanted to pursue Hector's demise further, but first he needed to know the answers to some personal questions about his two adversaries.

For a short while nobody spoke. Grant decided it was time to take the initiative. 'OK, now it's time for some answers. First, why did you call off your engagement the week before the wedding?'

'Right . . .' Danny looked uneasily at Suzie. 'There were good reasons for that.'

'Which were?' Grant demanded, getting firmly on the front foot. 'Oh, come on. You've already told me you were both prepared to murder your father, Danny. I think you can give me a straight answer.'

'OK, OK,' Danny conceded, looking awkward and, for the first time, vulnerable. 'If you must know, I'm gay, and even though I adored Suzie and she was the love of my life I knew I could never consummate the relationship.'

This came as a shock to Grant, but he collected himself

and shrugged as if to say 'Big deal.' Of course, he realized, this certainly provided some answers. But he was keen to stay on the attack; he had waited long enough, so he moved swiftly on. He asked Suzie why she had warned him off the Galvin family so firmly.

Suzie looked at him with disdain, wondering why she needed to be accountable to Grant, before deciding to play him at his own game. 'I was trying to put you off; to protect them, to protect Danny.'

'So there was no theft of the DVDs from Danny's flat and', Grant's voice was rising again, 'there was no DVD taken from the ladies' toilets at Heathrow when you kept me waiting?'

'No,' they replied in unison. Grant detected a slight reddening in Danny's face, while Suzie looked triumphant. Although he needed no confirmation, he certainly knew now who was running the show.

Before he could continue, Danny's attention was diverted by a text arriving on his mobile. He decided to share it with them. It was from Ivan Youlen. 'Meet me as soon as possible,' it said.

Despite his back pain Grant was now visibly calmer as he started to believe he could finally be free of all the anxiety and family guilt he had carried for over forty years. His mother was perhaps implicated as a possible accomplice to a very small extent, but he now viewed her lover, Richard, as the main culprit. And although he was an over-zealous, arrogant, self-opinionated medic who had overplayed his hand, at least he was no murderer. The fact that he never knew of Tom's medical condition exonerated him to a great extent, and Grant now thought his mother was simply a victim of circumstance. This he could live with, and he gave an unintentionally audible sigh. Suzie and Danny looked at him curiously, and he decided to tell them what had driven him to pursue this witch-hunt, as they viewed it, with such vigour over the past ten weeks. They listened politely, and Grant, for the first time, felt a trace of empathy from the pair.

But still he required more answers. 'Why did your father not press charges after your mother's botched attempt at poisoning him?'

Danny looked taken aback. 'Why do you think?'

'I don't know, but I could take a guess.'

'Which is?' pressed Danny.

Grant knew he could be on thin ice now, but he skated on. 'He knew he'd behaved very badly over the years and felt guilty about it – especially where the family was concerned.'

'No, it wasn't that. It was his role in Hector Wallace's drowning.'

'Which was?' Grant had been waiting for this.

'As I understand it, my father knew Hector was the sole beneficiary of his Aunt Agatha's estate. Dad had been hit very hard by his collapsed building project in Penzance, and that night in the pub he tried to get Hector to put his future inheritance into a dodgy scheme he was pioneering. He also saw it as an opportunity to get Ivan Youlen off his back. He knew Ivan was still very angry about his failure to pay Sandersons and the subsequent liquidation of the firm, which left his father Dickie unpaid and out of work. He feared what Ivan might do. So ripping off some of Hector's inheritance would have settled a few scores.'

'So this investment. Was it a Ponzi scheme?'

'That sort of thing, and he persuaded Ivan and Trevor Mullings that they would each receive a considerable sum of money if they could help him achieve his goal. After excessive drinking in the pub, it all got out of hand, culminating in Mullings and Hector taking messages in bottles on to the beach. Mullings had apparently persuaded Hector that if they wrote their messages in blood the Mermaid of Zennor would await them in the sea. It was all potty, of course, but they were as legless as the mermaid Hector was swimming after. Dad would have been the only one who wasn't pissed. He usually drank weak shandies in pubs. At that time he never lost control. His drinking problems came later.'

At this point Danny saw he had another message from Ivan, saying, 'Please call. URGENT.'

His friends agreed that he should ring Ivan back. Just then Grant saw he had two text messages of his own, from Caroline and Justyn. The former simply said, 'Sorry, Phoebe taken ill at school. Have to collect her. Are you OK? Do you want me to call the police?' Grant decided to share this with them. Suzie reassured Grant that Caroline had been entirely uninvolved in their conspiracy; she had acted merely as a facilitator to help with meetings between Suzie and Grant.

'I never suspected otherwise,' said Grant, who then read Justyn's text: 'Are you OK? Henry tells me you are getting grief from Desperate Dan?' He decided not to share this message in its entirety but explained that it was Justyn checking that he was OK. Grant replied to both messages, telling Caroline and Justyn not to worry.

Meanwhile Danny called Ivan, who answered immediately.

'It's Trevor, Trevor Mullings. He's got God.'

'Is that a problem?' asked Danny.

'Well yes. He's converted to being a Catholic and all that and tells me he must reveal everything at confession.'

'I see. I'll get back to you in five minutes.' He turned to the other two, explaining the gist of the call.

'Mullings must be silenced,' stated Suzie so forthrightly that even Danny was shocked. She was turning into Catherine de' Medici. 'We have to arrange for him to have some sort of accident.'

Grant was aghast, casting an anxious glance at her and thinking he was in the company of a psychopath. It was Danny who sought to rein her in. 'Look, Suzie, these old sins have reaped a rotten harvest. We don't want to create new ones.'

'And we don't want to start looking over our shoulders again,' she retorted, regarding Danny dismissively. 'Don't you see, a confession from that idiot Mullings could jump-start a whole new investigation. With modern DNA and cold-case techniques Father's name and reputation would get dragged into it, and your family's role in all this would be questioned as well.'

Grant realized what was at stake for her: her father's legacy. He now comprehended that what this clinical, rather cold and highly efficient woman was most concerned about was her late parent's reputation. He found it vaguely touching but delusional. He considered giving her a reality check, making her aware that her damned father, so exalted in her eyes, was the cause of the ruin of his parents' marriage. He couldn't clear his mind of Richard's ultimatum, delivered on the telephone to his mother with his brother in earshot and his poor father facing his final curtain. He said quietly to Danny, 'What was it you said about "old sins reaping a rotten harvest"?'

'What's your point?' Suzie shot back.

'My point is that your sainted father has a lot to answer for.' Grant spat the words out and let them hang in the air, waiting for reprisals but feeling much better for saying the one thing he truly believed.

Suzie looked stunned and was about to let rip when Danny stepped in to play peacemaker. 'Look, we've got to call Youlen. What do we say?'

Yet again, Grant was impressed at Danny's improved demeanour. 'Danny, I have to ask you a personal question.'

'Go on.'

'How come you've been so unpleasant to me of late but now you seem more like the old Danny?'

Danny gave him a half-smile. 'Ah,' he said, maintaining a steady look, while wanting to stay onside with Suzie. 'It's OK. I know what you mean, Grant. Ever since we met at the Spurs match in early May I've been trying to put you off. I've been playing a role. I had to keep it up. I knew you were seeing all the others – Caroline, Jenny and Nick, Justyn and Henry. I wanted them all to think I was a hard man so you would get the same message back all the time. Oh, by the way, did you enjoy your lap-dancing adventure with Justyn that night? The clergy seemed to amuse you, but you didn't half look sad in that casino!'

While relations between Danny and Grant were thawing, Suzie stared at both of them. She wasn't too keen on this turn of events. Much as she had adored Danny, she was frustrated by his homosexuality, which had ended their relationship, and now she was concerned that he was dropping his guard too quickly. 'How are we going to silence Mullings?' she fired with the rhythm of a machine-gun burst.

'Pay him off?' suggested Danny.

'He'll turn it down. If he's got religion he'll probably come out with some ideological crap about having visions of angels telling him not to accept unclean money,' she retorted with all the cynicism she could muster.

Wow, she's a hard cookie these days, thought Grant. Scratch the surface and you'll find cold steel.

'We've got to see him,' she continued.

Grant was glad now to be included in their future strategies, but privately he was harbouring doubts. He had no desire whatsoever to be drawn into Suzie's dark world, and his improving relationship with Brigit was his main priority. His sabbatical from Gilks and Silkin was due to end the following month, and he knew he had to get back to real life as quickly as possible. At dinner with Brigit they had both laughed about his obsession, and he believed he was in sight of closure. But that was before this morning's extraordinary events. He had gone from feeling he was a victim in a terrorist plot to moving in with his kidnappers, becoming sympathetic to their cause and going native in a Patti Hearst sort of way. He quietly resolved that he must extricate himself. He had discovered what he needed to know. His mother's role in events had been clarified, and it was time for him to move on and get back to the family home as soon as possible.

'You can count me out,' he announced, to the surprise of the other two. 'I can understand you needing to go on, but this whole episode has taken quite a toll on me. It has affected my personal life, and I haven't worked for three months. I am driving my sister-in-law crazy living with her and Glen – you remember my kid brother? My friends think I've gone cuckoo, and I've found out what I needed to know.'

Suzie fixed her hard stare on him. 'Well, goodbye, Mr Bleeding Heart. We go on, don't we, Danny boy? We'll have to see the weasel Mullings ourselves.'

'Yep,' replied Danny a little weakly. 'And probably Youlen as well.'

And so, after three hours at Suzie's aunt's flat, Grant said his goodbyes and shook hands with Danny, having rekindled some of the friendship they had enjoyed in childhood. He was never to know whether Suzie would have accepted a farewell kiss, as her aunt's keys were heard rattling at the front door at that moment. Mary looked extremely dishevelled for someone who had just had her hair done, and Grant smiled to himself as he registered that this was another deception in the elaborate hoax to which he had been subjected. It no longer mattered; he left the flat with a lightness of spirit he had not experienced for some years, and as he went to find his car he punched the air and released a loud 'Yes', the like of which he had last emitted when Jonny Wilkinson had kicked the famous drop goal to win the Rugby World Cup for England in Australia in 2003.

## 38

## PRESENT DAY

'Disaster!'

'Sorry?'

'Disaster!' repeated Caroline.

'Hang on,' said Grant, 'what's all this about?'

'This could be totally disastrous.'

'Why?'

'Because Danny has a gun, and, for all I know, Suzie may have access to one, too. She certainly had one in Cape Town, and her father used to keep one over here.'

'So?'

'So I'd say there's a reasonable chance that one or other might use a gun in Cornwall.'

Grant considered this for a moment and decided that Caroline might be right, however far-fetched the idea might appear. 'So what do we do?

'When did they leave?'

'Yesterday afternoon at around three. They should be there by now.'

'Actually Suzie phoned last night to thank me for setting things up with you. She told me about their trip to Cornwall and said they were meeting Ivan at his cottage in Mevagissey tomorrow at midday. I gather they were staying over in Somerset on the way, at the Castle Hotel in Taunton. Danny is driving an electric car, giving it a road test to decide whether it's something he wants to deal in, and the Castle has a battery-recharge facility. So we'd better get down there.'

'Where?'

'To Cornwall, you dunce.' Caroline was really fired up.

Grant had not wanted to hear any of this. He had moved on, discovered what he needed to know. He had high hopes of meeting Brigit later that day and moving back into the family home. He really didn't need or want any further distractions.

'Look, Caroline, Suzie and Danny have their own reasons for pursuing matters. I don't any more. I'm satisfied with the truth of what happened.'

'Grant,' – her voice sounded urgent – 'they're going into the lion's den, and they may be armed. This could be cata-strophic. We have to get down there as well.'

He considered her words for a while. He really wanted out, to resurrect his marriage with Brigit and to have his life back with her and the girls as a united happy family. He never asked himself why Caroline felt so strongly that both of them needed to get down to Cornwall.

'OK,' he said after a pause, 'let's drive down, but that's the end. There's a fork in the road ahead, and I intend to let it go, leave it all behind.'

'Yeah, yeah. OK,' replied Caroline. 'Where can I meet you? I'm sure Stuart will let me take the Porsche.'

'Let's meet at Fleet Motorway Services on the M3 at ten tomorrow. Then we can avoid the M4 and M5 by taking the A303, picking up A30 near Exeter. Do you mind driving on from Fleet?'

'No, of course not. That's brilliant, darling.'

'When Suzie was on the phone to you, did she say anything about our discussion yesterday?'

'No, what was it about?'

'I'll tell all before we get there.'

'I can't wait.'

Suzie and Danny had stopped at the elegant Castle Hotel in Taunton and enjoyed a fine dinner accompanied by two bottles of Mâcon. He had surprised her with his relaxed manner and his enjoyment of the elegant surroundings, even though he had been taken aback by her booking a double room in the sumptuous Garden Suite.

During dinner he couldn't resist raising the subject of the double bed.

'What of it?' said Suzie, shrugging dismissively.

'Well, you know. You're married to Frank.'

'And I would much rather be married to you, but as that isn't possible I'll just have to content myself with a cuddle tonight.' Suzie embellished the word 'cuddle' with air-quotes, fingers flapping by her ears.

'Don't you think it's a bit improper?' Danny asked, ignoring Suzie's diversion.

'Danny boy, you were – and are – the love of my life. It's not my fault or yours that . . .'

'Yeah, OK, right, whatever. We'll have that cuddle, but you won't convert me . . .'

He was sure he heard a sigh followed by 'If only . . .' but in truth they were both a little intoxicated.

Relaxing in their room after dinner, they found a television channel featuring a Nina Simone concert – she was perform-ing 'To Love Somebody'. Suzie stared unnervingly at Danny as Nina ripped into the chorus: 'You don't know what it's like, baby. You don't know what it's like to love somebody.' For the first time there was a palpable tension between them. Danny now also knew the role reversal was complete. Gone was his tough-boy-on-a-mission persona; he knew Suzie had taken control, much to his discomfort.

They arrived in Cornwall around eleven the following morning and checked into a B&B in Veryan. Their meeting with Ivan, at noon at his Mevagissey cottage, was already confirmed.

Meanwhile Grant and Caroline were about three hours behind, having met up at Fleet. They had discussed whether to ring the other two to advise them of their imminent arrival, calculating they should arrive about an hour after Suzie's and Danny's appointment with Ivan. Grant knew where the cottage was, up a cobbled street facing the harbour. Mevagissey had been the smuggling capital of Cornwall so it seemed appropriate that Ivan, dodgy as he was, should choose to live there.

As Grant drove along, he thought of Rudyard Kipling's poem 'The Smugglers Song', and some of the lines kept coming back into his head.

> 'If you wake at midnight,
> And hear horses' feet,
> Watch the wall my darling,
> While the gentlemen go by.'

Grant couldn't recall the exact words and refrained from sharing the poem with Caroline. He turned his thoughts to the problems of parking, as there was little chance of leaving the car anywhere near the cottage. This didn't worry him unduly, as he knew there was a car park on the left just before arriving in Mevagissey – and that was no more than ten minutes' walk from the cottage. The dwelling was up a little road to the left. A large black iron anchor was to be found outside number 83, a convenient cue to turn left again and approach Ivan's house, number 85, via a small square. The house was off the beaten track and out of sight of the harbour. He and Caroline had agreed that if she provided the vehicle and drove them down there, he would book and pay for their accommodation, and he knew exactly where that would be: a B&B near St Austell.

Caroline was driving Grant in her husband Stuart's Porsche, faster than she had ever driven in her life, skilfully slowing down for the speed cameras and hitting the accelerator pedal where there was none. 'Wheels on Fire', which Grant thought theirs probably were, blasted them on their way as they sped past Stonehenge. They remained silent, deep in thought, until they approached Exeter. Earlier in the journey Grant had revealed what had taken place at Suzie's aunt's flat. Strangely, Caroline absorbed it all in almost total silence, giving only the odd grunt here and there to indicate that she was listening. It wasn't until they were close to Bolventor, crossing Bodmin Moor, that Grant reopened the conversation.

'How d'you know Danny has a gun?'

'Suzie told me some years ago. He keeps it for protection in his desk in his office at the car dealership. I gather there was once a nasty incident.'

'And what on earth makes you think that she might be carrying one?'

'Well, she told me that she and Frank have a firearm at their home in South Africa. Despite living in a gated community with razor wire surrounding the garden, they reckon it isn't sufficiently secure. I've an idea she keeps one in England as well. I seem to remember her saying something about inheriting her dad's Colt 45 after he died and leaving it in the UK. Didn't you go to their house in Cape Town?'

'No, we met on the harbour front for lunch and then walked round some gardens.'

'Kirstenbosch?'

'Yes, that was it. Anyway, why do you think she or Danny might use a gun on Youlen or Mullings?'

'Think of the lengths the two of them went to put you off.'

'They certainly worked up quite a hoax.'

'They were determined to stop you.'

'Did you know?'

'No, I didn't, but I've pieced it all together now, and I know nobody goes to such lengths without having something pretty terrible to hide.'

'Well, it seems to me', Grant slipped into legal-summary mode, 'that Danny's sole concern was to protect his mother while Suzie seems fixated on preserving her late father's so-called good name and legacy.'

'That's about the size of it. From Danny's point of view, there's a lot to keep quiet about to protect his mother, not least the attempted murder of Paul.'

'Did you know Danny was gay?'

'I knew it was why the wedding was cancelled. Suzie phoned me the weekend before to tell me it was all off, as I was going to be a bridesmaid. We always remained in touch. And I have my own reasons for staying close to her.'

'How sad for all concerned,' Grant reflected. 'So what's the big deal with Richard Hughes-Webb's legacy?'

'Well, Suzie always adored her father. She saw him as a god. She thought he could stop the rain and bring the sun out into the sky. She even followed him into the medical profession. More significantly, she felt that he never got the credit he deserved for his research into heart disease.'

'Well, I'd say she followed her mother by becoming a nurse.'

'Yes but it was her father she adored. Apparently there were reasons why Suzie couldn't train to be a doctor, despite doing very well in her A-levels. I'm sorry, Grant, I know this is a difficult subject for you, but Suzie really thought her father was Jesus Christ Almighty.' Caroline spat this out with a trace of venom.

'So did he,' replied Grant with more than a little bitterness.

'But he's been dead for years, thank God – and what real damage can be done now?'

'Well, quite a lot actually. He was far too casual with the worm eggs, and he was indirectly responsible for Tom's stroke.'

'Yes, but he didn't have any involvement in Hector's drowning, and that seems to be the remaining issue now.'

'Didn't he?' Caroline stared ahead at the road as she pronounced this.

'What! I mean, did he?'

'I don't know, I don't know, Grant. All I know is they – Suzie and Danny – are going to great lengths to stop Trevor Mullings from talking, and I keep thinking there may yet be some revelation of great significance that, if it were to become known, could have devastating consequences.'

'Well, let's think what that could be. Say that Mullings reveals, in confession, that over forty years ago he helped get a man blind drunk and encouraged him to go for a late-night swim, taking messages in bottles, promising an encounter with a mermaid, and the following day the man is found washed up naked and dead on the beach. He relates that he was on an earner from a bent London businessman who told him that if he played his cards right and did as he was told he'd be cut in on a significant amount of dosh along with his mate Ivan Youlen. While this is all probably true and rather distasteful, Richard Hughes-Webb doesn't seem to have been involved in any way.'

'No,' admitted Caroline, 'but Suzie is obsessed with stopping Mullings from saying anything. Why else has she been so quick to organize the trip to Cornwall, talking about arranging an accident? This is the woman who was the catalyst for Alison Galvin trying to poison her husband. She is ruthless, Grant, really ruthless.' Her voice now took on a harder edge, causing him to glance across at her as she drove even faster.

'I thought you were friends. You were going to be her bridesmaid.'

'We were. I mean, to an extent we still are, but we are very different. Also, as I said, I have my own reasons for wanting to stay close to Mrs Suzanne – née Hughes-Webb – Barber.'

'Yeah, sure,' Grant commented absent-mindedly.

'No, I mean, I need to be involved. There is real danger now. You and I now know the extent of the subterfuge, all the shenanigans about the tapes, and you know about the DVDs, the theft at Heathrow that didn't happen and the way she delayed you because she needed to meet Danny prior to your arriving at her aunt's flat.'

'Agreed.'

'I'm afraid she'll stop at nothing now.'

'But it's the Galvins who have the most to fear.'

'Is it? Who arranged for the poison, and where did it come from?'

'I still think, Caro, that if Danny's mother wasn't still alive he wouldn't be so uptight about all this. I now think his hostile behaviour towards me over the past few weeks was designed to protect his mother.'

'I agree, but don't underestimate Suzie's influence over him. She adores him, but she wants to control him. I think she's still a bit obsessive about him, even now – in fact, particularly now.'

'Well, you would know, but ultimately it's all played out on a platonic level, and that must frustrate her. But, whatever, how are we going to handle the situation? They don't even know we're in Cornwall heading towards them.'

'OK, I've been thinking about this. Let's say they both have guns . . .' She left the foreboding words hanging in the air.

'Let's say they are walking into a trap,' suggested Grant mischievously, 'and when they get to Ivan's cottage they are ambushed by him, Trevor Mullings or even conceivably Ken Holford.'

'What?' said Caroline, stepping on the gas again as the Porsche ate up the A30. 'That's a bit unlikely, isn't it? Didn't he die years ago?'

'There is no evidence, no evidence at all, no cause of death revealed or final resting place identified. We only have Youlen's word that he is dead at all, although a local in a pub did refer to Holford in the past tense . . .'

'I think we can assume he won't be there. But as for the other two, I reckon we should text Suzie now to say we are on our way and we fear they're walking into a trap.'

'Let's not. I know where they're going, and if anything untoward happens we'll only be forty minutes behind them.' He checked his watch; it was now twelve-twenty, so the meeting should have started. Besides, it quite appealed to him to let the two of them have some aggravation; he had been on the receiving end of enough of it from them.

Caroline smiled in a way that revealed empathy mixed with affection, but she also seemed happy not to text Suzie. Grant found this somewhat disconcerting, ominous rather than comforting; he enjoyed neither her acquiescence nor her defiant grin, which lingered rather too long.

## 39

## PRESENT DAY

'West is where all days will some day end; where the colours turn from grey to gold . . .'

Some strange music was emanating from Ivan Youlen's cottage, number 85 on a little cobbled square that looked as though it had been laid with pebbles from the beach. After climbing up the narrow path from the harbour Suzie and Danny turned into the square, away from the sunshine that rippled light on the water below, which was enjoying an unusually high tide in Mevagissey Harbour. The music was not only loud, it was menacing – sufficiently so as to make Danny and Suzie pause a moment before knocking on the front door. They listened some more, and Danny noted the lyrics 'Into the West, smiles on our faces, we'll go'. He had an inspired thought and found Justyn's phone number on his mobile.

Followed by Suzie, he retreated several doors down the cobbled street and, relieved to get a signal, made the call. 'Justyn, Danny here. Suzie and I are about to go and see Ivan Youlen at his cottage. Don't ask why.' Justyn, sensing the urgency in Danny's voice, dispensed with his usual flippancy and on being quoted the lyrics recognized the song.

'It's "Refugees" by Van der Graaf Generator, a cult band of some distinction from the late 1960s and 1970s. They were great, one of my favourite bands, but it sounds to me as if Ivan might be expecting you, setting a bit of mood music,' warned Justin. 'I should be careful. The song continues along the lines of "West is where you shall spend the final days of your lives".'

Danny appeared shaken as he returned to Suzie.

'What did he say?' she asked anxiously.

'We could be walking into a trap. Justyn warned me that this music might have been deliberately chosen by Ivan to set the stage for us.' The silence that fell between them was dominated by the strains of 'Refugees', now even louder and more threatening than before, as they heard a chorus about 'Mike and Suzie'.

'In the summertime the August people sneered,' went the song.

Danny thought he had heard the words before. 'That must have been us,' he said, recalling how Ivan would have viewed them back in the old days: the grockles and other holiday-makers of yesteryear that invaded his county every August. They moved slowly back to the front door, still unsure of their next move.

'Let's wait a moment,' urged Suzie as she saw a vision that drained the blood from her face and filled her with astonishment and horror. She had been half expecting an ambush of sorts, maybe Trevor Mullings lurking around the corner or even the reappearance of Ken Holford, but never in her worst dreams had she expected to see the shadowy, skeletal figure she was sure she had spotted through the half-open front door.

It was her father's dreaded first wife. She had last seen her collapsing in the front hall at her family's holiday hotel back in 1972, and now she was here. She thought how unfair life was: Father long dead and Estelle still breathing. For Suzie, Ivan's modest home now resembled a cottage from hell.

'Give me strength,' she muttered before regaining control.

'Sssh, they don't know we're here. The volume of the music has seen to that. Let's move back down the street and wait and see what else Ivan might have in his horror show today.'

While Suzie and Danny were biding their time, Caroline and Grant had turned off the A30 and were hurtling at break-neck speed down the winding roads from Indian Queens towards St Austell. They were no more than twenty minutes away when Caroline dropped her bombshell. 'You know, Grant, I have my own reason for pursuing this. I need vengeance, too.'

'What? What? I mean, tell me.' He was all too aware that they would very soon be in Ivan's village. This was a very strange and inconvenient time for Caroline to bring some-thing up he was fairly sure was going to be significant. He recalled the foreboding he had experienced as a child on being prepared for very bad news, such as before being told of the death of his grandfather. He saw that disconcerting look on her face was leading somewhere, a place he instinc-tively knew he didn't want to go. His fears were to prove only too real.

'Yes,' Caroline continued, now in a distinctly dark mood. Grant had always considered her a very cheerful character, almost to the point of blandness, and he was alarmed. 'You see, Grant, it was Richard Hughes-Webb who suggested Daddy's electroshock therapy.' She said this in a girlish 'hey-diddle-diddle' sarcastic sort of way, and Grant feared a storm coming.

'Well, he didn't administer it. He would only have been trying to help,' he suggested lamely, although why he should now seek to defend Hughes-Webb fairly shocked him.

The Porsche swept through the winding roads to Meva-gissey, still travelling far too fast for Grant's liking. Caroline negotiated the bends at alarming speed, seemingly oblivious to danger. Grant gripped his seat, captive and fearing a further onslaught.

'No, he was playing God.' Her voice was hard and sharp. 'Richard Hughes-Webb talked to the doctor who arrived at the hotel, the doctor he summoned when Mummy couldn't get Daddy out of bed, and he kept looking at that depressing poem, and he suggested the treatment.'

'Well, he couldn't have known that it would . . .'

'Couldn't he? Couldn't he?' Caroline had been transformed into some kind of demented force, the threatened storm now unleashing hell fire. 'He should have known that Ernest Hemingway committed suicide in 1961 after receiving the same treatment. Just read what Sylvia Plath said in *The Bell Jar* about how the treatment affected her: how two metal plates on either side of her head were buckled with a strap that dented her head and how she had to bite on wire and how great jolts seared through her body, making her feel her bones were breaking. And didn't you see *One Flew Over the Cuckoo's Nest*?' she yelled.

'OK, OK, I'm so sorry. I had no idea you carried . . .' Grant had never seen Caroline like this and feared she was out of control. He thought of asking her to pull over so that he could take over the wheel.

'Baggage,' she responded, finishing his sentence for him as she floored the accelerator to overtake a tractor just ahead of the next hairpin bend. Grant, held his breath, terror-struck, as she completed the manoeuvre.

He recovered his composure and tried to sound calm. 'No, well, yes, but I understand. Just as I've spent forty years fearing my mother was implicated, possibly involved, in a murder because of a man with whom she had an affair as my father lay dying of cancer, you have spent forty years thinking Hughes-Webb helped kill your father. I do understand. I really do.' Grant knew he had to express sympathy while being assertive. She had released an elemental force that had raged away inside her for forty years. Why had she never mentioned it before? Why did she wait until now when they were almost upon the scene of a showdown?

'Yes,' she replied, calming down a little. 'Yes, you got it.'

Grant was palpably relieved as Caroline relaxed her foot on the accelerator, regaining a modicum of control. He sensed the storm had moved away, but he still feared her mood and now understood her motive for wishing to join him in Cornwall. For an uncomfortable moment he wondered whether she carried a gun as well.

'Just one thought,' he continued, aware that he could still be treading on eggshells. 'How come you could be friends with Suzie after what her father helped to do?'

'Keep your friends close but your enemies closer. I stayed in touch with her because I wanted to find out the truth, Grant. Just as you did. It's just that now you've got yours. I don't have mine. When you started this whole private investigation I didn't want to get involved. I thought I had moved on, but as it's unravelled I discovered I have the same fixation. You see, I had buried my resentment of Daddy's treatment for a long time. I was in denial, but I had always thought Suzie must know the truth – she was so close to her father. So now, here, today, I will get my confirmation one way or the other.'

'And that's why we are hurtling down to Mevagissey together?'

'Yes, I must find out. I must know why Daddy died!' Caroline was close to breaking down again, but she drove more calmly through the villages left ravaged by the closure of the china-clay pits. Grant decided diplomacy was not only the best but the only option.

'I understand. We are peas in a pod. We have both suffered torment. We both had to know, but we are very nearly there, and we need to think how to play this when we arrive.'

Caroline, calm once more, was mute. Grant was relieved that she appeared to be concentrating on the road.

## 40

## PRESENT DAY

Outside the Youlen cottage Suzie and Danny were still undecided as to their next move, their minds filled with fearful anticipation. The glimpse of Estelle Hughes-Webb in the doorway had changed the game. Suzie, normally so decisive in thought and action, was dumbfounded. She and Danny sensed they were walking into a trap. Although they had arrived ten minutes early, it was surely no coincidence that Estelle was there, even if she had not planned to be seen until later. And why was Youlen's front door open? The loud music continued unabated, and while the song had changed the band had remained the same. Danny, who had been feeling quite useless and was sweating profusely, dreading the confrontation he was sure lay ahead, decided to key in Justyn's number once more and relay the next song to him over his phone.

'On a black day in a black month at the black bottom of the sea,' boomed the lyrics.

Justyn urged caution. 'It's still Van der Graaf Generator, and this song is "Killer". There may be a clue here about Hector's drowning.' At that point the song became more frenzied. 'Death in the sea, death in the sea, somebody please come and help me . . .'

'Don't worry, and thanks, "Whispering" Bob Harris.' Danny hoped his reference to the veteran BBC disc jockey might ease the tension. At any rate he felt more in control for having made the call and having done something. 'I have a gun in the car,' he whispered to Suzie.

'So have I,' she replied, to his utter shock.

Feeling a bit like a latter-day Bonnie and Clyde, they raced back to their car to arm themselves with what turned out to be identical Colt 45s. Such was their conviction that they were entering a trap that they initially resisted asking one another why each had felt the need to bring firearms along. However, Danny's curiosity got the better of him. 'Where on earth did that come from?'

'Let's say it's another of Father's legacies.'

Slowly they walked back up to Youlen's half-open front door and after a moment's hesitation Suzie pressed the bell. Ivan appeared, unshaven and unkempt, wearing an ancient black roundneck sweater with holes at the elbows. His faded jeans were also well past their use-by date, but his ragged appearance belied an alertness more usually associated with a wild animal circling its prey. 'So you're here,' he said.

The visitors crossed his threshold in silence, and after refusing his offer of coffee they sat where he beckoned in his front room.

Suzie was the first to speak. 'Yes, Mr Youlen, we're here, and you know why.'

'Well, hum-de-dum-de-dum-de-dum,' started Ivan in an eerie vocal; it made no sense to Suzie, who just stared blankly. He continued, 'And now Trevor says he's found God.'

At that moment a thin and rather rheumy-eyed woman of advanced years, with a surprisingly nimble gait, walked into the room. She fixed her gaze on Suzie as she walked towards her.

'Don't you dare touch me!' yelled Suzie, jumping from her seat as Estelle approached.

'Well, still Daddy's spoilt little rich girl, are we? And still as brazen as ever!'

'Up yours,' said Suzie with a thunderous glare that meant more than Estelle could have known.

'Now now, manners, please. Daddy wouldn't appreciate you being so foul-mouthed.'

Suzie felt like slapping Estelle hard in the face but resisted, deciding to refrain from talking or even moving a muscle for a good half-minute while she fixed a steady and disdainful stare on the old woman. What struck her most forcibly about Estelle was the remarkable fact that she appeared completely sober, an unusual state of affairs. Estelle moved closer and leant over to whisper something in her ear. Suzie initially bucked half a step back then opted to listen. Danny was alarmed and wondered whether to intervene, but Suzie, observing this, made a calming gesture with her hand.

Ivan had been no more than a spectator until now but chose this point to break his silence. 'Welcome to the house of fun.' All three turned their attention to the clown-like figure, now wearing a frazzled straw hat that looked as if it had been in his family for generations. 'You see, the sins of the past have arrived at your gates.' Ivan calmly set out his demands to ensure that everything remained hunky-dory, as he put it. He wanted money of course, large life-changing quantities of it. It was blackmail by any name, and his trump card was not Trevor Mullings but the antique first Mrs Hughes-Webb standing before them.

During Ivan's monologue Suzie regained her equilibrium. She was not in the least bit phased by his demands and was plotting her own course. She asked in a conversational tone, 'So where does the fisherman Trevor Mullings fit into all this, Mr Youlen?'

'He didn't want that pompous arse Morrison digging the dirt, so 'e tried to put the frighteners on 'im in Zennor and had 'im followed to St Austell. Trevor walked into the sea with that piss-artist Hector and wasn't too keen on the boys in blue finding out – what with all the old cases being reopened from them days. Besides, no one wanted the piss-artist to drown.'

'And how does Mullings's new-found religious zeal square with that?'

'Oh, that was red herrings.' At this Ivan roared an odious laugh that originated from deep within the folds of his well-fed belly. 'Red herrings from Trevor Mullings, the fisherman!' His laughter increased and his face reddened to rival a ripe tomato, while the others watched in silence, not finding the joke remotely amusing. Estelle, recently seconded to Ivan's cause, appeared alarmed – but he wasn't finished.

'He's in another place, but I mustn't carp on about it or you might put on some kipper feet and skate over there. You can't miss him with his mullet. You see, he hasn't really caught God, but I'm sure he still catches cod!' With this witty *tour de force* Ivan nearly fell off his chair. But then, like the Joker in *Batman*, he swiftly turned deadly serious. His face looked contorted with hate. 'So you has a choice. Either you coughs all the readies or Lady Bollocks-Chops here does what she just told her daughter.'

Suzie looked so furious at the suggestion she was from the same bloodline as Estelle from Hell – as she and her brother used to call their father's ex-wife – that Danny feared she might lose control altogether. What especially troubled him was seeing Estelle whisper in Suzie's ear. He knew how volatile his friend could be and demanded of the elderly woman, 'What did you say just to her?'

'Never mind, Danny,' said Suzie briskly. 'We'll consider your proposal, Mr Youlen. Mr Galvin and I will go outside for a short while. I'm sure you'll grant us a few minutes.'

'Well, don't be too bloody long. Offers get timed out around here, you know.'

'We won't.'

Outside Suzie revealed the gist of Estelle's threat. 'Apparently the old bag has a doctor friend who's going to spill the beans about Father in *The Lancet*.' She looked distraught. All these years she had protected her father's name, and, as Grant had discovered, it was this that she cared most about; it defined her life. The thought of her father's reputation being severely tarnished now, even more than twelve years after his passing, filled her with horror.

'What the hell do we do?' asked Danny in a somewhat panicky voice. He knew he had no grip of the situation, nothing he could offer by way of a plan. He was now very frightened.

'Well, I'm not going to risk shooting her and having a murder charge against me.'

'No, but I might.'

'No, Danny. Don't even think about it. We guessed we were walking into a trap. We now know what it is: blackmail from Youlen using a threat from Estelle. I suggest we leave them for half an hour, let them sweat on it. We'll have a coffee by the harbour over there to collect our thoughts and decide what action to take.' As ever, Suzie took the lead, and there was no mistaking her tone. She meant business, whatever the consequences. Danny acquiesced without further discussion, feeling like a dog being led by his master.

# 41

## PRESENT DAY

Caroline and Grant pulled into the Park and Pay outside Mevagissey. As they alighted from their car they were greeted by seagulls screeching overhead. The cool autumnal air was in sharp contrast to their mood; Caroline's rant had seen to that. A pleasant breeze swayed through the palms and pines and seemed to escort them as they set off towards Ivan's cottage. They heard the deep thrum of a ferry's engine, and as soon as they turned the corner the harbour came into view. They didn't pass Suzie and Danny walking back towards them, although they missed each other only by minutes. Their conversation had become a little stilted after Caroline's outburst. There was also now every chance of her provoking an ugly confrontation with Suzie, a prospect Grant did not relish.

The two approached the open door of Ivan's cottage. Like Suzie and Danny before them, they were met by music with arresting and macabre lyrics. 'The killer lives inside me; yes, I can feel him move . . .' Neither recognized the song, but Grant, sensing some dark message, decided to ring Justyn.

'Hi, Justyn, can you listen to this . . .'

'Give me a break,' came the weary reply. 'This is VDGG again.'

'What do you mean, "again"? And what's VDGG?'

'Oh, the games people play . . .'

'No, seriously. What do you mean by "again"?'

'Well, I've just had Desperate Dan on the phone telling me that he and Suzie were outside Youlen's cottage listening to the lyrics of Van der Graaf Generator's "Death in the Sea" and so on from forty-odd years ago.'

'Thanks, mate,' said Grant, catching on. 'Speak soon.'

He turned to Caroline. 'Suzie and Danny heard the same music when they arrived. It's a band from the early 1970s. We must be wary. I wonder where they are. Inside, d'you think?'

Caroline, who had turned pale, agreed to wait a while outside the door. As the track finished they heard voices and waited for the next song to start, but no more music was forthcoming. They listened intently and could make out two distinct voices. One Grant recognized as that of Ivan; the other he didn't know, but it was clearly a woman's voice, sounding frail and almost ghostly as if from another era.

They could make out some words. She was complaining about someone telling people how to run their lives. 'He told me I was worthless, but it was my money that got him going in the first place, and you know how he portrayed me in the court case – as a drunk and a slut!' The voice trailed off.

Suddenly Ivan was standing on the threshold of his cottage.

'Well, well, what have we here? Another Awayday from the Smoke. So what did you do? Take a pound-stretcher from Paddington?'

Grant and Caroline, taken aback by Ivan's hostile tone, looked at one another for support before Grant recovered his composure. 'Well, hello, Ivan. How nice to see you again. I recall how charming you were the last time we met at – where was it? – the Lost Gardens of –'

'Shut it! I don't need any more of your pompous crap. Are you here to meet your friends?'

'*They* may be, but I'm here to meet *you*, Mr Youlen.' A low, menacing voice came from behind Grant and Caroline. It was cold and calculating, and it was unmistakably Suzie's. She and Danny approached the door of number 85 once more, but this time she was holding a gun in her hands trained on Ivan's forehead. An engine could be heard chugging in the harbour, and the seagulls decided this was the moment to increase their screeching overhead.

'Holy shit!' shouted Ivan, moving smartly back inside his cottage, shutting and bolting the door. His old straw hat fell on to the doorstep, blown by the draft of the slamming door.

They heard an eerie scream, almost certainly from Estelle, inside the dwelling; it sounded like a cry of shock. Just then Ivan appeared at the first-floor window brandishing a twelve-bore shotgun aimed at Suzie's head. All four stood outside, rooted to the spot, suppressing an instinct to run for cover. There was no mistaking the gravity of the situation. Suzie raised her gun towards Ivan at the window, but before either could fire their attention was diverted by the arrival of a petite blonde hurrying towards the cottage. It was Ivan's partner, Julie, a hotel beautician, who had returned home in her lunch-hour.

'What the . . .'

'It's all right, Julie. Let me deal with these grockles. Just back off. It'll be fine. Hunky-dory.'

'And don't call the police.' Ivan and Suzie uttered the words almost simultaneously. Momentarily each was surprised by the other's command echoing their own. However, they kept their guns trained. Suzie raised her eyebrows as if to indicate nothing had changed; Ivan resembled a disturbed wild dog.

As Julie backed out of the small square Suzie seized the initiative. 'I want that old crow out here right now, or some-one will get hurt.'

'What about my money?' bellowed Ivan.

'You'll get your money, Mr Youlen. Just give us Estelle!'

Ivan weighed up his options. He decided to play ball, ordering her out of the cottage. 'Yeah, all right. Get out there, you old bird!' He almost kicked Estelle down the stairs from where she had been crouching next to him, so certain had she been that Suzie would fire a bullet at her head. Estelle shot a look of disbelief and horror at Ivan, who cruelly teased, 'You're only useful as bait. I don't foresee a long-term relationship. What are you: a hundred next birthday?'

The door opened slowly and the fragile, wizened figure walked out into the glare of the sunlight. Her pink-tinged white hair looked as if it had just been toasted. Meanwhile Ivan maintained sentry duty on the first floor.

'You shouldn't treat an old lady like this,' she squeaked pitifully. No one was sure to whom she was talking, but any sympathy the onlookers had soon evaporated as she launched into an onslaught of her own. 'OK, Suzie, or should I say Suzanna?' she continued in the commanding tone Suzie had always loathed. 'You've had your fun, but you know your father wouldn't have amounted to anything if it hadn't been for me and my patronage. I paid for him to get through medical school, bought our first flat . . .' She paused to see what reaction she was getting.

'Go on,' said Suzie grimly.

'He was a fake, a complete fake. Did you know his real name was Richard Hurd, which rhymes rather well with what he was, don't you agree? But he had to be grander, so he changed it by deed poll.'

'Enough,' Suzie shouted, levelling her Colt 45 at the old woman standing four yards away. 'Now tell my friends what you whispered to me,' she ordered in a voice so low as to be practically inaudible.

'I'm going to get *The Lancet* to publish the truth about your father, how he played God, experimenting not just with animals but – and here's the headline for the esteemed medical journal – with humans, too!' Estelle's face glowed with triumph.

'Say that again and you're dead,' pronounced Suzie, spitting the words. Her voice remained low, but there was no doubting the threat.

'She's right, Suzie.' All were taken aback as they turned round in disbelief to see that Caroline had spoken.

'Oh, Caroline, per-lease.'

'No, Suzie. He *did* play God with humans.'

Suzie addressed Caroline but continued to aim her gun and cold stare at Estelle. 'Oh, for pity's sake, you stupid girl. We've all got our own stories to tell.' She noted how Estelle was enjoying the interruption.

'You didn't see him.' Caroline's voice was distraught. 'You didn't see him, my father, with metal plates attached to either side of his head, straps across his forehead and under his chin. You didn't see him in the hospital from Satan's own backyard. You didn't see him bite the wire brace as great jolts of electricity shot through his body.'

'So he had electroshock therapy. So did thirty thousand other people in 1970s' Britain. Get over it and move on. Don't cause a scene now, Caroline. You're being rather tiresome.'

'No, I won't move on. I *will* cause a scene. How dare you! How dare you! Your father recommended the treatment and – I later learnt from the doctor – helped to supervise it.'

The sharp crack of gunshot echoed far beyond the narrow cobbled street. No one in Mevagissey could have missed it. The deathly silence that followed was surreal. Even the seagulls went quiet. Just before she fell to the ground Estelle had been grinning from ear to ear, with a smirk so satisfied it further inflamed Suzie's emotions. But the shot hadn't killed her; she had simply fainted at the sound.

The bullet was buried deep in the right temple of Suzie Hughes-Webb. She had turned the gun on herself and was already gone from this world. Danny, Grant and Caroline froze in stunned silence, aghast and oblivious to Estelle rising slowly to her feet. Ivan appeared at the front door, still brandishing his twelve-bore. He took in the scene with a look of incredulity. From across the square came an urgent cry of 'Suzie!'

Only Grant recognized the great bear of a man running towards them as fast as his frame would allow, nearly tripping over the corpse of his beloved before crouching down and lifting her head to see the fatal wound at the side of her skull.

'Oh no, oh please God, no, no! Please God! No!' It was Suzie's husband, Frank. Grant approached him but was rebuffed.

'Why?' yelled Frank, as he cradled Suzie in his arms. 'Why?'

Words failed the others, but Danny spoke for Suzie. 'Estelle,' he spat, pointing an accusing finger at the old lady leaning against the door frame, the only support she could find. 'Meet Estelle Hughes-Webb, yes, the first Mrs Richard Hughes-Webb. She was going to trash Richard's reputation once and for all. She was involved with this pathetic specimen of human flesh here, Mr Ivan Youlen, in plotting a form of blackmail whereby she would reveal, through a doctor friend, details of Richard's experimental work on humans to find a cure for heart disease. In this way she was seeking to denigrate his pioneering breakthroughs. So what if he used humans as guinea-pigs? Her doctor pal was going to get all this published in *The Lancet*.' At this point, Danny, close to emotional collapse himself, realized that Frank was not listening.

'I came as soon as I could, Suzie,' wailed Frank, as grief overwhelmed him. 'I came as soon as I could,' he repeated loudly. He elevated her, supporting her upper body until it was clear, even to him, that she was way beyond the clouds and the stars already.

Danny had phoned Frank the night before they left London, as Suzie had unnerved him as well as Grant with her suggestion that Trevor Mullings 'must be silenced'. Frank knew his wife had access to her late father's gun in England and feared that she might use it. He had caught the first flight out of Cape Town the following evening and arrived at Heathrow at six in the morning. He took the eight-fifteen train from Paddington and arrived in St Austell shortly after midday, hiring a car there. He was devastated to have arrived at the scene seconds too late, as he was convinced that his police experience and knowledge of his wife would have enabled him to disarm her in time.

Grant called the police. Almost immediately the constabulary's cars could be heard, sirens wailing, rushing through the country lanes towards Mevagissey. They arrived almost at once, startling the assembled group, who didn't realize that the police had been summoned by one of Julie's workplace colleagues who had dialled 999 on hearing of the scene Julie had witnessed. On learning of the presence of firearms, the police required no prompting to race to the cottage.

Grant suddenly felt nauseous and retreated down the cobbled path to the harbour, where he threw up, before recovering quickly. Spotting that he had a signal on his phone he called Brigit. He broke down, and it was some while before she could calm him down.

Tony, Suzie's brother, arrived in London the following week for the inquest. It didn't take long for the Crown Prosecution Service to conclude that it was a case of aggravated suicide. Proceedings were initiated for the arrest of Estelle Hughes-Webb and Ivan Youlen for conspiring to blackmail, but Suzie's friends in the gallery were not over-exercised by this development. In the event, Estelle was released with no charges being brought. What interested Grant rather more was the look on Tony's face as the details of the scene at Mevagissey were played out during the legal proceedings. It was written large that there were family secrets known only to the Hughes-Webb family.

It occurred to Grant that Danny may have been party to a few of these secrets, since, after all, he had been engaged to Suzie. Grant looked across from the aisle first at the forlorn figure of Frank, his frame hunched forward; he looked numb and possibly sedated. He then glanced at Danny to his right, who was crying. As the proceedings concluded, Grant put an arm round his friend's shoulder and helped him out of the stuffy courtroom into the bracing morning air.

Once outside in the bright autumn sunshine the four of them gathered together as Tony, Danny and Grant arranged to meet for dinner that evening at a quiet restaurant off the King's Road in Chelsea. Frank made his apologies, saying he couldn't face a gathering of any sort; he was returning to Cape Town as soon as possible.

Grant, for his part, was caught in a cauldron of emotions – from guilt at Suzie's suicide to anticipation at talking to her brother that night, who he guessed might have some significant revelations to disclose.

## 42

## PRESENT DAY

At dinner that night the three men were initially subdued. Justyn had asked if he could join them, but Grant was concerned that Tony might feel overwhelmed if they arrived mob-handed. The last thing he wanted was to risk putting him off talking freely, as he suspected that this gathering might be his one chance to hear the full story.

He placated Justyn by saying that the two would meet up for a drink later that evening at Justyn's favoured West End club or his flat in Maida Vale. Brigit, meanwhile, had no problem with the old friends getting together on their own.

'It must have been Estelle appearing like that and winding her up that sent Suzie over the edge,' started Tony.

'But she had gone to Cornwall with a *gun*,' countered Grant.

'Well, so had I,' added Danny, which came as a shock to Tony but not to Grant.

They turned to study Danny closely for a moment before Tony inquired, 'Why?'

'Ivan Youlen,' he replied. 'Well, you know, Grant. He had hoodwinked us with some baloney about Trevor Mullings the fisherman catching God, so we were nervous that we were walking into a trap.'

'And did you know Suzie was armed, too?'

'No, not until we reached Mevagissey. I guess we both feared what might lie ahead.'

Tony listened in silence. He was aware that his sister had once used a gun in Cape Town, firing at an intruder on her property. His brother-in-law had told him about it when he had visited them in South Africa some time later; Frank had said that he had to take the gun off her, as he was sure Suzie was shooting to kill.

The three men were briefly interrupted while they placed their orders for dinner. The menus received scant attention.

It didn't take Grant long to return to the subject of Estelle's role in events. 'So why was her reappearance so distressing to Suzie?'

'Well, she knew,' replied Tony. 'She knew everything. Even though Richard had divorced her after only five years of marriage, she never let go.' He hesitated, and Grant noted Tony's use of his father's first name, recalling how Suzie always referred to him so formally and reverently as 'Father'. 'Estelle used to turn up at our home near Croydon and sort of stalked him. We christened her "Estelle from Hell".'

'We saw her performance in Cornwall in 1972,' interrupted Grant. 'I remember her demanding, "Has anyone seen that bastard ex-husband of mine?" I'm sorry, Tony. I can see this is very painful for you.'

Tony paid no attention to the apology, instead revealing that it was after that incident at the hotel that Richard had taken a restraining order out against Estelle to prevent her constant harassment. He continued to set out the family tale of woe until he arrived at the last piece of the jigsaw. 'You see, Richard was a control freak. Estelle believed he had both used and destroyed her. Their flat in London was a pretty plush affair in Belgravia. And she never missed an opportunity to belittle him by telling everyone she'd paid for it. They had a busy social life, and he was going through medical school – another thing she said she'd paid for. She started drinking heavily. He rather neglected her as a loving husband, and as her drinking escalated she became increasingly unstable. He was well aware of her mental and physical decline and knew she was having casual affairs, but this suited him fine because it gave him the ammunition he needed to sue for divorce.'

'Suzie told me some of this,' interrupted Danny, who had a strong suspicion he knew where this was heading.

'Ah, yes, I thought she might have.'

As Tony continued, Grant took the opportunity to observe him closely. He was a good-looking sort of fellow, no doubt attractive to the opposite sex. He was somewhat thick-set and lacked his father's height, but he was an imposing presence none the less. Grant knew he had been a good club rugby player and had once had a trial with the Harlequins. He clearly took himself very seriously. However, what particularly struck Grant was Tony's apparent lack of empathy. He delivered his story of unhappy family life in a flat, monotonous voice devoid of emotion. The tale he revealed was undoubtedly true and no doubt hugely personal to him, a burden he had carried through life, but he was setting it out as though he was detached from it, as though it were merely some inconvenient truth, someone else's domestic misfortune. He went on to reveal more about his sister's life, matters of which Grant and Danny had been unaware. Suzie had been bulimic during her childhood and had twice tried to take her own life. Nobody outside her immediate family knew about this because of the secrecy and closing of ranks deemed essential by the all-powerful Richard.

'You see,' Tony was now in full flow, 'my father thought he was at the cutting edge of advanced medical research, in terms of the heart and the brain. He was a great believer in trialling electroshock treatment and monitoring its results, and he had prescribed and administered it on many occasions.'

Grant was tempted to mention Richard's role in the treatment of Caroline's father, but he feared that Tony might take offence and clam up.

'The second time she attempted suicide Richard took full control. She had been very overweight as a child up to the age of about thirteen. She had as a pet an overfed border terrier called Aorta whom she indulged ridiculously. Later, when Suzie's eating habits went into reverse and she developed anorexia, Aorta suffered and would have won gold had there been a canine slimmers' Olympic Games.' Tony's remark was delivered without any humorous inflection, but Grant had to suppress an involuntary laugh. 'Richard used to call them Fatty One and Fatty Two, which didn't do a great deal for her self-esteem, as you can imagine.'

Grant recalled the spindly border terrier Suzie kept in Cape Town and guessed that lessons, no doubt of a painful variety, had been learnt.

Tony stopped talking as their food was served. When he resumed he had tears in his eyes, and with a twinge of guilt Grant felt he had misjudged him. No doubt he had been very fond of his elder sister, his only sibling, and seeing her in such a tortured state, bulimic and nearly killing herself, must have been incredibly upsetting for him during his formative years.

'It was just before Christmas,' Tony continued with bleary eyes, 'and she couldn't face the festival of food and television-watching. She disappeared. Just as the authorities were about to issue a national alert and a search party, a voice was heard whimpering in our neighbour's garden shed. Suzie used to see a lot of Gill, her friend next door, and had decided the best place to take an overdose was concealed in Gill's family's shed. It was Gill's father who first heard her and shouted across to me in our garden, where I was playing football with a friend. We had to smash down the door, as she had locked it from the inside, and we found her curled up in a foetal position emitting tiny moans. She looked half-dead. I will never forget the pleading look in her eyes. I'll never forget it,' he repeated. At this point he broke down.

Danny and Grant comforted him as best they could, until he was able to recover his equilibrium, apologizing profusely. He brushed their concerns away by raising his hand. 'Richard took total control, as usual. An ambulance delivered Suzie to one of those grim-looking mental hospitals that blighted the landscape in the 1960s and 1970s. Six weeks later she was delivered home. In her mind she felt she was coming back to a tickertape parade. She had gone into hospital wailing and broken, but she was returning smiling with a new confidence. She was, however, emotionally walled up. Her love and gratitude to our father knew no bounds, and that was the problem, you see – all she had ever wanted was his approval, and now she genuinely believed she was alive only because of him. In her head . . .' Tony hesitated a moment, 'she didn't just think Richard played God; she thought he *was* God.'

The others at the table fell quiet. Danny and Grant felt it only respectful to let Tony's heart-rending story be followed by a moment of silence.

'Thank you for sharing this with us, Tony,' Danny finally said.

'It must have been very painful to do that, even now,' Grant offered sympathetically. 'But we thank you. It now makes some kind of sense. How I wish I hadn't started the investigation. I feel very responsible, and I'm so sorry.' He went quite pale, and the others thought he was about to pass out.

'No, you mustn't think that. Don't think that, Grant. I always thought something like this might happen,' Tony said, 'as long as Estelle Hughes-Webb was alive, anyway.'

'Well, that can't be for too much longer. I'd say we've been a bit unlucky there,' Danny observed.

'Have we?' said Tony. 'To be honest, I don't bear her any kind of grudge. The real problem was Richard.' He spat the word out. 'He caused all this, spreading misery wherever he went.' He paused for a moment before adding, 'He deserves to have his reputation thoroughly trashed.'

'Hear, hear,' Grant found himself agreeing, in a murmur. Then a final thought occurred to him. He recalled that when Caroline had been haranguing Suzie about Ted's electroshock therapy Suzie had been downright dismissive, saying, 'We've all got our own stories to tell.' He now understood what she meant.

# 43

## PRESENT DAY

Grant left the other two at the restaurant. He felt they should have some private time together, knowing their affinity to Suzie was much closer than his own. Tony was departing the following day, returning to New York, although he was already making plans to return for a memorial service the following week. After calling Brigit, Grant headed straight to Justyn's flat in Maida Vale and yet again was glad of his friend's company and conversation. He related all that Tony had told them over dinner.

Finally Justyn asked, 'So how did Estelle know so much about Richard's medical affairs – in particular the Animal Life Science place and the shock therapy?'

'That's a good question. She'd never got over being discarded by Richard and – unusually for a wife in those days – being screwed financially in the divorce. His case against her was well documented, and his lawyer played a blinder. Let's just say that they played a few cards from the bottom of the deck. Estelle never forgave him and looked for vengeance for ever after.'

'But how did she find out so much about Richard's work?'

'She had a lucky break. She lived in St Mawes near Falmouth, and one of her neighbours, a retired GP from the St Ives area, had been encouraged by Richard to administer electroshock treatment. In fact, Richard was involved directly in some of the treatments. On being introduced to Estelle, and hearing her unusual surname, the doctor had asked if she knew a Richard Hughes-Webb.'

'Don't tell me,' interrupted Justyn. 'The doctor revealed the treatment meted out to poor old Ted Jessops.'

'Yes, sirree, and Caroline holds a major grudge against Hughes-Webb to this day. I had no idea and only found out *en route* to Mevagissey when Caroline was offloading her long-standing grievances against Richard on me. Anyway, Estelle from Hell never stopped stalking Richard after the divorce, even after the restraining order. Her doctor friend had learnt a great deal about electroshock therapy from Richard when he recommended it for Ted.' At that point Grant noticed that a call from Caroline was coming in, and, despite some misgivings, he decided to take it.

'So how was dinner with Tony?' She got straight to the point. Grant had phoned her after the inquest and told her about the evening's plan with Tony and Danny. He was, however, surprised to receive a call from her at one in the morning.

'It's a long story. I'm in the process of telling Justyn right now, but I think you can rest now, Caro. You found a justice of sorts for your dad.'

No sooner had he said it than he regretted it, but Caroline took no offence. She seemed to have recovered her equilibrium after the devastating events of the previous week.

'Thanks,' she replied with genuine warmth. Then she added, 'I guess we have no reason to see each other now.'

Grant glanced again at his watch, checking it really was one in the morning. 'Let's meet for lunch one day next week, perhaps in town. For now, how about "the season of all natures – sleep"?'

'I would really like that. Lunch, that is. I'm still too churned up for sleep,' she replied, hoping he might continue the conversation. Grant, however, was direct in concluding the call.

Afterwards Justyn was quick to give an opinion. 'She'd like to rekindle intimate relations with you.'

'I know, but that flame went out a long, long time ago.'

'Whatever. Anyway, I still don't see why Hector had to perish in the sea. And do you have a taste for Van der Graaf Generator now? "Death in the sea, death in the sea. Somebody, please come and help me."' Justyn bellowed out the lyrics.

'No,' replied Grant. 'But there is no doubt that Ivan was choreographing the scene that morning with all the ominous, dramatic music. He had chosen it for Suzie's and Danny's benefit, of course, and he probably thought he'd scored bonus points when Caroline and I arrived. However, I remain convinced that Hector's death was an accident. Paul Galvin was very worried about money after the failure of the house-building project, and he knew he had major enemies in the Youlen family. Then word got round that Hector's Aunt Agatha was terminally ill and that Hector would be the sole beneficiary of her estate. Paul put Trevor and Ivan up to getting Hector drunk, hardly a difficult thing to do, but the high jinks in the sea got out of control when Hector started swimming further out, saying he was going to give that mermaid a good seeing to. I think Trevor Mullings panicked and vanished into the night. He was very lucky no one thought to study your brother's last film.'

'What mermaid?' inquired Justyn.

'The Mermaid of Zennor, part of local folklore in west Cornwall. Evidently, drunken Hector had been persuaded that if he swam out with a message in a bottle, written in blood, he might get lucky with the mermaid. Incidentally this was the same mermaid that Ted Jessops was drawing on his deathbed.'

'Weird and sad, but how would getting Hector wasted

enable them to inherit Aunt Agatha's loot, particularly when she was still alive?'

'It seems it was Paul Galvin's ruse, attempting to get Ivan and Trevor to persuade Hector to invest his forthcoming inheritance in some dodgy scheme. Paul had offered Hector a "put-and-call option" for twelve months' time, claiming it was a preferential rate if he signed now. He knew the prognosis on Aunt Agatha was death by Christmas – and he wasn't wrong there; she died on 23 December. However, the drunken swim to find the mermaid was never part of Paul's plan. All that came from Mullings and Youlen getting smashed with Hector in the pub.

'So Paul had the option to "call" on the money any time before the following August, which he knew was a pretty safe bet. He conned Hector that, among other things, out of this fund Paul would pay all future holiday bills at the hotel and at the Office until the end of Hector's days, taking care of booking his reservation each year, negotiating his rate, sorting out all the extras and thus freeing Hector from all administration. So Hector's focus wasn't so much on his investment potential as on his future freedom and having the means to carry on going to Cornwall and getting pissed every night. Whatever happened to the investment, that was a hell of an incentive to Hector. All he had to do was exercise his "put" option for this to work, but he never got the opportunity. No doubt Paul would have presented him with a written document to sign ahead of his departure the next day. But do you want to hear the amusing twist?'

'Yeah, hit me with it.'

'When Paul contacted the solicitors acting for Agatha's estate, having seen the will advertised in the *London Gazette*, he regaled them with tales of his "put-and-call" option and he was stunned to be advised rather curtly that her debts exceeded her assets. She had run up huge credit-card bills, had bank loans outstanding, and even her house was mortgaged to the hilt.'

'What the fuck!'

'It turned out she had been a "Name" in a Lloyds of London insurance syndicate and had suffered several years of successive heavy losses, which continued even after her death and eventually wiped out all her capital and plunged her estate into debt. Evidently Agatha hadn't taken out an Estate Protection Policy. She refused to change her extravagant lifestyle and for the last few years knew she was on borrowed time anyway. The reason she was so keen for Hector to find a partner was her fear that that she would leave him in the lurch. Hence his message "Tonight I am not alone". It was his drunken attempt to give her the good news that at least he had some new friends to offer support.'

'Sad for Agatha, and it would have been tragic for dear old Hector. But, still, it is quite funny.' Justyn couldn't suppress a giggle nor Grant a chuckle, and soon they were both laughing uproariously.

Grant continued. 'Just imagine Paul's face! And, you know, the probate lawyer to whom he spoke asked him for details of the "put-and-call" option, suggesting he might owe money to Agatha's estate!'

This was too much for them; they were pleading with one another to stop laughing. Justyn was rolling around the floor, while Grant had to hold his ribs.

Justyn was the first to get a grip. 'I guess Paul Galvin got his comeuppance, but I'm glad Danny reverted to being the nice guy we always knew. I suppose he thought he had to play a part to try to put you off and prevent Suzie coming to London. Did I ever tell you that he shared this flat with me for a while a few years back?'

'No!'

At that moment Grant saw he had a call from Suzie flashing up on his phone. Startled, he answered, only to hear Tony's voice. 'Hi, Grant. Just for the record I don't care if you let the full story about Richard get out. His reputation doesn't deserve protection, and Estelle doesn't deserve to go to gaol.'

'Oh, fine, if you're happy with that, yeah, sure,' muttered Grant, relieved that he had not received a phone call from a ghost. As he concluded the brief exchange it occurred to him they might never speak again. He now felt very sorry for Tony, who had witnessed some extreme scenes in his childhood and who had now lost his only sister in such a tragic way. He understood now why Tony had told his family's tale in such a detached way: he had clearly anaesthetized himself from it all, its impact having long since dulled his capacity to respond emotionally.

## 44

## PRESENT DAY

Justyn interrupted his reverie. 'One other thing. Who were the Spooks of Zennor you kept going on about?'

'Friends of Trevor Mullings,' Grant replied. 'He didn't want anyone reinvestigating Hector's drowning and, according to Ivan Youlen, was tipped off that I was in Cornwall and on the case. He was very concerned that advances in DNA might implicate him in Hector's death, so he hired a couple of old biddies he knew to put the frighteners on me. They did a pretty good job, too, I have to admit. Fusing the lights in the pub and stroking my face in the dark really gave me the creeps. They were also the DJs from hell on the jukebox. Can you imagine Arthur Brown at full throttle when you've just gone to sleep? "I am the God of Hellfire and I bring you . . ."'

'Great. I would have got off on that,' Justyn teased.

'Furthermore, I know now that they – the Spooks – put off a dinner arrangement I had with a former colleague from my firm, Ian Fothergill, who was about to leave his home in Truro. When he phoned the pub to ask directions he was told dinner with me had been cancelled, while I was told that he had phoned to cancel our meeting. I think they earned whatever Trevor paid them.'

'Another thing, why didn't Suzie just shoot the old bird?'

'I'm sure she was tempted, and for a few moments we all thought she had, but Estelle's threats were now out there for others to exploit, and I guess Suzie knew that, which was why she tested Estelle's intentions by asking her to repeat to all of us what she had whispered in her ear. She knew the retired doctor in St Mawes was a very unwelcome contact for those seeking to denigrate her precious father. Besides, no doubt Caroline's outburst destabilized Suzie further.'

'One last thing,' continued Justyn. 'When you last went to Cornwall, who tipped off Trevor Mullings? You only got to Ivan Youlen after seeing Trevor at Porthcurno and being told that Ivan was in the St Austell area.'

Grant stared ahead and after a gaping silence of some twenty-odd seconds, tried to speak, but no words flowed.

Justyn repeated the query.

'I have no idea,' Grant finally admitted.

'I suppose, then, it must have been me.'

The atmosphere between them changed in an instant, as Grant felt a 'someone's walking over my grave' sensation wash over him. 'Why?' he inquired in a low, shell-shocked voice after a pause that seemed to last an eternity.

'Because', started Justyn, after further deliberation, 'I knew the weasel Mullings knew rather more about poor old Hector's drowning than he made out. I wanted to get him rumbled before you got to him, so that he would incriminate himself. I guess I was trying to flush him out. I suspected from what you told me that you thought Hector's death was self-inflicted, that it and he were both irrelevant, and I needed you to take it seriously.'

'Oh, cheers,' interrupted Grant, 'so you had me half frightened out of my wits. And how did you track him down?'

Justyn saw the look of betrayal on the other's face. 'Sorry, mate, I didn't intend to scare you, but I figured you might get further if Trevor knew you were on the case. I was only look-ing to warm things up for your investigations. I suspected his involvement all along when his name and address came up in the report Dad and Clive received from their private detective. I also recall Henry telling Mark Vernon about the last part of his film, where he captured Mullings and Hector waddling off to the beach.'

'So did Mark give the police that information when he reported what you and Robert had said?'

'I have no idea, but the lack of justice for Hector, for a dear friend, has been on my conscience since he died.'

'Well, you could have told me you alerted Mullings.' Grant was still angry. 'He might have fled the county.'

'Yeah, maybe I should have done, but I never thought Mullings would quit Cornwall after all these years. I mean, where would he go? I doubt he's ever been out of the county.' Justyn got up to pour them both a coffee, recovering some of his usual jauntiness as he hummed, 'Death in the sea, death in the sea, somebody please come and help me . . .'

'Hang on a moment, did you just say "the weasel Mullings"?'

'Yeah,' shouted Justyn from the kitchen. 'That was the name Hector gave him. Never stood his round, apparently, and when he did he put it on Hector's tab.'

'Oh my God!'

'What now, Grantie?'

'Oh my God! What a fool I've been. Suzie called him the weasel as well. Now I know the meaning of the rhyme!'

'What rhyme?'

'Half a pound of tuppenny rice, half a pound of treacle.' Grant was in full flow.

Justyn returned to the sitting-room with two coffee mugs. He looked at Grant in alarm. They both heard it.

'That's the way the money goes . . .'

Neither Grant nor Justyn were singing. They heard the

door to the outside of the flat slam shut. As the door from the corridor into the sitting-room swung half-open, a cold draught swept in.

Their mouths were gaping, both scared to move.

'Pop goes the weasel.'

Justyn dropped a coffee mug. It smashed on the floor by his feet. Grant sat terrified in his seat.

The figure of a well-built man moved from the shadow of the dark hallway into the room. They instantly recognized the intruder. Standing before them was Danny.

'Calm down, guys. It's only me.'

'Jesus Christ, Danny. You scared the shit out of us!' exclaimed Justyn.

'Well, you didn't answer the bell, and I still had the door keys from when I used to live here. I figured you guys would still be up talking. By the way, the weasel was Mullings.'

It took a while for the other twos' heartbeats to calm down, but soon the three relaxed. Grant made a conscious decision to feel less resentful of Justyn; he knew all along he had been very fond of Hector, and Grant now understood why Justyn felt the need to draw Trevor Mullings into the inquiries. Grant also knew that Justyn had been his one true ally, and he wasn't going to fall out with him now. He felt further vindicated about taking his mad few months out of normal life, as he had discovered that both Caroline and Justyn shared his sense of unfinished business to a lesser degree. He had been the driver, obsessive about this 'cold case'. But even though his two friends were not propelled by the same fear that had tortured him for over forty years, he now recognized that they, like him, had maintained a burning sense of injustice about what happened in 1972. His sorrow and horror at Suzie taking her own life was yet to sink in, and he suspected there would be trauma ahead. However, he now knew she had tried to kill herself twice before, and, even though he wouldn't allow himself to say 'third time lucky', he was aware that she had been damaged for life by her childhood and, in particular, by her father.

As Grant put on his coat to depart, he could see the other two were far from ready for sleep. 'Don't get so pissed you start looking for mermaids in the sea!' Danny let out a schoolboy's guilty laugh, while Justyn rolled his eyes to the ceiling, struggling to conceal a half-smile.

## 45

## PRESENT DAY

The interior of the quaint Norman church was illuminated by the strong autumn sunshine that poured through its stained-glass windows. A trickle of mourners became a procession as the starting time of two-thirty approached for the 'Service of Thanksgiving for the Life of Suzie Barber'. Old friends and acquaintances nodded in recognition, with their faces set in looks of grim concentration.

The church didn't exactly fill up. Tony and Frank sat in the front pews either side of the aisle. Danny arrived with his partner, Oliver, and they took seats behind Tony. They were joined by a middle-aged woman sporting a 1970s' punk hair-style, who hurried into the church as the doors closed; she turned out to be Danny's sister, Sharon. Tony glanced back and saw Grant with a woman he presumed to be Brigit. He beamed a warm smile at the mildly surprised Grant, as if reassured by his presence. Caroline caused the door to be reopened, and on spotting Grant she squeezed in next to him, on the other side to Brigit. The churchwarden reclosed the door and was visibly annoyed to see it immediately reopen. In filed Nick Charnley and his sister, Jenny Poskett, soon joined by Justyn with his on–off girlfriend, Clare, and his older brother, Henry. They took seats behind Caroline, Grant and Brigit.

The churchwarden shut the door firmly again as the organ music stopped, awaiting the formal start of the service.

Although there was only a sprinkling of other friends, the contingent from Suzie's past sufficiently swelled the congregation so that the small number of pews, no more than a dozen on each side, now seemed fairly full. Attention was taken by the door creaking open yet again. This time a frail, elderly lady, her hair and head shrouded in a veil, stepped across the threshold. Grant froze, as he feared a final appearance of Estelle, but on removal of the veil he was mightily relieved to recognize the features of Suzie's Aunt Mary. Grant recoiled slightly as he recalled the last time he had met her in such unpleasant, highly charged circumstances at her Bayswater home, where Suzie had revealed her disturbing true colours.

The congregation sat in silence to await the arrival of the vicar. It was now more than five minutes after the appointed time, and such was the tension that it felt more like the hiatus caused by a delayed bride at a wedding, with the bridegroom fidgeting and getting neck ache from constantly looking behind him. Once again the church door crunched and croaked open, disturbing the prolonged tense silence. If the appearance of Suzie's aunt had been a dummy run, the assembled mourners were now confronted by the real thing. The gaunt, antiquated figure of Estelle stepped forward, assisted by a formally dressed man of middle years whom the assembled mourners assumed to be a chauffeur, butler or personal assistant. In any other situation an audible gasp would have been heard, but the congregation was too respectful of their surroundings to react.

This was the moment many had feared. Frank and Danny exchanged anxious glances as Frank rose to his feet; simultaneously Tony stood up as well, motioned with his hand to Frank to sit down and proceeded to the pulpit at the right-hand front of the church. There was no evidence of a vicar, and there was no one even to announce the traditional singing of a hymn to initiate proceedings. Instead Tony addressed the congregation with the words of Henry Scott Holland's 'What Is Death?'

> 'Death is nothing at all.
> I have only slipped away into the next room.
> I am I and you are you
> Whatever we were to each other
> That we still are.'

And so it continued until Tony finished with the poignant lines:

> 'I am waiting for you,
> for an interval,
> somewhere very near,
> just around the corner
> All is well.'

The last lines were spoken in a barely audible whisper as Tony broke down. He climbed slowly and awkwardly down the steps from the pulpit. At that point a rather deranged-looking vicar with long, curly white hair strode to the front of the church from the left of the congregation. He announced joyfully, his eyes bulging as if he was exercising them, 'We are here to celebrate the wonderful life of Suzie Barber, and I ask you all to sing the first hymn from the booklet, "Mine Eyes Have Seen the Glory of the Coming of the Lord" . . .' at which his own eyes seemed to widen further. At this Danny's partner, Oliver, gave an involuntary giggle which was largely drowned out by the singing of the hymn.

The service continued on rather more formal lines with hymns and prayers, but Tony was unable to deliver the address he had prepared as a tribute to his sister. His face was awash with tears, and a number of those sitting close to him saw his distress. Ironically the man Grant had previously deemed without emotion was now weeping openly, revealing his true feelings in plain sight. Suzie's widowed husband, Frank, motioned to him, offering to step into the breach. Tony politely declined the offer, as he did Danny's overture. Surprisingly, Tony beckoned to Grant, inviting him to step forward and read the eulogy. Grant reddened momentarily but then responded and was handed the script. He climbed up the steps to the pulpit, paused and advised the congregation that he was reading the words written by Suzie's brother, Tony.

'My sister Suzie was born on 15 October 1955 in St Thomas's Hospital, the first born to Richard and Yvie Hughes-Webb. I arrived in the world a little more than two years later . . .' For several minutes Grant told Tony's story of Suzie's life and of a brother's love for his sister, with no mention of mental instability or suicide attempts or anything remotely controversial. This was until he read out the astonishing sentence 'Our father was not a bad parent; he was a terrible one.' Grant stared at the text he was holding, as if looking at a gun he had just fired that had killed someone before thinking, Oh no, I can't have done this!

The assembled mourners gave a collective gasp. Grant, whose chin and jowls had wobbled in a sort of tango, now felt his face go crimson. He stopped abruptly. He couldn't bring himself to articulate the next line written by Tony: 'You see, he played God.' Grant ignored this and instead ad-libbed, 'And we will all cherish Suzie in our memories and miss her very much.' He eased himself down from the pulpit, and the eccentric cleric took centre stage once more.

'We will now sing our final hymn, "The Day Thou Gavest, Lord, Is Ended", oh yes!'

The congregation ripped into this with vigour and volume, relieved to avoid further tension and embarrassment. Several people cast skewed glances at Tony, who had now composed himself and was singing as if his life depended on it, his lungs belting out for England and St George.

Thoughts now turned to the après-service hospitality, and Tony wasn't alone in wondering whether Estelle would be joining them at the designated hotel near by. The congregation slowly departed the church to the strains of John Lennon's 'Imagine'. The vicar had informed them that this was Suzie's favourite song and declared 'Imagine Suzie is here with us!' The assembled looked sheepish and tried to ignore this strange request, averting their eyes from the clergyman. The first person to walk down the aisle out of the church looked steadfastly ahead. The fresh air blew hard against the autumn trees, now displaying the classic colours of the season, gold, russet and copper. Tony made a beeline for Grant who had become stuck in the middle of a random, mundane conversation between Brigit and Caroline.

'Grant, I'm really sorry to have dumped that on you, and well past the last minute of the last hour . . .'

'Don't worry.' Grant smiled warmly at Tony.

'It's just I've always respected you, and I know how Richard affected your life, damaging your family, and I couldn't . . .'

'It's OK, Tony. For both of us it's a case of revenge being a dish best served cold. Great choice of song at the end, by the way.'

'Yes, Suzie played it constantly when she came out of hospital. I think it gave her a sense of calm at that time. What a weird vicar though.'

'Are you sure he's a vicar?' Grant's flippancy got the better of him.

They were interrupted by burly Frank joining them,

announcing in a rasping, hostile voice, 'If that woman follows us to the hotel I may not be accountable for my actions . . . !' They both knew to whom he referred, observing the wizened, ancient figure with pink hair crouching on a stick near the church, her companion nowhere to be seen.

'Ah, Anthony,' she began as she walked towards them. 'I wanted to come to say sorry. It was a wicked thing I did. You see, the hate I've held in my heart for your father for most of my life has been the reason of my failure . . .'

Tony moved forward and held her tiny, bony right hand between his, observing her closely before replying, 'It's all right, Estelle. You're forgiven.'

But Estelle's eyes were elsewhere, trying to focus on a row of gravestones behind him, looking past him as if he hadn't spoken. The wind had whipped itself up into a gale, stirring up the autumn leaves that covered the graveyard into a blizzard of muddy brown. Through the flurry of dancing leaves she shouted, 'Look! I think there's a man over there.'

Grant and Tony turned to see where her eyes led. Justyn and Danny rushed to join them, as they shielded their eyes with their hands to see better. A hooded man came briefly into view some thirty yards away. Then a bottle came flying through the air, crashing and shattering at Grant's feet, revealing a rolled-up piece of paper that rocked to and fro in the wind among the shards of glass, beating like an open heart in an exposed, shattered chest.

Grant bent down to read it.

'What's it say?' yelled Justyn.

'It doesn't. It's a drawing . . .'

The others present spoke as if with one voice: 'Of a mermaid?'

Grant nodded.

Justyn made to give chase, shouting, 'I'm not having this. Hector doesn't deserve this!'

He was grabbed by Grant, who failed to hold him. Justyn wriggled free but was brought crashing to the ground by Tony, the former rugby player, with a shoulder-barging tackle applied to his right thigh.

It was Grant, however, who was first in Justyn's ear. 'Let it go. It's over.'

# SOME AUTHORS WE HAVE PUBLISHED

James Agee • Bella Akhmadulina • Tariq Ali • Kenneth Allsop • Alfred Andersch
Guillaume Apollinaire • Machado de Assis • Miguel Angel Asturias • Duke of Bedford
Oliver Bernard • Thomas Blackburn • Jane Bowles • Paul Bowles • Richard Bradford
Ilse, Countess von Bredow • Lenny Bruce • Finn Carling • Blaise Cendrars • Marc Chagall
Giorgio de Chirico • Uno Chiyo • Hugo Claus • Jean Cocteau • Albert Cohen
Colette • Ithell Colquhoun • Richard Corson • Benedetto Croce • Margaret Crosland
e.e. cummings • Stig Dalager • Salvador Dalí • Osamu Dazai • Anita Desai
Charles Dickens • Bernard Diederich • Fabián Dobles • William Donaldson
Autran Dourado • Yuri Druzhnikov • Lawrence Durrell • Isabelle Eberhardt
Sergei Eisenstein • Shusaku Endo • Erté • Knut Faldbakken • Ida Fink
Wolfgang George Fischer • Nicholas Freeling • Philip Freund • Carlo Emilio Gadda
Rhea Galanaki • Salvador Garmendia • Michel Gauquelin • André Gide
Natalia Ginzburg • Jean Giono • Geoffrey Gorer • William Goyen • Julien Gracq
Sue Grafton • Robert Graves • Angela Green • Julien Green • George Grosz
Barbara Hardy • H.D. • Rayner Heppenstall • David Herbert • Gustaw Herling
Hermann Hesse • Shere Hite • Stewart Home • Abdullah Hussein • King Hussein of Jordan
Ruth Inglis • Grace Ingoldby • Yasushi Inoue • Hans Henny Jahnn • Karl Jaspers
Takeshi Kaiko • Jaan Kaplinski • Anna Kavan • Yasunuri Kawabata • Nikos Kazantzakis
Orhan Kemal • Christer Kihlman • James Kirkup • Paul Klee • James Laughlin
Patricia Laurent • Violette Leduc • Lee Seung-U • Vernon Lee • József Lengyel
Robert Liddell • Francisco García Lorca • Moura Lympany • Thomas Mann
Dacia Maraini • Marcel Marceau • André Maurois • Henri Michaux • Henry Miller
Miranda Miller • Marga Minco • Yukio Mishima • Quim Monzó • Margaret Morris
Angus Wolfe Murray • Atle Næss • Gérard de Nerval • Anaïs Nin • Yoko Ono
Uri Orlev • Wendy Owen • Arto Paasilinna • Marco Pallis • Oscar Parland
Boris Pasternak • Cesare Pavese • Milorad Pavic • Octavio Paz • Mervyn Peake
Carlos Pedretti • Dame Margery Perham • Graciliano Ramos • Jeremy Reed
Rodrigo Rey Rosa • Joseph Roth • Ken Russell • Marquis de Sade • Cora Sandel
Iván Sándor • George Santayana • May Sarton • Jean-Paul Sartre
Ferdinand de Saussure • Gerald Scarfe • Albert Schweitzer
George Bernard Shaw • Isaac Bashevis Singer • Patwant Singh • Edith Sitwell
Suzanne St Albans • Stevie Smith • C.P. Snow • Bengt Söderbergh
Vladimir Soloukhin • Natsume Soseki • Muriel Spark • Gertrude Stein • Bram Stoker
August Strindberg • Rabindranath Tagore • Tambimuttu • Elisabeth Russell Taylor
Emma Tennant • Anne Tibble • Roland Topor • Miloš Urban • Anne Valery
Peter Vansittart • José J. Veiga • Tarjei Vesaas • Noel Virtue • Max Weber
Edith Wharton • William Carlos Williams • Phyllis Willmott
G. Peter Winnington • Monique Wittig • A.B. Yehoshua • Marguerite Young
Fakhar Zaman • Alexander Zinoviev • Emile Zola

 **Peter Owen Publishers**, 81 Ridge Road, London N8 9NP, UK
T + 44 (0)20 8350 1775 / E info@peterowen.com
www.peterowen.com / @PeterOwenPubs
**Independent publishers since 1951**